About

Andy Loughlin was born in Manchester but grew up in Southport where he lives with his wife. A lawyer by profession, his interests include reading, gardening, cinema, tackling logic problems and sampling real ale, although not necessarily in that order.

The Silent Hive is his first novel.

The Silent Hive

Andy Loughlin

Published 2009 by arima publishing
www.arimapublishing.com

ISBN 978 1 84549 399 8
© Andy Loughlin 2009

Printed and bound in the United Kingdom

Typeset in Garamond 11/14

Swirl is an imprint of arima publishing.

arima publishing
ASK House, Northgate Avenue
Bury St Edmunds, Suffolk IP32 6BB
t: (+44) 01284 700321
www.arimapublishing.com

For Maureen

PART ONE:

Time, like honey, is sweet.

CHAPTER 1: *Out Of Time*

I'd been dreaming again. They're strange, dreams. Sometimes I even try to figure out what they mean. But most of the time I just dismiss them. Some envelop one in a shawl of security, as idyllic but improbable scenes drift as randomly as blossom; others are crammed with menacing scenarios, some recognisable, most unreal and beyond one's grasp. They're scraps of memory that are torn from the pages of routine. They exist as part of an incomplete set. And on waking in the morning, the images linger patchily, their accompanying words echoing in the lull, whilst insipid sunlight filters through the curtains of the mind to dispel the confusion and the new day beckons just like it did before, and always should do.

But something was different; I woke to blackness and a loud, almost incessant, shrieking that was molesting my senses from all directions. Then my vision was clouded, and, through a blur, I saw the rapid motion of something dark and heard a flutter. I rubbed my eyes, my sight clearing just in time to see the flapping wings.

The bird had gone.

My senses were returning, storming my mind, but the pounding of my aching head was the most dominant awareness. I felt as if I had been to Hell and back. Where *was* I? Wrestling against drumming temples, I stared at my surroundings. I had slept, but for how long I didn't know. Odd. I couldn't even begin to guess. And the dream; a girl, a bus, unjustified panic, running, somewhere a telephone, surely an emergency of some sort- the usual inanity…but all *this* seemed real now, and my recuperating was no longer purging itself of wasted thoughts. I *believed* I was awake, though I couldn't recognise my environment. All the trees stood motionless, not even the slightest rustling came from their leaves. They were still and straight and silent and identical like undertakers. Everywhere seemed tranquil. But it wasn't an icy calm, because I could feel the sun warming my face; at least *something* felt familiar. I was aware, too, of a heaviness about my thighs. I tried to stand, and my legs struggled with the effort, buckling slightly, bound in a cordage of exhaustion. I sat again, very slowly, waited for a moment, and then made a further effort. On the second attempt I conquered the pain and stood. But that damned dream was still going through my head; that girl, the running for the bus- a bus that wouldn't stop, of course…I felt no compulsion to delve further into that dream to investigate those events, as the bestirred tends to do for those first blissful moments. I cast it from my mind because now I needed answers. So where was I and how had I got here? There was nothing to be gained from standing around. I needed to move- no, *shift*- myself. I had to force myself to set forth and walk in an attempt to find some answers.

Determinedly, I hiked for a while- twenty minutes or so, but it seemed longer. I had probably covered about a mile before the trees began to thin out. It had just turned twelve- fifteen, although my watch- fast- said twelve- twenty- six; the piercingly- blue sky was singeing the landscape with a breezeless uniformity, and the sun was hotter than a grate. The small lakes that I passed, their levels low, dazzled in a silvered sapphire like scored glass. Before long, the stunted shrubbery began to peter out as the landscape altered and soon I reached barren rocks, a grimy cream in tone, which projected from the earth like worn teeth. From the rocks I combed over peculiar gentle hillocks, lush with a fur of moss until I came to flatter terrain that stood stark, barren and unspectacular as an earmarked construction plot. And just as unpopulated.

Spotting a river in the distance, I walked on whilst trying to stay in the shade wherever possible. The air was pitched with birdsong and the intermittent humming of bees and other insects, but only then did I realise that, beyond and above the trees, there was nothing in the sky. Indeed, the lack of human presence on the ground was compounded by the stillness of that unbroken blue. Imagine scanning a cloudless sky on a fine day and seeing no trace of a plane! But there wasn't one. There was nothing. Romancing liberally, I likened it to the Fifth Day of Creation! A butterfly skipped past me at that moment, then another fluttered to catch up and the pair tumbled with acrobatic delight before disappearing from view. Nearby were a few wasps, gorging selfishly on some swollen fruit.

I grew frustrated and my anxiety increased until I could feel little knots form in my stomach. Fear? No, hunger surely, for I was ravenous. I sat down next to some apple trees and began to shake. But that was due to nerves, the type that rise, like a trapped tide, from the trough of the stomach and turn to a feeling of sickness by the time they reach the throat. Where was I? Was I mad? Was I dead? Could this be Heaven, and I a soul now passing over? Or nothing but a dream? Perhaps earlier I had been wrong to eliminate such a suggestion; what if my mind were *pretending* that I was awake, and this was in reality a jaunt through dreamland? Hence I found myself sitting there and trying to think of the sort of things that a dreamlike state wouldn't allow its designer to recall. And I could. I remembered my family, the street where I live, nearly every detail- noteworthy or trivial- of yesterday- even a trifling telephone conversation- *and* all the items in the previous morning's post...well, those that I bothered to read. In fact I could recollect *every* moment from yesterday until *it* happened. There was the walk on the moor, and the weather changing suddenly from summer sun to torrential rain. The downpour had been so bad that I'd crouched beneath a small precipice to shelter. All I could recall is that I'd wanted to stay at that refuge and sit it out until it cleared. But it didn't abate, I'm sure it didn't. It was incessant. I must have knocked my head- that was it- and wandered aimlessly. My clothes were dry though. I felt my face; it was tight and bristly, a night's growth. Even between shaves, a few grey ones were always visible nowadays. Normal for my age I suppose...or so they say. But my thoughts were rambling as I was avoiding the issue, shoving it into a corner. Had I slept at that very spot where I sheltered? Had anybody seen me? People should be looking for me now, asking questions. That was a certainty.

At last I reached the river whose bordering trees, seasonally garbed, were thrusting from its banks at peculiar angles and painting the water in burnets and greens. Sitting on a stump in the middle of an explosion of daisies and buttercups, I scanned the course of the river and tried to collect my thoughts before setting off again. Fortunately the walk became shadier, the air soaked with the smell of sweet violet, and only for fleeting moments did I feel the sun warm my head when I passed through gaps in the foliage. My few meagre rations had all but depleted, and I decided to save the last of my boiled sweets until I found a shop and a payphone. However, every step was echoed by strange doubts, and every branch I pushed from my route had become a brambly barricade to reality. Those uncertainties were beginning to nag me, jibing me like tricksters, and, like a whiff of discord in a crowd, I sensed that something was wrong.

And I was right.

There are some revelations in life to which one's forced to reconcile oneself. They're embraced into one's existence like a friend, and only when acceptance dissolves into rationalisation, and reasoning melds with realisation, does one question that which is apparent.

There *was* nothing remarkable about the structure itself; large and square and buff block harsh concrete. Generally bland, its design wasn't vastly different to many other buildings in any townscape. But...but something else *was* different, and it was then that a cog in the engine of logic- that hidden mechanism that sifts all that the eyes absorb- cranked on its bearings. But what had caused my eyes- and thoughts- to become immobilised in dubiety? It was that dull edifice that greeted me at the fork of the river. I stared, and soon jolted into heightened awareness, as concerns began to wing like birds from the backwoods of my mind. Although I couldn't, at that time, understand any of it, there was clearly something wrong as I read the carved stonework. I read it again. Then a third time, even rearranging the words and numbers- something I always do when my nerves are fuelled. There was something illogical too, as the sign, cresting the ruins of the concrete, read boldly but simply:

ENTRY (ENGLAND: COUNTY 32a – AD 2078)

I felt my gut wrench with a sensation of nausea; there was a feeling that all wasn't right, an instantaneous hunch that familiarity had become sealed in a vacuum. I had to ignore the wording that had been chiselled into that stone. I had to hurl it from my mind…or at least worry about it later; I was adept at doing that.

With much unease, I decided to enter the building. A stout lock, which at first appeared to bar my way, simply crumbled, the rust flaking like tobacco beneath my fingers, staining my hands orange. So much of the building had fallen into decay that I did not need my torch, one of the few provisions I had on my person. I walked down the stone steps with some trepidation and saw that the floor had partly disappeared and had been replaced by useless earth. Fibrous strands of lichen had begun to explore the old blocks, and cobwebs hung resolutely against the walls, many of their own occupants long gone too. Everywhere I looked I saw weeds and soil, and in places were little putrid puddles. Suckers had penetrated the walls in an attempt to re-establish their territory. But there was nothing else to see. I explored room upon room, and saw that, instead of a staircase, there existed the remnants of four strange plastic tubes- lifts, I decided, to the first and second floors. There were fragments of broken glass, now a tawny colour with the years, but not a single artefact remained that could give me a clue to the purpose of this building or what had happened to it. The feeling of biliousness grew all the more real, griping in my belly, straining like a brick in a sling, and the insane logic pinched at my mind incessantly: I had a building, a *starting point*, and a date…no, not a date…a set of numbers that *resembled* a year.

But in reality, I had nothing. I had just a further mystery upon which to ponder; another problem, and apparently nobody with whom to share it! I moved out of there. Whatever answers I sought wouldn't be found at that spot, and I decided to continue by choosing the right- hand channel of the river. *'Keep doing the logical thing'*, I had said to myself, said it many times. By now, some four hours had elapsed and I knew that I should have to be thinking of nightfall.

After trekking dejectedly for another couple of hours, I decided to rest for the remainder of the evening. I'd been fortunate enough to chance upon a small brick building where I could lay my head, and the roof was intact too. I have no idea of its purpose, as it was too small to live in. Besides, who would want to live out here anyway, the very middle of nowhere? A stream ran behind the building, and, with trepidation, I seized the opportunity to drink and then had a brief wash and sat awhile in despair. All too soon, darkness began to fall, although it was still uncommonly warm. I perched myself on a rock and watched the naked sky transmute from blue- grey to blazing carmine as it spanned the spectrum of hues cast by the setting sun.

Then it came. Under the quilt of a new moon, I sat alone in a landscape devoid of street lamps, car headlights and shop illuminations. This was a blackness that froze my veins and chilled me to the bone. I moved inside, lay down and faced the doorway; eyes shut or open, it made no difference to my fear for the silence was boundless, and with every breath I seemed to imbue life into formless imaginings that lurked in that inkiness.

Then, somehow, I fell asleep.

My mind became unleashed as it set out on its expurgation. But this time there were no random everyday things. Now I had a kaleidoscope of patterns, colours and indeterminate objects filling my thoughts. And those trees that had greeted me were no longer still as they danced in that crepuscular theatre like a blue- fingered forest symphony. It seemed that nothing made sense anymore, especially in sleep.

I don't know what woke me but I stood, and through the corner of my eye I saw a light guttering hazily some five to ten miles away. It couldn't have been natural, and I realised that somewhere, perhaps along the river, were people. I couldn't do anything about it then, but the next day I'd find them. I lay down again, and, despite my enervation, dropped off.

I always used to imagine that, should I ever have been unfortunate enough to be cast ashore on a desert island, which, on the face of it, always seemed implausible, with just a coconut tree for company, I would still know whether the day in question was a Friday; that special feeling can only be experienced on that one day, almost sacrosanct to the worker! I awoke to the new day and realised, for probably the first time in my life since infancy, that it made no difference whatsoever. Today all that mattered was to find nourishment and seek out the origin of the light in the night, with the hope that one would lead naturally to the other. The sun, steadfast in this unknown land, had risen and was still where it should be in the sky, serving the new day. I could already feel its warmth, despite my wristwatch telling me that it was only ten- thirty. I filled my two reusable plastic flasks with water- unfiltered and uncomplicated- from the stream behind my shelter, placed them back in my bag, uttered a few words of self- encouragement and strode out.

A little over three hours had passed when I saw something that always fills me with fear. I don't know whether it was the shock that it didn't lunge towards me, or simply the fact that it was there at all, that agitated me more.

It was a dog.

Having never been a lover of dogs, and even having taken carefully placed steps in order to avoid them in the past (those steps increasing in proportion to the particular animal's size), I was aware of my fear. But, conversely, the dog, a healthy- looking mongrel of some sort, was one of the most welcome sights I could imagine. It simply sat there, in the middle of my pathway, panting; no barking, just a steady panting. It was black all over, and certainly too well fed to be a feral animal. A problem presented itself: it was sitting quite calmly across my path and I needed to go forward. I had to dispel any qualms that I may have had about stroking it. It sniffed me, wagged its tail and proceeded to lick my hand. In the midst of all the crowded commotion, I had, I hoped, clutched at regularity's robe. It even seemed fitting to name him after the day itself, and so, like the visitor left behind on that far- flung island, 'Friday' he was christened. We walked together for what must have been several miles, and sometimes he would quicken his pace, almost breaking into a trot, and then stop- as dogs do- and wait for me. But all the while my suspicion grew stronger- I was *following* him. Thus my excitement was no longer due to my new friend's company - I was in a state of constant anticipation, because Friday's presence had given me renewed hope of some form of human contact.

Up a modest hill I followed him; in normal circumstances it wouldn't have been an achievement, but now my legs were beginning to suffer. Each step seemed more laborious than the last, and my thighs had begun to twinge dully. The final few steps were the most arduous, as if my shoes were encased in lead.

Just a bit further until…until…*accomplishment!*

At the crown of the hill, with a fresh breeze kindling my face in defiance of the heat of the late afternoon sun, the scene that awaited me seemed to root me to that very spot. It felt as if a pair of steel hands was clutching at every muscle in my body, locking them into place. Even my jaw seized- I never thought that it were possible- in an awful, frozen vice of mixed emotion. There, at the bottom of that slope, past the trees, enclosed by a wall, the end of which I couldn't see, stood an array of glittering structures. An assortment of coloured domes and what appeared to be metal roofs twinkled and glittered in the late afternoon sun. In some places, minarets rose above this gaudy canopy, just as the grandest trees dwarf the rest of the forest. The sight ravished me, distending my disbelief. Then an isolated cloud passed across the sun, causing the whole vista to alter in hue, almost as if I were watching the tinctures of changing leaves at an exaggerated rate of acceleration.

A nearby bee distracted me, but only briefly.

My thoughts turned to Friday, and I looked down to see that he was already tearing down the side of the glen.

CHAPTER 2: *Light Through The Trees*

I could barely keep pace with Friday, who seemed only too familiar with his route. I ran through the trees, careering down the ridge, kicking my way through the vegetation, in a frantic effort to obtain a better view. But my progress soon became hindered on account of the denser foliage, and I decided that the sensible thing to do would be to survey my surroundings from higher up. It wasn't easy to find a suitable tree. The silver birches offered no accessibility; far too flimsy I thought, despite their unusual girth, so I turned towards a tree that I couldn't identify, with strange lined bark and vivid green axe- headed leaves. I reached for the first firm bough and lifted myself, positioning my foot firmly on the broken branch below. The next limb seemed to be within reach, and I hoisted myself upwards. I struggled, for it had been many years within the past three- dozen or so since I last undertook such a venture. But gradually, I edged closer towards the lower leafage. Sweating, and with my pulse throbbing healthily, I rested at an appropriate spot. From my vantage point, I could see that the town wall was partly screened by laurel bushes and all manner of trees. That new landscape was decorated with a vibrant display of shrubs such as rich red azaleas, vivid purple rhododendrons and clusters of blue- white hydrangeas that obliterated the ground this side of the perimeter. Friday had vanished, and I assumed that he was now within the walls of the town in friendly company. Such fair-weather friendships!

There was no point in staying where I was, for within those dwellings lay the answers to many questions. Forsaking any thoughts of danger, I decided that I should approach the place. Perhaps I should note here that neither ground nor wall bore any sign- or none that I could see- that told me its name. I descended the tree, branch by branch, perhaps more nimbly now. Excitedly, I placed my right foot on the ground, followed by my left, let out a brief sigh of accomplishment, rested my left hand against the trunk, mopped my brow with the back of my right hand and turned around.

That was when I saw her.

At first there was nothing peculiar in our meeting- she looked shocked, certainly, but she stayed calm. She scanned me up and down, suspiciously I thought, and frowned as she stared at the top of my head. Perhaps acknowledging the fact that she had the advantage in the situation, she opened the conversation, greeting me in a taciturn way:

"Hola," she said.

That was all; just that one word.

I was oblivious to her greeting, for all I could see before me was someone undoubtedly tangible, yet, at the same time, imaginary; a person whom, taking into account the events of the last thirty hours, could almost have been a vivid illusion.

"Hello," I replied. I stretched out my hand, sweating. Would she understand the gesture? To my relief, she held it, but there was no grip, merely a feeble palming. But it felt right. I offered my name, though she just stared at me for a moment, seemingly transfixed by my hair and facial stubble. Finally, after a silence, she responded, and I learned that she was called, unusually, "Lincoln". Of course, it might have been "Lincon", "Linkun" or suchlike, but my mind had already settled on the conventional spelling. I cleared my mind and took a deep breath.

"That's an unusual name," I said, as if I were pretending that everything were still normal. Needless to say, the situation was far from ordinary as, at that very moment, I stood, a man confused, at the outer limits of a potentially hostile environment, exchanging greetings with a girl from…from where? I felt, however, that the feeling was very much one- sided.

I couldn't help but stand transfixed by the sight of her. She was extraordinary. A black hue covered the area between her eyebrows and lids, whilst her eyes were as blue as bright jewels. A charcoal- coloured smudge was striped across each cheek, and her dark hair dropped like an onyx waterfall to her shoulders where it lay delicately against the two slender straps of a cream- coloured singlet that only just contained her ample breasts. Her body was toned, youthful and golden in its tint. Her middle was wrapped in a cloth, much resembling a chamois (but not leather I thought) and around her waist she wore a caramel- coloured belt that was roughly hewn from a cotton- type fabric and which fastened with a round buckle. She was equipped with a range of small instruments, for their ends poked out from little pouches that were stitched onto the belt. And as for her bare legs, they seemed to stretch an infinite distance from her slender thighs to beyond her tanned shins, whereupon she was clad in somewhat unsophisticatedly- shod ankle- boots. The texture of her footwear, though similar in shade, suggested that it was not the same material from which her belt was fashioned. And across her shoulder, where a bow and quiver would not have looked amiss, was slung a large sack. I realised that I was scrutinising this striking young woman, surely a goddess of the greenwood, in a way that must have appeared quite rude; I felt my own thoughts had been paraded atop a carriage for the world to dissect.

"You have followed the dog?"

It could almost have been a statement, but I took it to be a question for I could tell that she was still nonplussed.

"Yeah, I…I stumbled across the dog and decided to follow him. He's a- a fine animal," I replied, unnecessarily formally with nerves.

"He had gone for his run, but he always returns. He has gone back now. You are not from Mentarea, and it is said by many that nobody lives in Otherland. I know your name now, but from where have you come?" she asked, continuing to gauge me, her face equably receptive and not displaying the vulnerability that surely should have been present.

How could I even begin to answer the woman? Where *was* I from? Her question was perfectly reasonable, and I was just grateful that she could speak English, as her greeting suggested Spanish. As regards her accent, it was hard to discern, although I thought that I detected a hint of a very gentle southern intonation. And as for any doubts concerning the whole chance encounter, I had to concede that I left *those* behind yesterday. Ludicrous thoughts could abound now, totally unrestrained by conventional parameters. They could catapult about my mind like a bluebottle around a lampshade, even though I had already decided that whatever was happening to me was certainly palpable. A quizzical look had now manifested itself on her face; she seemed to be studying me in even more detail, obviously bewildered by my clothes and general appearance. By her standards, I was certainly overdressed. What could I tell her? Tell her the truth, of course; just tell her the truth!

"There was a storm," I uttered. "I arrived here yesterday. I…I really don't know any more than that. I need help though, because I don't know what's going on."

But yesterday belonged somewhere else; it seemed so long ago now that my words came across as futile until she shocked me with her response.

"Yes," she said, and paused. "There was wind, but not a storm, and the people of Mentarea took shelter. But there was little rain. Just wind. We expected *much* more rain. Perhaps rain will come, but not yet."

She spoke with a calm precision, and her words flowed as smooth as liquid metal. So *she* had sheltered from the weather too; her words had triggered a wild notion, and I began to elaborate on the fantastic and the inconceivable. Somehow, in this future, the year as yet unknown to me, a storm would rage, no….*had* raged. Whilst the people of this Time sought sanctuary, I too took protection in my own Time. By some strange, unexplained happening, I had been swept, by an unwanted and wayward circumstance, from my period into another Time and, it seemed, even another place. I had read of Time misplacements and other outlandish occurrences, but, like most rationally- minded people, had paid no attention to them. But no, what *was* I thinking? I began to believe that I was playing a pivotal role in some huge joke. I noticed her reasoning stare, similar to that of an inquisitive child, as if she were trying to penetrate the thoughts that whirred about my mind and sift the probable from the absurd. I had to attempt some sort of explanation, as I was in danger of being seen as a wandering fool.

"I slept several miles from here and have been walking all day. This place must be the origin of the lights that I saw last night. I'm not from this Time and I don't belong here…something's happened to me, but I don't understand fully yet. The storm, I think I travelled with the storm from another Time…somewhere else."

She was silent for a moment, ruminating on my words. Then:

"I know of the story," she interjected, gently fingering a loose hair from her decorative face, "of the travellers who came before with a storm. Like you, they wore strange clothes and were said to be from another Time. There were two of them and their words made no sense either. But they came with illness; they did not live. You speak strangely too. But you do not look ill. Instead, you look- *hungry*."

She paused.

Two travellers who died? Was this my fate also?

A bee murmured; it hovered around her head, but she wasn't irritated by it. In fact, she seemed oblivious to it, totally engrossed with my being there in front of her. What must I have looked like to her, unkempt, clothed in jeans and t-shirt and climbing down from a tree? But, somehow, her next words put me more at ease:

"Come with me."

"To…to that place?"

"To Mentarea," she answered.

I could still hear the sounds from her town and the tiredness of the past two days made me only too willing to accept her summons.

"Come," she directed again, as if to remove any doubt from my mind. I did not really feel that I had any choice for I wasn't going to turn now and retrace my steps.

"There are many to meet and there is much to eat," she continued rather equably.

In the encouraging peace of that mellowing day, amidst the flowers in all their glory, and with a sense of diluted thrill coursing through my whole body, I allowed this mysterious girl to guide me, like a lantern in my gloom, to the gap in the hedge, over a stream and on through a break in the stone wall.

CHAPTER 3: *Hospitality And Honey*

I hadn't seen it, and it was only the prompt action of her hand gripping my forearm, the second time that she had touched me, that prevented my being hit by the small manned obovoid conveyance that sped past us, propelled a few inches above a bright track of some sort.

"Thanks," I said. There would be so many occasions when I would need to be heedful. This was a new world, and with the obvious exception of the natural sights that I had witnessed so far, there would be so much that was unfamiliar to me.

She hadn't answered. Maybe she felt slightly uncomfortable at having reacted the way she did, but I was grateful and thanked her again. Still she didn't respond, but continued to escort me with a look that vacillated between intrigue and anticipation.

The vehicle stopped about eighty yards from us, and two women dismounted. I watched as they walked into the nearest building and noticed that, as far as I could tell, their appearance was similar to that of my companion. The building that they entered was white, flaking in places, with a copper-coloured roof, and I noticed that most of the buildings were off- white or pastel shades, but they all appeared to have either metallic or immensely thick, clear roofs.

I looked back and was surprised to see that a small crowd had gathered nearby, some of them clearly fascinated by my emergence. The men were dressed in almost identical designs and shades of linen attire, the women much the same in their looks and dress as Lincoln.

"This is a visitor to our town, and we will make him welcome." She told them my name, and, once more in that engaging way, said, "Come, for there is much for you to see. But first you shall eat and drink as I am sure that you must await such refreshments."

And thereupon she did a rather quaint thing- she scooped her arm through mine and led me through the busy streets of that town. It was virgin territory to me, and I compared myself, in an asinine way, to a tourist on a day's excursion to an unfamiliar resort. I tried to assess my surroundings and noticed before long how the people travelled around their town in those odd miniature vehicles, resembling a fairground ride in their design but having the same purpose as city trams (for that is what they appeared to be). I reminded myself to ask Lincoln later about their means of propulsion, for at that moment I was eager to investigate the array of other queer sights. Thus we continued with our walk, I befogged and tongue- tied, and she, apparently content with her credence of my tale of misplaced centuries, escorting me quite pragmatically and seemingly ignorant of the stares from the more bemused onlookers.

But within ten minutes we had arrived at a vast lime- coated structure, not dissimilar to the unattractive shopping centres of my own Time.

"This is where we shall eat," she affirmed, "and you shall also meet my people".

She obviously trusted me, and was only too willing to lead me inside.

It seemed odd to enter a building without any interaction with a door. There *was* no door. As I thought about it, I had spotted none on any of the buildings during our walk. Many had openings, but each was bereft of door or glass. It's marvellous how the mind can observe such trivialities when panic should reign supreme! As we entered through the ornate archway, my escort rolled a thinly- slatted wooden jalousie and clipped it to two hooks above her head. She urged me into a room beyond, a vast hall full of tables, chairs and cupboards. And, thankfully, people! The hall was fresh, too, and the off- white marble floor added to the coolness. It had been an unusually hot day, I thought, overbearingly hot, the sun companionless in a cloudless bed. And that storm! What weird natural phenomena now existed? I wondered if our slow dismantling of our ozone layer, always a subject of dispute amongst the scientists, had not now resulted in some extreme weather conditions. Presumably the heat had dispensed with the need for doors, but surely there had to be crime. Everywhere had crime. Or did it? Misdeeds had been perpetrated ever since the Bible told us of the Fall of Man. However, such irrelevant thoughts were not assisting my predicament. I *had* to keep my mind from thinking such-

"Ho!" sounded a powerful voice.

In front of me stood a man who was roughly my own height and build, but he was completely bald. In his early fifties I reckoned, he had piercing blue eyes that looked out from neat and very dark eyebrows. He wore shorts and sandals, and, like the fibrous tissue of a leaf, a vest made from some sort of flimsy cinnamon- coloured netting, all of which gleamed cleanly against his sun- darkened skin. His stare penetrated so fiercely, and petrified me to the spot, that for a moment I thought the Devil himself had been raised before me. His eyes bored into mine for what seemed like an age, and I felt as if I were on trial waiting for him to pass sentence on me. My mouth was dry as I struggled to swallow.

"You are the strange one."

To him, evidently.

And then he smiled, a warm smile that met the corners of his eyes.

"Yes," I replied, croaking apprehensively. Other than forgetting the bizarreness of the whole situation for a second, I can't understand why I should have chosen that moment to quip, "News really does travel fast around here".

Ignoring, but probably not through rudeness, my comment, he introduced himself:

"I am Edis, a Harvester and Overseer of the crops."

I told him my name, the catch in my voice still present, and held out my hand. His smile morphed into a lame grin; he clearly didn't understand the gesture. It must have been pure chance that the oddly named girl, Lincoln, had placed her palm in mine when we met.

"Come and sit", he said, and with a casual curl of his left hand, he directed me to a large wooden table.

I sat down on a metal chair, which I thought (somewhat irrelevantly) to be a strange contrast with the old wooden table. Lincoln patted me on my upper arm- perhaps to bolster me- and pointed to another chair, diagonally opposite me, where she would sit. Then she walked around the table and just stood by her seat. Behind her was another room and I caught a glimpse of someone walking past the opening carrying something. I presumed that the room was the kitchen. The fellow, Edis, sat across from me and to the left of Lincoln. He reached to the centre of the table for two beakers. They looked like crude pot and, I fancied as I took one from him, were brittle in their construction. Then I began to be aware of faces examining me, although I tried to avoid catching anyone's eye as I scanned the room by looking above their heads to the tops of the stark walls (which needed repainting). And higher still was a clear pyramid that flooded the room with light, supplementing any natural light that shone through the wall apertures.

"Bring us wine, Lincoln," Edis said, snapping me back to the moment.

"I will bring a full jug," she responded very obediently and also quite cheerfully. She walked from her chair and snaked between two nearby tables to a stone pedestal. Her submissive manner caused me to experience a fleeting feeling of unease, but I was in no position to have an opinion on the social aspects of this period, for I was the stranger here and I had to remember that. The girl was either in some form of paid employment, or else she was- I shuddered privately at the very thought- a slave! But *why* should I even care? Just an incidental thought, as arbitrary as a reflex action.

Back she came. Then, addressing me:

"Do you wish for wine?"

"Wine? Yes…yes please."

Lincoln poured some into my beaker and. Then she leaned across the table to Edis's beaker and pointlessly I found my eyes straying to the exposed contours of her breasts.

"I've a lot to ask you, but I think that you'll have questions for me also," I suggested to Edis.

Edis seemed oblivious to the wine that Lincoln was decanting into his beaker, and he merely regarded me with that same look, a look that was more probing than contentious.

"Yes," he answered. "Where- are- you- from? I know that you are not one of us. I know also that you have come from afar. Your clothes are…they are odd…you have hair; men have not had hair since the Passing, and you smell almost…like a *flower!*"

A man laughed at his words. I realised that he may be able to smell a deodorant or aftershave, although after two days I didn't think it would be possible.

"I know something else, too. Am I not right?" he enquired, as Lincoln sat down beside him.

"I think you do. I'm from another Time."

First the girl, now him; to how many others would I utter such nonsense? But that phrase he used, "*The Passing*", had set me thinking.

"You mentioned 'The Passing' just then. Please can you explain that to me. What's happened here? Where are all the things that I know…..*knew*….what is this place?"

"This is our town. We call it 'Mentarea', a name passed down through the generations. Has Lincoln told you that already? You asked what has happened."

I sat as still as a snapshot and he drew a long, slow breath, before continuing.

"There was a plague, many times ago, and most of our forefathers died. It is all…" He glanced to the floor, and then looked up again. "It is all '*a long time ago*'. Those words! They can be a preamble to a happy memory, or used to signify reluctance to discuss a sad one."

He swigged from his beaker, and I did the same, having forgotten, uncharacteristically, that I had the drink in front of me. It was potent, much stronger than any wine I had drunk before, and I coughed as the liquid whacked the back of my throat. I tried more, this time a fairly generous gulp. It was good. I wanted to see if Lincoln was drinking the same stuff, but I didn't want to look uninterested in his talk and I was fascinated of course.

"But what caused the plague…what carried it, I mean?"

"Rattus Norvegicus," he said calmly.

I was surprised to hear his use of the Latin term.

"Rats!" I exclaimed.

Then I paused.

"Yes, rats. The germ they carried was obscure, and it could not be defeated by Man. Man may not have created the recipe, but he supplied the ingredients and Nature created the result. Ultimately, only Nature could conquer it and its carriers."

"Rats again. How could *that* happen again? We all expected the atom bomb or …or a rogue meteorite. Rats! My God! Defeated by an old enemy."

I shook my head slowly. Perhaps they'd had a score to settle and the next time they had been prepared. Man's indifference to poisoning his surroundings had resulted in a terrible toll.

Edis continued, a dour expression on his face:

"We have learned this rhyme from previous generations:

'Rattus Norvegicus was its name;
We thought it came to steal our grain.
Instead it played a stealthy game,
And caused the plague of death to rain.'

Across on the next table, a child's eyes lit up on hearing the 'nursery rhyme.' I nodded:

"You could add another line, *'And we all fall down again.'* We had an old rhyme too, Edis; *'Ring-a-ring o' roses…'* It was composed in similar circumstances and would've been meaningless to most people of future generations, but known verbatim by children everywhere in…*in my Time.*"

I had said those words; I must be madder than I thought. Should this be pure fantasy, I would play along.

He elaborated:

"As the temperature on the earth increased, so too did the severe weather. Storms led to flooding and as the waters rose the rats sought solace above the ground where they could breed, roam and spread their disease."

"I'm guessing that the world was unprepared. How many died worldwide, is it known?"

"We do not know. All we know is that small and unconnected groups survived, finding isolated and abandoned towns and building their defences accordingly against the Plague carriers. Now you understand the reason for the wall. As our forefathers became the strongest group, people came from afar to live here and they would wait by the wall for permission to enter. But after many periods of bright moon, all journeys began to cease. So we remained here in this town. We have grown as one since then. We have used the materials that were left to us, and we look after each other. We have all we could desire. Could we ask for more?"

I did not know if this man, Edis, wanted me to answer. But I *did* respond.

"Since Time began, every man's wanted more than he has."

"*No!*" he contradicted me. I felt as if his eyes could have seared me with their glower. He continued: "Everyone *did* ask for more, but perhaps your people should have asked for guidance and protection instead."

I didn't relish the thought of heated discussion with this fervent and passionate man, and could already feel my body beginning to quake from released adrenalin. A silence ensued. Lincoln stood again, perhaps feeling some discomfort. Nervously, she rubbed her bare midriff.

"You do not need to leave. Sit, do," Edis said.

She sat down again. Little tints of light danced across her hair, and her face glowed a healthy copper. But now my senses were beginning to feel dulled by the wine, but despite the effects of the alcohol and my sheer exhaustion, the queerness of my surroundings and the fascination of the conversation were preventing me from succumbing to a much- needed slumber. Eyes wide, I shuffled in my seat, as I knew that I had not asked my obvious question, and enquired very calmly so as not to trip over my words:

"What year is this?"

Like a wary hound, Edis's face tightened.

"The term 'year' no longer means anything. Why should it be of use to us, other than to know that we work less in shorter suntimes? The Earth began again- you need to remember that now. The Passing began in Two-one- two- zero. But, as I am sure that you will be interested, I will ask that you be taken to the copper plates that show a number of 'two-zero-six-zero'. You must *also* remember that the plates themselves are very old, perhaps as old as twenty- five of the periods that it takes for a child to become an adult."

I was shaken by this rejolt as I did a rough calculation and surmised that I was somewhere in the early Twenty- Fifth Century!

How much more could I endure?

Lincoln had been sitting quietly, her ear attentive all the time. Occasionally her eyes would intumesce, and I noticed that her facial gestures, particularly the deportment of her chin and the flashing of her very white teeth, seemed to echo Edis's. It crossed my mind then that there may be something more to their relationship. But that was irrelevant- why I even thought such a thing at that moment, I don't know.

"Now you must eat," stated Edis. "You are not too tired to eat?"

"No- no, of course not. I'm hungry."

"Good, then we shall feast and you can meet some of the others."

'*Feast!*' I wondered if he had noticed my ears tauten at that very word.

It was almost a cue for Lincoln to rise from her chair and walk to the kitchen (for that's what I had gathered the room to be).

"I meant to ask who's in charge here; you must have a leader or ruler?" I ventured. "I think I should see them."

He looked surprised and his tone changed to that of mild refute.

"No, there is no-one that leads. If there were, would you be sitting here now talking with me? There are no kings and queens of old. There is no minister in his prime."

He stopped, and appeared to be trying to compose himself. It would certainly have been a solecism to acknowledge his unintentional play on words! Then he breathed:

"There is no *need* for such a role anymore, and no man nor woman here would be deserving of such power, nor even wanting such a burden. I have told you that we all care for each other, but there is more that you need to understand. We are a society of *workers*; I am a Farmer, one of many, and Leo, who will join us soon at our table, is a Cook. Lincoln is a Gatherer- fruit, leaves, mushrooms and anything that needs gathering. *You* are an unexpected find!"

He paused. I heard a blind tinkle in the evening breeze.

"We have Men of Science, Medicine too."

He patted his chair.

"And Recyclers of Metal. We have many who make clothes."

I became quite aware of my own clothing.

"Each works at their own skill. Look at this table…I could go and sit with Jeth and he could move to another table where he could drink from another beaker. But we all eat the same food and we dine in the same room. We work together as one; collective interaction."

I nodded, adding, "They say that's the first significant accomplishment of the Natural World."

"That is undoubtedly correct- in such a way are problems analysed, solutions pooled and obstacles overcome."

He could have been reading from a manual.

"No one group has authority over another- that is how we survive. We all need one another. Society had to adapt, and we could not afford the mistakes of the past. We do not hoard wealth, for we have no need of it. As I speak, forget what you know and let your thoughts roam; without wealth and aspirations there is no jealousy, and without envy there can be no crime. If there is no crime, there is no need for any punishment more severe than the chastisement of an unruly child. But I speak of no wealth! Foolish words for we are rich, of course, in the good things of life. Wealth is all around us; the finest foods, the most palatable drink and, of course, crops that thrive under a golden sun. Your lingering diseases of old have gone, and destruction of the Earth ceased so long ago."

I nodded, a perverse logic stinging me like a slap, as I said, "*I will restore unto you the years which the locusts have eaten.*"

Frowning, "Your words make no sense."

"They're not mine, but they're appropriate."

He arched an eyebrow:

"The wine finds favour with you I think!"

And he proceeded to refill my beaker.

I realised why Edis had looked as he did. Here existed an evidently successful society without hegemony and my question obviously had stirred an innate bitterness that he harboured in his breast. I felt certain that all these people would feel the same way; my generation, and many afterwards, had snatched all that was laid before us- we had acted like the spoiled child as we grabbed what we could without a thought for anyone else. Always, somebody would clear up after us. And always, of course, there would be a dessert course. Why should *we* have cared about the next- but- one generation? No point in saving for someone else's rainy day. We hadn't been *borrowing* the Earth from our grandchildren, as many had philosophised; we'd been helping ourselves- not merely dipping our fingers, but jemmying the whole drawer. What damage could we possibly inflict during our brief sojourn on the planet? Who, but a ridiculed few, really cared? We were as spores in the rolling acres of eternity. Always the

Earth would spin on its rotational axis, always, turning solidly, but eventually, for whom? We reaped the knowledge of centuries. Global communication and travel had shrunk the World, Science had advanced beyond all expectations, we were living longer, the West no longer knew hunger and many serious diseases had been eliminated. But what legacy had we been creating? We thought we were right, and we elected leaders who failed to prevent our slow dismantling of our own greatest inheritance, Mother Earth. And, I conjectured, after more decades of defiling our planet, we left ourselves exposed to something that had prospered whilst we grew obese on our greed and wanton in our neglect. And I began to wonder how we could have been so unprepared for something that would completely alter the course that Humanity was destined to take.

I was prevented from asking my next question by the sudden appearance of a small and animated procession of people that emerged from the kitchen. Lincoln led this curious band of newcomers, and she carried in both arms a huge wooden platter of food. At that moment, I believed in all honesty that I had never felt such hunger. And, if I wasn't mistaken, I recognised a familiar dish, its smell whisking me to childhood evenings of gravy boats and misted windows.

"Apple pie?" I braved, snatching at the opportunity to lift my thoughts, as a slender pair of bronzed feminine hands placed a sizeable pastry dish before me.

"Apples yes, but grapes, blackberries, herbs and dogspaws too", a resonant male voice sounded.

I looked for its source and noticed that the voice came from a tall, angular man of some sixty or so years in age. Clothed in a similar garb to Edis, the veins under his skin were so pronounced that they mapped an almost geographical route from his shoulders to the backs of his wiry hands, where they dispersed into a delta towards his bony knuckles. The structure of his whole face seemed to comprise a series of disproportioned triangles, like a badly- drawn cartoon character, his cheekbones pulled taut by some invisible wires, and his chin reaching in an opposite direction to a sharp point. So this was Leo the cook.

Edis affirmed by quizzing, "Leo prepares a good table. Am I right?"

"Well, this meal will certainly satisfy my hunger. But what are …er…dogspaws?"

"Have you *ne-ev-ver* tasted the dogspaw?" Leo asked, looking slightly incredulous, as a woman placed a candle near the centre of the table.

"The dogspaw grows in the forest and ripens under the sun. Throughout its brief flowering, Lincoln and many others work until moo- *oon*time to reap the fruit. *Ha!*" he boomed. "Never *tasted* the dogspaw!"

Despite his appearance, he had the demeanour of a full- bellied, port-blooded giant of a man, and he seemed the type who would hold a leg of mutton in one hand, and, whilst devouring it, give me an encouraging slap on my back with his other hand. He shrugged his thin shoulders, and with his parting words he seemed to almost mock me: "Enjoy your meal."

And I could have sworn that I saw him smirk.

A group of fifteen other people, consisting of twelve women and three men, joined us at the table. Lincoln seated herself back in her chair. She gave me a glance, as if to check that all was well, and then Edis began his introductions:

Ike was a wine-maker, and, thumbing a chink of normality, as one does in the middle of a wild dream, I found myself praising him for his excellent grape! He was clearly the eldest of the group and, as if to make up for the colour his hair would have been had he had any, he had eyes of a griseous tone.

But Edis's next words were unexpected.

"You have met one of my daughters, Lincoln."

My first impressions now flawed, I twitched.

"Now meet the other."

Gale, like Lincoln, was another finely shaped girl, and from beneath her neat chestnut fringe shone a pair of inky blue eyes that seemed to study me with curiosity. Her hair tumbled to her shoulders, where it kinked, just fractionally, as it touched the two slender straps that suspended a row of tassels that just preserved her modesty. Omas, younger than Ike by about ten years, was a Man of Medicine. Most of the other women, who ranged in age from about sixteen to thirty, shared Lincoln's trade. They also had a similar mane of dark hair- although none as deeply black as Lincoln's- and it caused me to ponder upon why the men were all hairless.

A bowl was placed in front of everyone, and Leo scooped out great helpings of the pastry- crowned fruit hash. I was handed a wooden spoon and I observed that the design of this basic utensil had remained unaltered after more than four hundred years. It was truly an outstanding meal, although it possessed a strong flavour, as if laced with a liqueur. I began to feel relaxed; the dogspaw obviously had peculiarly intoxicating qualities. Afterwards, two of the younger women left the table and disappeared into the kitchen. They emerged a moment later carrying between them a large metal crucible that they placed on the table. Steam was rising from it and I could see the little beads of moisture on their foreheads. But a sweet smell had permeated my nostrils.

"What *is* that?" I enquired.

Edis explained, his eyes burning as brightly as the wick in the pot of wax on the table, "That is honey. You will discover that it is part of the very life- blood of our society, for it has many features. This is just one of its benefits."

And the two young women, whose names I was never told, began to dole out huge ladles of the sickly piping stuff. Lincoln must have anticipated my next question, for she reached to one of the jugs of water and poured it over my dish. Everyone else was doing the same thing. And I watched as they ate large dollops of the cooling syrup. I tried a mouthful, but that was enough for me. I recall being content, conversely so, to just watch aghast as Lincoln savoured every draught, the treacly residue glistening on her lips.

"Why do you eat so much of it?" I asked, risking offending my unusual hosts.

"Honey has healing properties, and our Men of Science and Medicine have learned to use it, and the plants within the forest, for the purpose Nature intended. I think there is much to show you of …*our* Time."

Yes, there would no doubt be much I could see, but I was shattered and, without thinking to keep myself in check, I let out a huge yawn which seemed to amuse most of those at the table.

"We shall find you a rest- mat for moontime."

It was a curious expression that both Leo and Edis had used to describe the night, but I was past caring about any further puzzles for today. All awareness was disappearing rapidly from my mind, draining like the failing sunlight outside and drenching my senses in shadow. I needed no further encouragement; I just wanted to sleep.

"Lincoln will show you to your cell," he continued.

My God, a *cell*…whatever next…was I a prisoner here, or was it just an idiom, another illustration of the changes that had encompassed me in this uncharted province?

CHAPTER 4: *In The Darkest Hour*

Lincoln beckoned me to follow her, and, having excused myself from the assemblage, I accompanied her to a hallway to the left of the kitchen. She stepped inside. I followed and she stopped.

"Now you have met all of my family, for our mother is gone."

"Gone? Died, you mean?"

"Yes, she died."

I had met this girl just hours earlier and now she was sharing such personal details with me.

"Ohh...I'm sorry. When?"

"When I stood and she could clasp my face to her waist."

She lowered and hovered her hand to illustrate. Her eyes had begun to film over and- surely not- *had altered in hue to a dark blue*. She forced a somewhat crooked smile and said, "Come."

I walked with her down the corridor that was lit by intermittently placed lamps that cast enough light for me to snatch glimpses of my surroundings. The passageway seemed uneven. As I ran my hand over its surface, I felt that it was hewn from a rough plaster that seemed almost out of place in the finely- aligned walls of the structure that I had entered more than three hours earlier. A green luminescence pervaded our route, and I stopped to look at one of the wall- mounted lamps in an effort to fathom its power source. On closer inspection, I noticed that the light was flickering, pulsating rhythmically, and I peered over the rim of the frosted shade. I could have been forgiven for blenching at the sight- inside the shade and working diligently whilst manipulating a piece of foliage, was a handful of strange looking beetles, each emitting a bright green glow from its abdomen. Lincoln had stopped to wait for me, as she seemed to understand my desire to investigate such unfamiliar things.

"Blaze- beetles; the more they eat, the brighter they glow."

"*Blaze- beetles*! But what the...no, never mind."

A few yards further on, she pointed, and I was aware that the light had altered in hue. We were entering a vast open area that was awash with the glow from a galaxy of candles, each one quivering and twitching in that yawning chamber.

She spoke:

"This is where the town sleeps; we call it the Chapel of Rest."

Standing there in that peaceful and soul- warming place, and hearing her call it by its totally unsound epithet- a name obviously passed down throughout the generations so that its original meaning had become lost-the tiniest flicker of warped amusement darted through my mind.

The space was huge. A large stone circle, connected by numerous railed ramparts, lay at its centre. Downwards, it stretched into a deep chasm – some forty feet or so, I hazarded- and, gazing in that gothic half-light, the view left me feeling somewhat giddy. Upwards, I estimated that we stood a distance of about eighty feet from the crystal roof. The whole area was divided into cubicles, and I could not begin to guess how many hundreds- maybe more- of these sleeping bays there existed.

"*The cells!*" I uttered.

"Your face shows the concern of a child. Why?"

"I just know a cell to be a *prison* cell...when your father spoke, I thought I were to be incarcerated as some sort of punishment," I attempted to explain to her. I needed no more shocks, and sighed simply then asked, "Lincoln, where will I *sleep*?" That was all I really wanted to know at that moment.

"Come," she directed me again. "You will stay in the cell next to mine."

She took my arm again in that rather reassuring way, and led me to a flight of hard steps. But before ascending that staircase, she snaked her hand to a row of fabric- fronted cubicles, the blinds to several of which were furled. I stopped to look inside one. There stood the most functional latrine that I had ever seen- well, in my own country, anyway- comprising just a stone block with a circular hole in its surface. Adjacent to it was a curved stone sink- cracked, I noticed- with a small drinking-fountain, which doubled as a tap, above it. Some soap lay in a dip, and two or three other outlets from the repaired piping projected at differing heights. However, if my description sounds less than salubrious, I should add that the lavatory/ wash- room was spotlessly clean and delightfully sweet- smelling. The room itself was immersed in orange candle glow.

"These rooms are lit all through moontime, as is the staircase," she reassured me.

We climbed to a ledge some forty feet up, where she stopped and took from the pocket adjacent to her belt- buckle a small metal utensil, shaped like the "7" of a lamb- chop bone, which she then promptly raised and slit the fabric of the cell that was immediately in front of us. She pulled the canopy apart and, holding it aloft, motioned me to enter. As I did so, the fabric flapped against my cheek, and it felt tacky as it glanced my skin. Lincoln followed me and then said, "Watch."

She then replaced the cut flap against its counterpart and I stared in disbelief as the two sides fused, blended- almost *melted*- to become one again. Without further ado, moving to the foot of my 'bed', she repeated the process on the cell's left- hand wall. She then said rather convolutedly, "May the moon keep you in sleep."

Her eyes now jet, she made a face between a frown and a grin before stepping through the fresh opening. She sealed the wall in the same way as the 'door'. The process was not unlike the fastening of a zip on a canvas tent awning.

So there was I, alone once more. Oddly, there was no pillow on my 'bed', so I rolled my weatherproof coat into a rough cushion, and prepared to lie down on that mattress of reeds. As I shuffled over onto my side, I began to think just how far I had come- how inexplicably far- in an unfettered thread of time. Yes, that was it- nothing more than a strand of time, its elasticity stretched irreparably. There is a strange anomaly that, no matter how exhausted one is, or how well one anticipates that one will sleep, one will often awaken suddenly after just a few hours. I don't know what stirred me, for, strangely, I had not been dreaming. Although I did not have a headache, I had developed a raging thirst. Past experiences in my life meant that I was no stranger to this condition. The night was dark; I could hear no sound, and I wondered what time it could be. I flicked the button on my torch and my watch told me that it was now a little after three. I shone the beam around the space. Strange draped walls, not quite real. Shining almost. At that instant, recognition of my surroundings was as far away as the new dawn. But then came revelation by torchlight, as I began to recognise the chamber into which the girl, Lincoln, had led me some time earlier. Grasping my rucksack that I had placed next to my 'pillow', I rooted for my flask. The water had become warm and tasted almost stale, but it quenched my thirst. Then I took another sweet from the crumpled paper bag. Although I had no desire at that moment to leave the cell, I considered how I should exit once daylight usurped the thin slither of moon. Whether somebody would call to rouse me, or I should sit in this womb crying for release, perhaps waiting for a man in a white coat to return my sanity to me with an illegible prescription, remained to be seen. The small hours of the morning and already I was fretting about my new day!

*

It was the sound of viscous fabric being disjoined- perhaps no louder than a plaster being ripped from shocked flesh- that woke me, and I finished rubbing my eyes in time to see Lincoln executing the same curious process that I had witnessed late last night. She was clad in the same scanty white cotton top into which she had changed the day before, the familiar loincloth about her waist, and I noticed how radiant she looked in the raw streak of sunlight that passed through the overhead clear dome and seduced the gigantic place with a morning ambience. And her eyes blazed bright blue again!

"You are well rested?" she greeted me.

I was grateful that I had slept in my clothes!

"Good morning," I said, forgetting that such a term had probably disappeared into obscurity. "Yes, I slept well". There seemed no point in telling her that I had woken briefly.

"You are to join us for a meal this sun...for there is much more for you to see, and we shall hear of your Time- we hope that *you* will want to tell *us* many things also, although I should like it if only *I* could hear of... of such things," she said, flicking her dark hair.

"Thank you, I'm certain that it'll be as tasty a meal as yesterday," I predicted, "and I'll answer any questions that you- or anyone else- may have about me."

"Our food is always good, and later this suntime you shall have a choice of fare," she promised, giving a little smile, and I truly believed that she wanted me to be pleased.

"But first, there are boiled eggs for you."

She turned, took a pace to the side, bent down to retrieve something, straightened and trooped back to the cleaved fabric holding a circular wooden tray on which stood three eggs, each sitting snugly in a wooden cup, a slab of bread, a pot of sauce and an odd- looking drink.

"May I enter?"

I sat up, and leant back against the only solid edge, the concrete wall of the strange complex.

"Of course...please...yes."

So in she came.

"Lincoln, your eyes changed colour when you left me last...last night. Do you wear lenses? No, not that...but how?"

"Ohh, I have seen your wonderment. Why do you not know? The eyes of a female change between sun and moon."

"What! How? I mean *why*...how?"

"It has always been so," she replied so meekly.

"No it hasn't. Something to do with the sun, the heat here, I don't know."

She looked to the tray and I felt that she wanted me to begin.

It was a modest, but much- welcomed, breakfast, although I was unable to discern the flavour of the sauce into which I had dipped my bread. The drink, I would learn later, was a coffee substitute made from the seeds and leaves of an obscure yellow flower.

Lincoln had waited calmly whilst I breakfasted. When I finished, I slipped on my shoes- they seemed strangely ill- fitting now. She eyed them curiously. As I tied my laces, I glanced at her sandals. There was a thin strip of fabric banded around her toes, stretching up her foot to a neat buckle, and a piece of cord tied around her ankle. And was that really bamboo on her soles? Then I told her I was ready. But before we left, I did something that was completely futile, more out of habit than vanity I should hope, and I noticed how Lincoln stared incredulously, fascinated by my act; I had run a comb through my hair! She asked to hold it and I placed it in her hand. I noticed again how thickly, but precisely, her hair grew and I could only guess that these females had no need for such a device. She gave it back to me, smiling approval. I sensed that she felt rather satisfied with herself for having studied this unusual object. My thoughts turned to the torch and bag of sweets in my rucksack, as well as the currency of my Time, but I thought that she might appreciate being shown those items on another occasion. She raised the strange partition above my head, and I ventured out onto the communal balcony.

A set of railings, some four feet high, scrap metal that had been welded together asymmetrically by the 'Recyclers of Metal', had been placed at the edge of the terrace, obviously for safety. Below us, on the huge circular stone 'island', people were milling around in much the same way as theatre- goers during an interval, perhaps greeting each other at the start of the new day, and most were heading in the direction of any one of several doorways. I surmised that each of these doorways led to a tunnel just like the one along which I had been led.

"Come," she said in that familiar and unruffled manner, and led me back down the stairway. She waited whilst I attended to more personal matters. I should have loved to shave as, with three days' growth, I must have been looking rather scruffy- compared to the other men, anyway!

I was surprised when we didn't retrace our steps from the night before, but instead she escorted me towards a large stone entryway. We walked for several feet, turned a corner and emerged into glorious mid-morn brightness.

CHAPTER 5: *Life And Death*

"I shall show you around our town," she said, and I anticipated that it would be a fascinating morning. "We shall travel on a magnasule," she continued, and gestured towards one of the peculiar carriages that had almost hit me the day before. The little capsule- shaped vehicle lay motionless on one of a pair of metal tracks several yards away. Lincoln marched purposefully towards it; she bent down, flipped it onto its side, and slid a metal catch that lay on its flat and rusted underbelly. She then pulled the carriage back to her and released her hold. In an instant, the contraption floated upwards by about four feet. For the first time I noticed that, aside from her almost impenetrable beauty, Lincoln possessed a feral agility, bordering on being lupine in nature, as I watched her place both hands on the side, propel herself upwards and clear the edge of the vehicle in one fluid movement. The craft wobbled and tirled whilst she reached inside to a hidden control, which lowered her to a distance of a couple of feet.

"Come," she invited me, and I joined her in the carriage.

With another flick of a switch, we were about seven feet from the ground.

"Lincoln," I urged, "you really must explain to me how this works. What's moving us, and why don't we fall?"

"The magnasule is powered by sunlight. Magnets control the height at which we travel above the magnarail; polarities repel, and we rise. They attract, and we drop to the ground."

I was wondering about the existence of some form of feedback circuitry and had expected to be told more- *anybody* would- but from this well- intentioned girl's apparent simplistic point of view, that *was* really all there was to it!

We were travelling at a fairly slow velocity, and I assumed that the speed was for my benefit in order that I could view the many sights of the picturesque environment. It was one of the most unusual things that I had ever experienced. About us lay the queer structures and delicate minarets that I had witnessed from the summit of that hill only yesterday. At one point, we passed so close to the wall that I noticed that odd stones had strange patterns and even traces of lime on them, and further on, set unceremoniously into the wall, was a hideous and weathered old gargoyle. The builders had obviously used recycled materials, just as our medieval masons salvaged Roman stone to incorporate in the construction of their churches. But it was not a time for noticing such architectural details, as people pointing, staring or just simply grinning at us distracted me continually. Small children ran gaily, as they always have done, a dog lounged ahead of us in the late morning sun, next a cat in the shade, and people thronged the footways of this busy community. New clothes and various acquisitions were draped over shoulders, whilst reed baskets, brimming quaintly with fruit and vegetables and other wares, swung from bare brown arms. As well as people, the whole area too was alive with an aroma which was difficult to describe- it was a pleasant, earthy smell, the type of clean and untainted natural redolence for which one would need to search in my own Time; it seemed to douse my senses as it swirled about us almost like water round a plughole. In the bustling crowd, a woman dropped an orange. She never even noticed. It bounced, just once I think, and rolled. Lincoln did something with a control lever. We were slowing down. I saw a boy scuttle to pick up the orange as Lincoln spoke:

"The falcon above us lives in that old tower."

"Eh?"

I looked up.

"There is no bird that flies as fast. Ohh, to move like the falcon!" she breathed.

The bird wheeled purposefully and glided gloriously into a small aperture. Then I scanned the crowd again; it was a shock to see that the boys, seemingly heavily outnumbered by the girls, were hairless likes their fathers and I turned to Lincoln, with the intention of asking for the reason for their baldness. But no sooner had my jaw begun to move than I felt the magnasule jerk very slightly and then we stopped. Lincoln pressed a small control and we descended gently to the ground. The instant we left the vehicle, two young boys approached and grabbed the opportunity to use it. We crossed the metal track, and I took great care to check on that occasion. Lincoln gestured towards a semi- circle of caverns, their low tiled roofs pocked with dark green mosses and yellow stone- crop, that lay several yards from us adjacent to a large mesh enclosure full of clucking hens. Each of the chambers protruded from a central campanile. As we walked towards the chambers, I observed that each one was stacked with everyday provisions and utensils. We were, I assumed, on the main thoroughfare of this town. Lincoln attracted my attention to one grotto in particular that was filled with clothing and proceeded to usher me to it. Everywhere lay piles of clothes, but the range of styles and colours was limited mainly to shades of brown, beige and white, although I did notice one or two other colours, such as olive-green and berry- red. She looked me up and down for a moment, emitted a fizzle of satisfaction, and then proceeded to select a pair of sandals, some flimsy sleeveless vests and two pairs of slack cotton shorts. She then took a bag from the shelf, and placed the garments inside. I told her I that I was grateful, and we turned to leave, although there was something I had to query.

"Lincoln," I said, "in my Time you'd have needed to pay for these items."

A look of perplexity crossed her face.

"Money…" I thought about Edis's words. "I mean, something in return, a trade…you've just taken these goods…that would've been theft."

"No!" She looked somewhat bemused. "Remember the words of my father; here, we all provide for each other. The person who fashioned these clothes may have already enjoyed the berries that I gathered, and when I go to collect the mushrooms from the forest, it may be boots made by his own hands that protect my feet from thorns," she reasoned, perhaps inflexibly. I couldn't really argue with the spartan logic of these people; practical and reasonable certainly- successful, undoubtedly- but definitely not a sound concept for my Twenty- First Century Western civilisation.

As we exited that well- stocked clothing outlet- I can think of no better terminology to describe it- a familiar sound distracted me, and I jerked my head sharply to see Friday bounding in our direction. He leapt at Lincoln with alacrity, and having greeted her, he turned to me for similar attention.

"The dog remembers you!" my companion said.

"Does he have a name?" I asked her.

"No-o-o…he is a dog…a dog has no name!" she replied quite seriously, as if I had asked an absurd question.

"In my Time, Lincoln, all pets had names… dogs, cats, goldfish…" I elucidated.

"You would name a dog? And a cat? *Humph*! Why? And a fish made of *gold*?"

"Well, it's true, and I've called this dog 'Friday', for reasons that I may explain to you sometime," I said, still amused by her last words.

So we spent another half- hour or so browsing those little grottos, Friday following close behind. Lincoln picked up an assortment of essentials, including fruit, a rather smart basket and a glass bottle. She seemed taken aback when I offered to relieve her of her load.

"Why should you wish to do such a thing for me?" she asked, almost suspiciously.

"Well, I feel slightly useless walking about empty- handed, whilst you …" I chose my words carefully, "…you have shopp…things to carry."

"But I am strong and am without injury," she remonstrated.

"I know that. It's just something that a man likes to do for a woman." I had regretted my offer.

She paused for a few seconds and I watched as her brow gradually loosened, the tiny lines around the corners of her eyes all but disappearing again.

"Yes, I will let you carry these things." Her next words confirmed my thought: "But no man has ever asked such of me before."

We continued on our tour of the town, and I enjoyed looking at all the unusual buildings, including one odd edifice made entirely from red sandstone, and, under the ceaseless assault from the elements, the stone had become so worn that it had morphed to resemble a stodgy cream. The building was, Lincoln explained, their granary. As she pointed to the different structures, I learned that people no longer lived in houses, as I knew them, but just shared the facilities of the conurbation. By far the most prominent structure was the huge domestic complex in which I had eaten and slept, comprising the Great Hall, as Lincoln called it, and, of course, the Chapel of Rest. It served the whole town, she told me. Like the proudest city landmark, its patchy whitewashed walls never appeared to be far from our sight, and I conjectured that it must have been about half a mile square. It was colossal. The circle of 'shops' I have already described, but the dozens of pretty towers, with their roofs of metal and crystal, were a designer's dream and would have rivalled many of the finest creations that I had known from my bygone era. Lincoln explained that they predated the advent of The Passing, so I was able to date them to a period between approximately 2020 and the year that Edis said the plague started, 2120 AD. She also said that, rather sadly I thought, most of them were now disused. They had been the houses of a long- ago generation, and they remained remarkably well preserved. Wisteria and clematis had crept up the walls, and other plants, including jasmine and wild roses, had seeded themselves around the bases. Some of the structures had been given a new lease of life as workshops, and Lincoln pointed to one, surrounded with crates of fruit, where a man was busy loading some small sacks onto a sturdy one- wheeled cart. These fascinating constructions had become like parting words, the last entries that Man of Old was to leave in Society's journal. Furthermore, I reflected on what had happened to all the technology that had advanced relentlessly once the silicon fuse had been lit towards the end of the Twentieth Century, finally exploding in the early years of the next Millennium. Of course, we had been travelling too fast as each day saw an improvement on the previous day's invention. Where was it going to end, many had wondered. Changes, always changes; so- called improvements, even to the smallest of things. I used to find myself disapproving of many of the slightest changes, such as how *many* times a toothbrush could be improved. What other innovations had awaited us? The New Dawn had brought with it, eventually, a pestilence, and with that Disease had come the suffering of a bloody Apocalypse. The rats were all gone now. Like the human exterminator who arrives to poison their lair, they too had visited with a purpose, done their fetid deed, and fled, their aim achieved.

Perhaps it was good that Lincoln interrupted my thoughts when she did:

"Come. I will show you inside one of the towers."

We had stopped by a most charming structure. Built from what I believed to be Portland stone, the tiered steeple rose some sixty feet into the air from a square base. Again, there was no door to open, and Lincoln took the three weathered steps to the entrance in a single stride. Naturally well ventilated, and also pleasantly light, the large room into which I followed her had at one time, I supposed, been an open- plan living area for a family of the Future. Placed clumsily in the centre of the room stood a sturdy metal ladder. But it was no traditional ladder- it resembled a fireman's pole with functional joists protruding at regular intervals.

"Come," she smiled, and proceeded to ascend that strange staircase. I have already remarked on Lincoln's agility, and it came as no surprise to me to see how nimbly she clambered up that post. She disappeared through the orifice above, and I climbed to join her. She was standing next to the opening with a grin on her face as I caught up with her; I think she realised that I was slightly in awe of her light-footedness. The room was now much narrower, and we were now standing on top of the base. Cobwebs hung from the ceiling, and old twigs and pieces of straw littered the ground. Some of the lime still clung to the walls in places, but in other parts there were signs of decay where the stonework had chipped. I wondered about the people that had lived here, and even when this house had been constructed. Would this impressive building have been the home of a rich man? Unlikely though, unless most of the folk had been wealthy, because I had already spied many more like it. How had people lived just before the Passing? And what had happened to make a future generation all move into a gigantic complex, living and functioning as one? There were many questions to which I doubted that I should ever discover answers. I reflected on the time that must have passed since these monumental dwellings had last been inhabited. It was indeed an unparagoned feeling surveying the room at that moment. There was I, an invader from another Time, a trespasser from the wrong neighbourhood, standing at a stranger's hearth and imagining the ghosts that once drew breath. But to Lincoln, who positively radiated vitality, *my* presence must have held her in an unearthly embrace. For me, in no more time than it takes to snuff one of Lincoln's candles, about four hundred years of Mankind had gone. Those years were vanished, and only the faintest trace of their vapour was left drifting on a silken breeze.

"Shall we go up again?" I asked.

But she just said once more, "Come."

I went first up that quirky pole on this occasion with slightly more confidence. The third level, or second floor, apart from being narrower still, was much the same as the previous one. The designer had, however, had the foresight to install larger windows (the glass had long since gone) and Lincoln was right about the view, even from this one higher floor. Down below, I could see the unassuming folk of Mentarea going about their uncomplicated lives: a rather hefty middle- aged man was struggling with two sacks of goods, two young girls were strolling along, gesticulating as they talked, a small boy was darting between his parents as they walked and two men, somewhere in their thirties I imagined, appeared to be engaged in a deep conversation about…well, about whatever such men did talk about here. And then Lincoln said with more than a hint of intrigue:

"Ahhh, I see Gale!"

I moved to the edge of the aperture where she was standing.

"You must have sharp eyes," I commented.

"Sharp? Eyes cannot be sharp. How can they be so?" she challenged, and again her celeste eyes crinkled in that girlish way.

"No, no…they're not sharp like a knife…they're healthy and strong eyes- you have good eyesight. It's just something we say…*said* in my Time!"

I followed her pointing finger and could just discern Gale. She was chatting to a male friend.

"It seems your sister may have an admirer," I quipped.

"Yes, Gale speaks with a man, Jose, who causes her to have good thoughts."

I wanted to ask Lincoln if she had a man in her life, but decided against such an intrusion. Although I tried to discard such a thought, I actually found myself hoping, like a preoccupied schoolboy, that there *was* no- one.

"Come," she commanded, changing the subject. "Let us go to the last level. From the top you can see for a great distance."

Up we went again, this time into a very small 'attic'.

"I was thinking, Lincoln," I said to her as we stood together on the highest floor of that tower, "if I'd lived in a house like this in my Time, I should have been considered an eccentric...odd, quirky...because I know of no house that was designed like this."

"Tell me of your...*howsse*," she said, as if she had been waiting for such an opportunity.

"Oh...small, two bedrooms- somewhat like your sleeping cells- an old- fashioned kitchen, piles of books everywhere. But it was built of brick, and it was therefore an investment!"

I thought of how hard I had laboured to acquire that little place. It was better than some, inferior to many, but it was mine. Now, I had gleaned, no one individual possessed more than another.

"Could you live here?" she asked.

"Well...it would need some attention, but it's not a bad place."

I crossed the floor.

"And the view is fabulous! Are they open to offers?" I laughed.

She batted her eyes, a chink in her enamel.

I looked through the open aperture, across the expanse of buildings, over the farmland and aloft the wall to the boundless rolling hills that breasted the horizon.

"What *is* out there, Lincoln? I saw hardly anything; does no- one *ever* go?"

As she stood by me, her arm glanced against mine and I caught the scent of her sweet aroma.

"It is Otherland. I have told you that no-one lives there. We do not know what exists, for there is no need to go there," she said quite glibly.

"I wonder...," I sighed, my hopes somewhat crushed.

We spent a good fifteen minutes or so just gazing from the apertures, and pointing to the other towers and distinctive features of the town.

And then Lincoln said, "Come. You will eat with us again."

We descended the tower (which I found to be far easier than my ascent) and strolled to the nearest magnasule. Lincoln repeated the starting operation, and, once again, like a sprightly kevel, boarded the vehicle in her supple way, then motioned me to climb aboard. Within a few minutes we were back at the main complex.

As we walked back down that familiar corridor, the daylight seeping in sparingly, Lincoln asked me, "Do you like Mentarea?"

"I do, yes," I told her. "I've never seen a place like this before, and I'm grateful to you for showing me around."

"What is your town like?"

I hadn't anticipated that question, although it seemed only reasonable that she should wish to know.

"Busy, noisy. Forever altering, too, although never for the better. Very ugly in places, very beautiful in others. I've seen a lot of beautiful things since I arrived here."

I felt my voice brandle, and I was aware that I had flushed slightly. I was enjoying my day, masticating every minute, and, perversely, I felt a surge of disappointment as we reached our dining area!

A tempting smell was drifting from the kitchen, but before I could ask Lincoln what we would be eating, I saw that a man had shot from the nearby table. Lincoln stopped and I did too. Still clutching his beaker in his left hand, he paced from his seat before Edis had even spied us, and fixed his gaze on me. He nodded slightly when he saw my hair and stubble growth.

"You are the Storm Traveller!"

It was not a question, but an exclamation, and I had, it seemed, been rechristened!

"Y-e-e-ss."

"I am Isaac, a Man of- ahem- Science."

I told him my name, although Edis had obviously already furnished him with that information.

"Come and tell me all about you," he cried, and walked back to the table. He was a small man, perhaps five feet six, and he had a ruddy complexion that spread, like madder on a yarn, to an incubating dewlap. Little purple marks dotted his cheeks and forehead and I recognised the effects of a man who clearly enjoyed his drink. As if to confirm my suspicion, he held his beaker towards Gale and, without his even saying a word, she topped up the container with a generous splash of a golden liquid. His hand swayed slightly, and he was unmindful of the fact that some of the juice had spilled onto the marble floor. Gale emitted a little sound of impatience, picked up a cloth from a side table, and, as unflurried as a conjurer's assistant, proceeded to mop it up.

Lincoln walked to one of the stone pedestals, poured two vessels of the drink and handed one to me. Isaac had turned to resume his seat, and Lincoln and I joined him and the others at the table.

"Tell me of your travel here. My knowledge needs to grow, and you can water the seeds that were sown when I fastened sandals around younger feet," he began as soon as I sat down. He spoke in an almost theatrical manner. I sipped from my beaker; it was an unsweetened cider. Strong, too, no doubt!

"Well, where should I begin?" I asked.

"I am referring to our two visitors from long ago; I believe that they came to us in the same way that you are here this sun. I presume that you have been told of them already?"

"Yes, Lincoln's mentioned them."

He shuffled and pointed his hands towards me in classic listening mode.

"Begin do."

I hesitated.

"Ahem...*before* the sun vanishes!" he said.

"In my Time, I went walking. I like walking, it's always been a form of...er... relaxation to me."

"You walk to relax? Ha! I prefer to sit!"

Upon which he waved his hand with impatience, as if to swat an invisible fly.

"So two days ago, I had gone for a walk in the countryside, and I crossed an area of moor..."

"Crossed an area of...*maww*!" he squeaked.

"The moor...yes, it's an area of uncultivated land. Surely you've such a place today, perhaps not far from here? You see... I don't even know *where* I am. Your town, Mentarea, didn't exist in my Time..." I knew that I was digressing, so continued. "It was a sunny day, just like today- well, cooler- with barely a cloud in the sky. But unexpectedly, the weather changed, and the sky darkened. It happened so suddenly."

"And what did you do when the sky changed from blue?"

"Just looked for shelter. I got pretty wet. I found a rocky outcrop, but I don't recall much after that. I just remember a tingling sensation in my hands, and an intense headache, as if the atmosphere were...well...*charged* in some way. You're asking me to explain the unexplainable..."

Isaac's head had been bobbing rhythmically all the time.

"As I have intimated, I have gaps in my knowledge. Reverting to the two strangers; when they came, I had youth. I am a much *older* Man of Science now," he added. Despite his advancing years, he exhibited a mixture of frustration and eagerness, like the child in the sweet shop who is too small to view the delights on the counter. "My colleagues who witnessed the events of that time have now crossed that mysterious murky river that flows between Life and Death. But I remember it as if it were just two moons ago! Those strangers were of an age close to mine at the time- young! With covered legs and darker colours, they were dressed like you. Also, like them, you appear to have traversed innumerable ages in the time it takes me to...to what...Ohh...to choose a wine! How...can it...be so?" he asked, almost wretchedly, and I believe that he knew that those cavities in his knowledge would remain unplugged.

I prepared to answer him, but the situation slipped further into unreality, and, at that instant, I felt like the train passenger who is snatched from his motion- induced bliss. Misquoted gleanings and hypothetical snippets, often born in that fertile soil of pub conversation, tumbled like white rapids through my mind. Here, an atomic clock on a plane...there, the circumnavigation of the globe at- what was it? - twice the speed of light?...everywhere, the river of Time with its tributaries...

Isaac tutted, shifted his hands at last and spread them on the table.

"All I know, Isaac, is that I came...came on a storm."

"You came on a storm. So be it. There is obviously nothing more to say about your journey here."

He sighed with disappointment, stood, walked doggedly between two tables to another room and disappeared inside. He emerged a moment later carrying something and placed a roll of tattered cloth in front of me. He undid the old rope and unfurled the bundle. Spreading as awkwardly as the feathers on a wounded sea- bird, the ends of the mothy old cloth unrolled and curled against the table- top. I was stunned by what I saw. Battered, but still instantly recognisable, were two military hats; to be precise, they were soldiers' helmets- Brodies from the First World War!

Lincoln looked slightly perturbed when she saw my reaction, and I regained my composure quickly. Isaac clearly looked expectant, and I supposed that he must have waited some forty years for answers:

"These are from your Time? Later…earlier? Do you *recognise* them?" he shelled.

"Oh yes, I recognise them."

"Well…?" he almost yelped with anticipation.

"They're helmets that were worn by military men. Isaac, your two visitors were soldiers! What happened to them? I know that they were ill, but how long did they live?"

"*Souldyers*…you must explain."

"*Explain?* Surely you…"

I stopped as he began to drum his fingers noisily on the table.

"A soldier is someone who fights for his rights, his beliefs…his freedom," I tried to clarify.

"Do you hear his words, Edis?" he asked as turned to his stern friend.

Edis frowned, but said nothing.

"You will tell me later why anyone would fight for his…his…freedom," continued Isaac. "We are all free- why should anyone fight like two boys tussling over a toy? Those Men of *Fight* were ill from gas. That is what they told us…that is almost all they *could* tell us. We made them welcome. We fed them. We watered them. But they lived just long enough to manage a meal. Then they died; one first, and the other followed. I talked with other Men of Science about the strangers. Where did they come from? How did they arrive here? Did their journey kill them, or was it something made by the hands of Man- the gas- that ended their lives? They are gone now, but they left us this."

And he placed another parcel before me on the table. The second parcel contained the personal effects of the men: two canteens, a diary, an engraved pen, some coins- foreign, I noticed- and a handful of other items. I learned that the soldiers had been called Hugh Chadwick and Edward Jones. Those two poor men- *barely* men- were lost forever, or "missing in action" their mothers would have read. But the last item that Isaac removed interested me the most. Bound in leather, and clasped with a minute bronze hook, was a small bible. It was a sobering thought to realise that there remained possibly one such volume throughout the whole of the land.

Our discussion was cut short again as a large tureen of thick steaming soup was placed before us. There followed an even bigger pot of stewed vegetables and possibly dumplings. Then next to them both was deposited a dish of what looked like cold bread pudding, topped with sliced fruit. A pitcher of wine, similar in size to a Methuselah, was positioned in the centre of the table, and I knew that I would soon be sampling another delightful meal. Lincoln was true to her word about the choice, and I opted for the lumpy soup. Various other guests sat with us, although I noticed that Gale had seated herself at an adjoining table. Gradually the great communal hall began to fill with people, and it reminded me of a busy school dinnertime when one hears the cacophony of a myriad of utensils as they clatter against the crockery. Last night had been a more restrained affair.

Lincoln sat across from me this time, and, though graceful in many ways, she clearly lacked refinement at the table. In fact, nobody seemed to bother when morsels of stray fruit slipped from their plates to the table surface.

Another hour was spent in conversation with Isaac and Edis who continued to ask about the Great War. It was clear that they found the whole notion incomprehensible, and, as they were ignorant of timescales from a period so long ago, I sensed that they believed initially that I had been witness to those catastrophic events in the Earth's history.

"Why did you not share what you had and live together as one?" Edis's question was almost infantile, and yet, as happens so habitually when grilled by the youngest of children, I struggled to find an answer. I told them what I knew of that war and also the Second World War and the Holocaust. Then I recounted the events of later conflicts. After a while, their questions and demands ceased, and they sat in at the table in a sort of stupefied silence, Edis wearing an expression of wide- eyed incredulity and Isaac's glassy pupils peering at me from his ripened face. Despite the horror that had spewed from my lips, Edis still wanted to show me the graves of those two unfortunate casualties of war.

And thus our conversation ceased. Edis stood, and said, "Come and see where they lie, they who escaped that carnage only to die in another Time and Place!"

Lincoln, who had moved to join her sister and a girlfriend, returned my smile- concernedly, I thought- as Edis and I walked out of the Hall, leaving Isaac alone at our table tilting his beaker. Edis pointed to an idle magnasule, and instructed me to accompany him. Although he was not as adept as Lincoln at climbing into the machine, we were, however, soon skimming above the track. It seemed that no sooner had we set off than we were slowing down again, such was the speed of these little machines. We had been travelling northwards, and had now reached the perimeter of the town for I could see the loose stones on top of the old wall. We dismounted, and walked through an arch within a hedge. It was difficult to fathom the stunning sight that I saw at that moment. Twinkling, dazzling and all appearing to dissolve into one another as they morphed in the afternoon haze, lay a field of coloured glass rods, looking rather like upturned wine bottles.

Edis seemed to have been anticipating my reaction as I asked, "What are they? They are… beautiful."

He met my eyes with that intense stare again: "This is where those who have gone before are put. As Isaac said, they have 'crossed the river'. But no- one may wade back from this river bank."

"May I go in?" I asked.

"Enter do," he said quite solemnly, but, I thought, rather proudly too.

This was a cemetery, but there was no decay here, no sense of death. Each one of those crystal tubes shimmered in the light, and I crouched down to inspect one more closely. I read the name 'Erid', and a symbol etched into the glass near the top caught my attention.

"What is that for?" I asked.

"It is a piece of hemp. This man, Erid, was a Maker of Clothes."

"But where's the rest of his epitaph?"

Uncharacteristically, Edis looked confused.

"His personal details, you know…facts about him."

"There is no more to say. This is the grave of a man called Erid who made clothes. The long rod tells us that he passed many a moon here in Mentarea."

"And the short rods?"

But I didn't really need to ask that question- they spoke for themselves.

"They are the graves of children. The smallest are for those newly-born." A mist clouded his eyes and his face appeared to darken, like a flash- fried fillet, with a downcast look.

"There is a child of mine- a boy- in this place. The mother of my other children lies here too. But I should have no sadness, for my daughters live."

"Edis, you are right- you *should* have no sadness, for Lincoln and Gale are fine girls."

Just silence, and then:

"Walk with me through this place," he bade me.

Having thus spoken, he turned to face the opposite direction again and began to follow the little path. As we weaved in and out of those peculiar glass sceptres, Edis continued to explain how the green- tinted glass denoted males, and the crimson represented the females. I could not help but remark on the disproportionate number of young male graves and I ventured to ask him of the reason.

"Our forefathers destroyed the good Earth," he replied resentfully, "and they were dealt their punishment in the form of a vile plague, carried by obscene creatures, against which they were weak. Yes, Man endured. But Man had become feeble. Survival is the first instinct, and later generations tried to regain their place as rulers of the planet. But it was not to be, for our newborns floundered. Only after many generations did strength appear to return, but then it was too late for the Male. He was not strong, and the Female began to outnumber him. He suffered from genetic disorders, and I am sure that you have seen how the people stare at the hair on your head and face. Only we who are old enough to remember the two strangers...*soldiers*...have ever seen such a sight before; for everyone else, it exists only on the copper plates. Our foulest legacy is that most of the new Males are born barren. Yes, we survived, but for how much longer? Now ask the question, 'do we once more rule?' Would that we could blossom like the apple- tree, bloom like the rose and grow strong like the bee. Instead we are becoming no more than the withered fruit that lies discarded upon the ground. Our lives are good, and every new sun is spent in toil and relaxation. We are grateful for what we have here, but, within several more generations, our numbers will have waned and I wonder if there will be anyone left to tread this arid path upon which we stand and talk now."

I could think of no words to say to Edis. He had spoken from the heart, and I realised now that my innermost thoughts had been poised like an eager combatant, ready to wage war on reason, as they had prepared to sway my convictions and lead me to misjudge these people. For yesterday my thoughts had been of a past that had gone now. Vanished completely. And I had understood that these people resented its destruction. But, in my eyes, their future hadn't looked *bleak*. I'd been wrong, though; they had every right to reject their past- *my* past- for what had they been left. A cruel curse had descended upon them long ago, and it seemed that Mankind, or what I knew to be left for there was no evidence of any human life outside of this town, was doomed to perish in perhaps another hundred years. Ergo, their future was as frangible as a tissue on a wave.

"It's hard to believe it's come to this; a long journey since those first biped ancestors of ours stood up and walked out of Africa."

"I know not of such a place, but perhaps we are almost back where we started," speculated my companion.

"Perhaps, yes. But I don't really think we'll follow the same path of knowledge again."

How sad that those coloured rods should shimmer in truculence of the grey future in which they would play so final a part!

As the gravel crunched beneath our feet, he rescued me from my melancholy by saying, his arm outstretched, "There lie our strangers!"

We walked over to two glass spheres, not rods, perched nobly on top of a mound of gravel.

"So those two brave soldiers, who witnessed such horror, now lie peacefully within the walls of this beautiful town. Edis, they'd have loved to live here. Perhaps they thought they were dead when they arrived-compared to the hell they were living through, this would have been Heaven."

I stooped and patted the mound with my hand. I should have liked to speak with those two young men, but the touching of those chippings was the only contact that I could have and the simplest comfort that I could offer them. We sat for some time amongst those graves of glass, saying very little. We strolled for a while, and Edis showed me the graves of his wife and son, then we sat again. I realised that Edis, like most people, found it a place of contemplation. I didn't like to intrude upon his thoughts. It was only when I noticed that, with the departing daylight, the peculiar little structures no longer gleamed and shone, that I wiped my dusty hands on my jeans and nudged Edis to suggest we return to the town.

I wasn't particularly hungry that night. I offered Edis and Lincoln my apologies and requested that I be excused from the meal. His talk had upset me, and I felt it better to retire to my little cell earlier than yesterday with a view to starting afresh the following day.

CHAPTER 6: *Stale Bread And Fresh Fish*

"It seems our Storm Traveller was tired," the voice said. A nonsensical dream was flowing through my mind, a strange train of thought rebounding aimlessly like one of those little rubber balls being lobbed from wall to wall, and the obtrusive words that I heard seemed out of place. It was Isaac's voice, and he stood by my mattress whilst munching on an apple.

"What time…" I began, but then realised where- and *when*- I was.

"Your dreams carried you to a place of beauty and peace?" he asked in his rather aberrant manner.

"I was dreaming, although of what I couldn't tell you," I replied. I rubbed my eyes to allow them to adjust to the fresh light of the early morning. Isaac was dressed in an olive- green shirt, and wore a cream-coloured pair of shorts with matching sandals. I looked around, expecting to see Lincoln. But she wasn't there.

Isaac must have read my thoughts, for he said, "It is just I that comes to greet you as you waken, and welcome you to the new sun!"

"Well, good morning to you too, Isaac," I said.

Breaking the granite silence that ensued:

"Ohh…you're here for a reason, aren't you?"

"Yes," he answered, "for soon you shall see the remnants of long ago, and maybe you can tell me more about the many things that you shall see this suntime." He placed the core of the apple in his mouth and swallowed it. He then said simply, "When you are ready, follow me to the Great Hall." Then he turned and, like a churlish infant, strutted straight out of the little cell that had become my bedroom.

I dressed as fast as I could in my new clothes, put on my sandals and ran out of the room. I spied Isaac in the distance. I walked at a brisk pace and eventually caught up with him. We arrived at the Great Hall, and I was faced with the sight of a congregation of several hundred people, all enjoying a breakfast of fruit cocktail. Lincoln, Edis, Gale and the others whom I had met were nowhere to be seen initially, although that is not to say that they were absent from the room. Isaac and I took our places at one of the less occupied tables, and he reached for the huge basket of fruit that lay in the middle of the surface. I helped myself to two apples, as big as globes, a pink grapefruit, and a pear and poured a large beaker of orange juice. Isaac took a similar helping of fruit, but, instead of the juice, he poured himself a plenteous beaker of wine. He put it to his lips before even tasting his food, tipped it, and took a generous gulp of the potent liquid.

"Aahhh…strong is the wine that wrestles with the bitter iron of addiction," he theorised cryptically. "Enjoy your food," he said, "for soon I shall lead you from this place."

And so, in between large quaffs of wine, he told me more of the copper plates, the strange boxes, the writings on the wall and all the various oddities that lay in a chamber of memories within Mentarea. I *did* enjoy my food, and I drank three or four tumblers of the flavourful juice, matching Isaac measure for measure with his wine. His cheeks soon became flushed, and he seemed impatient for me to finish. No sooner had I swallowed my last segment of grapefruit, than he said simply, eyes shining, "Let us go forth."

I rose from the table, and started to follow him out of the room. It was then that they must have caught sight of us, for two familiar figures stirred from one of the tables that was situated about fifty feet away and hastened after us. Gale looked as splendid as I remembered her, but Lincoln, that dear Lincoln, looked quite radiant. She was dressed in her loincloth, as usual, but wore a towelling band around her breasts and a delicate chain of pretty orange gems around her neck.

"The Storm- Traveller may find some things of interest in the dark and unexplained void wherein lie the mysteries of Mentarea," Isaac said enigmatically to the two sisters.

Lincoln smiled as she studied me.

"I made no mistake when I chose your clothing."

"They're a good fit, Lincoln. Cool, too."

Thereupon, we all four left the main complex and headed around the side of the building. In response to my request, Isaac attempted to explain the basics of magnetism, mobility and pressure, although any failure in his words was surely due to my inability to grasp the concept! The sisters immersed themselves in feminine talk. A couple of minutes later, and once again that gives some idea of the sheer size of the complex, we reached a door- lead, I thought- set resolutely into a recess in the wall. I was surprised to see such an everyday item as that door, as I had seen not one since my arrival. Isaac bent down, as, peculiarly, the door stood less than four feet high, grabbed one end of the handle and instructed me to do the same. He then proceeded to turn the stock, and I pushed as hard as I could. I was sweating, but Isaac, out of condition through drink and weight, was sweltering. With a steady pressure, an idle groan, a reluctant click, the door eased and we sat down on the ground for a brief respite. Lincoln looked concerned and offered me a welcome drink of water. Then we returned to the lead door and pushed it inwards with some effort. Gale loped to the edge of the portal to peer in, but Isaac snapped at her to stand back. I had begun to see just how irritable the man could be, and I felt rather sorry for Gale as I remembered how she had mopped up his cider only the day before and had received no grace from him.

"Can I go in?" I asked, rather wary of my escort's quick temper.

"Yes, yes," he replied crustily.

I walked through the opening and entered a huge room that stretched for about a hundred yards, and was some twenty feet in height. It was lit partly with a dismal daylight, and tiny particles of dust swam about on the leaden shafts of light that crept murkily through several heavily- frosted thick glass blocks; I assumed that this particular glass had survived on account of its sheer density. The air was fusty and I coughed as the dryness assailed my throat. But as I grew used to the stagnant atmosphere of the place, I began to notice that it was stacked with all sorts of objects. Shelves remained where they had slipped and tilted, their contents tipped and tumbled. Crates and small boxes were stacked against walls, and cracked vessels and broken household implements were deposited around the floor. The scene was reminiscent of the cellars of a church- hall, wherein one used to find the outmoded props from productions and unwanted benefactions from forgotten bazaars. Right where we were standing, there lay a pile of tin sheets. Inquisitively, I reached for one, wiped it with my hand and noticed that it was a picture. Not a conventional picture, but almost screen-printed in different metals. I spat on my hand and sponged the surface again, and only then did I catch a glimpse of gleaming gold. I tried again as I was even more curious, and I noticed that the gold had been laid in intricate strips across slim strands of silver. I rubbed it harder, and, like lifting the grime from a light bulb, the picture began to reveal itself as a detailed cityscape. It was no city that I recognised, but, from its general appearance, I surmised it to be Eastern European. I have no idea when such a picture was created, but I do know that, should I ever have owned such a fine work of art, then I should have been considered a wealthy man. Isaac could give me no clue as to its origin, and I picked up another one. Repeating the process, I recognised various metals, amongst them copper and silver. I also saw the comforting sight of St Paul's amidst a cruelly- altered London skyline. I cleaned another, then another. But all the creations were damaged around the edges and corners, and I felt a sudden pang of sadness.

"Your face shows no happiness," Lincoln perceived. "Why?"

"Why? Well, it's just…" I thought about it carefully, before continuing, "just that such beautiful creations should be seen in all their glory."

But I didn't catch her eye, for I was not that brave.

"But what use are they? What were they for? Why did people from long ago make these?" he asked rather anaemically. My interest had become the trigger for Isaac to fire his questions at me without pausing to reload.

The very fact alone that he had used the word "make" meant that it would be almost impossible to try to explain the concept of art as a medium of pleasure to a man like Isaac.

"Well Isaac," I answered, "a long time ago…in fact, many *moons* ago…people liked to depict scenes and display them. They brought happiness to people when they looked at them- like Lincoln's jewellery- or studied them." I was trying my best, but these people of the Twenty-Fifth Century lived for each other. They ate, drank, worked- I could not deny that they worked hard- and shared. But art had no place in their world. It had no place because it served no purpose. They wanted fruit, sandals, basic clothes, wine, honey, baskets…but certainly not paintings.

Isaac twitched his head with impatience, and I sensed- no, *hoped*- that he understood to some extent.

"Yes, yes. Let us move on," he prattled. He was clearly a man who possessed excess time for neither person nor thing and could flit from one topic to another, like a poorly- scripted drama. I placed the picture back on the ground, and followed Isaac and Gale as they penetrated further into that dank and decaying room. Lincoln was content for me to go ahead of her. Isaac halted by a tiered display, and reached with both hands for a large discoloured square-shaped object. As he dragged it from the shelf, a spray of dust dispersed before our eyes. Gasping, he placed it on a small wooden table that stood next to our little group. Then he wiped his brow, exhaled and flicked a dead spider from the top of the strange box.

"And this, my strange friend from long ago…can you tell me the purpose of *this* object?" he ventured.

I looked, and casting the first notion from my mind, I shook my head and said, rather disappointedly, "No."

"Ha! So we now have something that is not from your Time but dates from before my Time. A mystery from our dark past!"

However, there *was* something familiar about the object, and I attempted to relate it to the rapidly expanding technological growth that I had witnessed in those years immediately prior to my...my *disappearance*. Once again I spat into my hands, rubbed them, placed them onto the surface of the object, and streaked them across it. The glass, or whatever it was, began to reveal itself, and I saw before me the clear face of a screen of some sort. Yes, that's what it was- a screen, but not flat as I expected it to be. There were ridges on the surface, and I noticed a strange array of distorted metal shapes- triangles, ellipses and so forth- beneath the thin transparent frontage. Not instantly recognisable, I guessed nevertheless that the object was a latter- day conduit of information, a very advanced computer monitor.

I coughed before I spoke:

"Well, Isaac, if only you knew what you have here in your possession."

"What is its use?" he barked.

"I *think*," I answered, "that this is a means by which information and images may be displayed mechanically. I don't know what these circles are here," I pointed to the display, "but I should think that this particular medium had advanced enough to display a type of three- dimensional image...a hologram. That's just a guess, though."

"But what *is* it?" he tried again, and this time quite curtly.

"Isaac, my friend, this is part of a computer, part of a machine that can work things out, quantify matters, interpret queries, formulate sums and simplify seemingly impossible tasks. There should be more to it, another part..." But then I wondered, for I was thinking of early Twenty-First Century concepts of computing. I turned my attention back towards the object before me; *what was I thinking?*

My hands moving furtively around the casing, I tried to feel for a power source, but my efforts were in vain. Should the monitor have been just *twenty* years ahead of my Time, I would have had no means of operating it. But *here*...here in this Babylon of the Future, where the only real inspiration lay in addressing each new day, the object possessed as much use as the cardboard in which it probably would have been packaged. Yet Isaac was looking for an answer and I spent the next twenty minutes or so in an attempt to explain the basics of computing, whilst Gale and Lincoln listened attentively. Or perhaps they were just adroit at shrouding their boredom. However, my words didn't flow freely, and I felt like a frustrated evangelist, as all the while my brain tried to interrupt their exit with its constant thoughts- thoughts that balanced the scales somewhere between despair and futility.

"A machine better than the brain! Oh no, I think you are mistaken," Isaac said mockingly.

"No, no. I'm not," I replied, as diplomatically as I could.

"Ha! 'Simplify the most difficult of tasks'! And all you have drunk this fine sun is orange juice! Did you seize *my* beaker when my head was turned?"

I just shrugged at such an abstruse paradox, and realised, with more than a hint of self-righteousness, that I had been witness to the computer's unanticipated obsequies.

Nevertheless, we continued, and we crossed again from dreary half-shadow into a needle of cheerless light. Lincoln said suddenly, "The plates...we must look at the plates!"

"Well," said Isaac, "perhaps you can tell us more of the people on the copper plates."

I followed his pointing hand towards huge piles of thin, warped sheets of metal, and he added, "But not too much, for I fear that we may have chosen unwisely with our names." For the first time, he chuckled.

I walked over to the stacks of panels, and, crouching down, I lifted the top one from the piles. It was covered in a thick film of dust, and I flipped it onto its other side, not knowing what to expect. Tilting it carefully in both hands, I veered it towards the direction of the tainted sunlight, and peered over the edge of the frame. I saw lettering and was startled to see it was familiar. There was an A, next an L followed by a B...then...it looked like an E- now an R-...E-I...I-N. No further clue was needed, for, as I wiped away the grime, I recognised instantly the etched face, the wild hair and the eyes that belied his genius, which gazed concernedly from the plate. It was a picture I had seen a thousand times; it was the face of Albert Einstein. I turned over the next one, and soon saw the familiar bearded face of Leonardo da Vinci, although smut and abrasion had left just the letters L-E-O-...R-D-...N-C-I visible. I placed it on top of the first one, and reached for another- Christopher Columbus- and then another. Eventually I moved three or four at a time until suddenly I found a sequence that displayed names of American Presidents. By this time, I was engrossed, although not so that I didn't hear a gripe of impatience from Isaac. I saw the name and face of Wilson, then Carter, Johnson too, and…it *had* to be there…yes- the shrewd eyes, steadfast brow…*Lincoln*. I looked towards Isaac.

"Your names…your names arise from here. This vast collection of etchings, which must depict hundreds of your famous forebears, means nothing to you, does it? These are eponyms- names have been stored, read and handed down simply as they appear, hence your own name."

"But Storm- Traveller," Isaac went on to say, "you *know* of these people, and you can tell us more about them. Who *were* they, and why have their names been recorded in copper and left here?"

"Isaac," I said despondently, "there's so much to tell of all these people, for each one achieved greatness in his or her own time. I can't tell you of them now because there is just *too* much to tell you. The first Isaac that springs to mind is the scientist whose full name was Isaac Newton. You should remember the name- *Isaac Newton*. He was from this country- *our* country- and he contributed so much to mathematics, physics and even astronomy. As for your second question, Isaac, I can only surmise that the earlier generation, either before they perished or maybe having survived the Plague but perhaps fearing some further tribulation, took the time to store these records lest they should be discarded and be unknown to Mankind for evermore. But at least you now know that you are named after an earlier Man of Science. And you, Gale, I imagine that your name's derived from that of the reformer who became a famous nurse. Gale's from *Nightin*gale, *Florence* Nightingale! She organised the sanitary hospitals in one of the wars of the Nineteenth Century - yes, there *were* other wars," I said, turning to Isaac, "prior to the ones about which I told you and Edis; she lived until a pretty good age, I seem to recall."

"Did you meet her?" Gale asked, smiling in her seriousness.

"No," I laughed, "oh, no."

Finally, I turned towards the girl who had become my friend- no, more, a female Achates- in this absurdly uncomplicated Time; the girl who, even with her face half-obscured in the gloom of that room, possessed an excruciating and potent beauty.

"You bear the designation of a leader, a famous man who was ruler of a nation, a man who commanded his people through a civil war and declared all slaves free. A great human- being!"

"A leader," she mused, brushing the dust from her palms. "I wonder what it is like to lead."

I rummaged through the piles until I felt I could take no more of the dank air that was clearly beginning to irritate me. I wanted to leave, to escape into that untainted atmosphere and inhale plentiful draughts of the revitalising air.

"Isaac," I said, as I cleared my throat, "this frowy air doesn't agree with me. I'd like to leave now."

He looked disappointed, but I noticed that the two sisters seemed unconcerned by my request.

"Oh, very well," he tutted. "Perhaps we shall return again soon."

I nodded, but knew that I had no desire to revisit this museum of decay and ignorance. Whatever answers I sought, I knew now that they lay elsewhere. He immediately directed Gale and Lincoln to leave, but the latter remained and thoughtfully passed me her flask of water. Selfishly, I all but finished the container. Gale took the lead, Isaac followed, and I could clearly hear him griping with dissatisfaction, and Lincoln and I walked close behind. After a short time, we were at the doorway. We each lowered our heads again, and once more were back in the refreshing sterile shadow of our familiar surroundings. I turned my face towards the sky and gulped welcome breaths of fresh air. As if from nowhere, a delightful and most unusual butterfly- African, or possibly Asian- bright green with peacock- blue lunulate markings on its wings, flew past my face and hovered about the open doorway. But, sensing its impending doom lest it fly into that dreary vault, Lincoln's hands thrust out and she cupped them resolutely over the unsuspecting insect. I felt certain that she must have crushed it, and I looked at her with some consternation. But, realising my surprise, she calmly unclasped her fingers to display the graceful fragile creature perched quite contentedly upon her right palm.

"This butterfly will enjoy its short life, and see more wonders, if it stays in the open air," she said serenely. She walked a few paces away from the door, held her hand aloft and blew gently onto the little thing. It twitched, flicked its wings once or twice and took flight. And no sooner had she moved her hand, than another one, almost identical, flew past in dainty pursuit, much to Lincoln's delight.

"I have items that I wish to acquire at the market," Isaac said, perhaps in retaliation to my having disappointed him, and then, rather rudely, "so I will not be seeing you again this suntime." No sooner had he finished his words, than he turned, scraped his sandal clumsily in the dry gravel, and marched away brusquely towards a vacant magnasule.

"Well," I said as I turned back towards the sisters, "Isaac doesn't seem very happy." The man was, I thought, as stubborn as the final screw in a rusted hinge.

"Do not worry," Gale reassured me. "Isaac is often that way. He drinks, but I think you have noticed that in your time here. Am I not correct?"

"Yes, I'm aware of it. I know that you all want answers, but I don't have any."

"But you have told us much already," said Lincoln in earnest, "for now I know that a man existed who was a leader, and, although my father has told you that nobody leads anymore, I am proud to share the name of Lincoln. And Gale has been told of her name too."

"Given enough time," I reflected, albeit half- heartedly, "I could tell everybody in Mentarea the origin of their name!"

"No," laughed Gale, "there are other things to do- *we* could go to the market too, for new clothes! I have seen a bracelet that I like."

"*No!*" Lincoln said quite firmly. "It is too soon to visit the market again. No, this new sun, let us...let us *fish* instead!"

I was somewhat surprised to hear her say that for I'd seen no evidence of any fish or meat so far. Whilst I had surmised that they were a vegetarian society, I had also assumed that I should never taste fish again either.

"That sounds like a good idea to me," I enthused, perhaps woodenly, because, after all, what could be a truly *bad* idea here?

"Come with us, Gale," Lincoln said. "Let us go to the water together."

The two sisters led me across the nearby magnarail towards a clump of trees and shrubbery opposite the vault, and we continued down a wooded incline to the bank of a chattering fast- flowing stream. We were in a glade straight out of the pages of some enchanting work of children's fiction, a delightful little glen where sunlight crept discreetly for fear of spoiling the bewitching quality of the place. Great boulders, glossy and featureless from centuries of erosion, leant against the earth, jutting from the water like the bleached bones of a slain giant. The water, perhaps three feet at its deepest, cascaded and tumbled around them, whilst little pockets of dark moss grew from crevices on the shaded sides. On we walked and into sunshine and on it gushed to a lone old willow that stood like a silent sentinel, one of its leafy arms twisting staunchly to the water where two blazing blue dragonflies larked just above the twinkling surface. I wondered whether it might not be the very same stream in which I had washed on that first day, or at least if it connected with it. Past the aged willow the water rushed, to a collection of fallen boughs lying on a protruding rock, as if a huge beast had broken from its cage and tossed the bars to the ground. And beyond that rock it flowed, laughing and gushing, rushing beyond the rock to somewhere else.

"So this is where you fish?" I asked, my hand on the rock.

"Yes, one of many places," said Gale, and she walked to a nearby flat stone, almost like a natural table- top, from where she retrieved a functional looking meshing that had been weighted down with two large pebbles.

"Watch us," said Lincoln as she took the other end of the net. She stepped back from her sister, unfurling it as she did so. Then the two girls removed their footwear and proceeded to walk into that rather inviting brook. As I watched the girls standing resolutely in the middle of the water, the net outstretched between them, I began to wonder about their ages. I estimated that Lincoln, the more confident of the two, was about eighteen or nineteen, Gale just a couple of years younger. I continued to sit at the water's edge in a state of total relaxation, just enjoying the sight of those two girls and listening to the intermittent business of a hidden bee.

"Now!" cried Lincoln suddenly, and, simultaneously, using both hands, they folded the net into a parcel. Then they scooped the trawl from the stream. As the water poured out, I could see that they had caught a substantial number of fish- perhaps ten or twelve- in barely any time at all and certainly using the minimum of effort. I stood up as they paddled excitedly back to the bank.

"Looks like a good catch!" I said.

"There are many," Gale replied as she and Lincoln threw the net to the ground. The haul of fish writhed about on the wet webbing, and I peered to inspect them more closely.

"Peculiar fish...they're a strange colour...what are they, Lincoln?"

She wore a mask of bewildered blankness as she looked towards her sister, Gale merely mirroring the former's puzzlement.

"They are just...fish," she replied rather stiffly. A few stray droplets of water clung resolutely to her drying legs.

"Of course, but what *type* are they? They're an odd purple shade- I've not seen anything like them before," I continued.

"Do you look for '*gold*' fish?"

She seemed to enjoy reminding me of our conversation from the day before, and I nodded as if to endorse her misguided ridicule.

"They have no name, they are simply fish," echoed Gale.

I could see that my question was pointless, for the girls were genuinely bemused by my interest. Here the sun shone, bees made honey, dogs barked, birds sang and fish...well, fish were just fish that were caught in nets. Gone from the country, I suspected, were the salmon, trout, perch and other such common varieties. I don't know what type of fish the girls had caught, but there was one thing of which I could be certain- they would taste good.

"Now come and try," Lincoln coaxed me, and retrieved the net once more. I discarded my sandals and splashed into the stream with her. The water felt sharp as it gushed bracingly around my ankles, and I followed Lincoln out towards the centre where the coolness rushed past my lower thighs. She touched my wrist to tell me to stop as she passed me one end of the net, and she edged about two feet away from me in the direction of the other levee. Then we repeated the process that I had watched from the embankment. After about two minutes, we had stopped a little group of fish from swimming any further and, on her instruction, we hoisted the net from the water, folded it and returned to join Gale.

"Now I shall try again," said Gale digging me in the arm, and I noticed that Lincoln, inconvenienced whilst placing the fish into a cloth sack, looked slightly irked by her sister's suggestion. It was the first hint that I had seen of any sibling rivalry. So I found myself standing once more in the middle of that stream; mercifully, my session with Gale yielded a smaller haul than on the previous occasion with Lincoln, for I truly believed that Lincoln may have been jealous had we caught a greater number of fish! Further stints with Lincoln ensued, with some long breaks in between, and, as I stood with her again, net poised in hand, I wondered how many people had gathered in that stream over the years. That brook had meandered faithfully throughout the centuries, and I likened it to a city's eldest surviving occupant, a bystander at memorable occasions, its constant burbling and purling now coherent words as it wove many a tale of all whom had graced its old waters.

A late- afternoon sun had now warped the shadows that were rippling calmingly on the stream's surface. This was my first chance to consider the time of year; by the time on my watch coupled with the shadows' length, I believed it to be July- this despite the fact that I had departed my century in June! I stood patiently with Lincoln, and, looking at her, I believed that her thoughts seemed far removed from catching fish. She had become self- conscious suddenly, her left fingers fiddling with the orange gemstones around her neck, and I ended the moment by prompting her to pull the net; but this time her movement was just that little bit more awkward. In what was destined to be our final haul that day, we resulted in our best catch yet as we pulled some twenty or so fish from the water. Our pickings rich, we decided to return to the town where the fish would be deposited in the kitchen for the benefit of whoever wanted them, because, as I had seen already, that was the way in which they lived here.

I had seen remnants from a bygone era, and familiar sights that day. And from the stagnant environment of that musty old storeroom, I had been taken to the freely- flowing vitality of a healthy stream. From there I had learned how to fish in the most beautiful and simple way known to Man. And, now coursing as deep and lively as the very water that we had fished, were my thoughts of Lincoln.

CHAPTER 7: *A Blossoming Friendship*

I had passed an untroubled night, and, no sooner had I dressed, than Lincoln appeared perched in my doorway. Her black hair shone like molten pitch, her pupils floated on chalky pools, her cheeks were a healthy coppered- bronze and through semi- parted lips her teeth etched a slim white line across her face; I fancied that she was one of those rare females that possessed such consummate beauty that she could emerge unruffled from the deepest slumber. She was dressed in a similar exiguous top to the one that she had been wearing when we met and slung low around her waist, with nudistic decency, was her loincloth. Her trusted and packed utility-belt sat tidily on top, just dipping fractionally to her right hip. I noticed that the buckle was in relief in places, and I reminded myself to ask Lincoln about it. She was obviously an early- riser, for she had already prepared a breakfast and a full pitcher that she carried on a large salver. But still she remained positioned in the opening (I have called it such, but, as I have intimated, once closed, the unit became a breathable, sealed structure, with no visible means of entry and exit) and again I realised that she was awaiting my invitation before she entered.

"That's a welcome sight," I greeted her. "Won't you come in?"

She smiled, glided effortlessly into the room and placed the tray gingerly onto the little wicker stool. I noticed her hand jewellery that consisted of brilliant blue gems set into ornate webbing connected from rings on her middle fingers to bracelets on each wrist. I could not help but admire them, finding them similar to the Indian finger bracelets that I had seen worn by many of the girls in Delhi. Then she sat on the floor, her long limbs outstretched and began to toy with the tips of her hair.

"I want you to enjoy it. There are apples, oranges and grapes. There is also honey mixed with crushed oats. But the main delight is cooked fish from our work at the stream."

"I can't wait…"

"First, enjoy the juice of the nettle and the dandelion," she said as she reached for the jug and began to pour two beakers of the strained green warm liquid.

I tried a little sip of the drink, and found its taste to be not unlike that of herbal tea. It goes without saying that I should have traded my house for a pot of fresh tea at that moment, but, of course, that could not be so.

I eyed the fish, and Lincoln picked up the little double- headed spheroid utensil and slid it into the food. She squeezed the handle and the upper head clamped over the lower one, holding the fish. She spoon- fed me that first piece. It tasted much like cod, but there lurked too an indeterminate flavour, perhaps akin to jacket- potato skins. But, aside from the unusual taste, it was superb!

As we dined, I took the opportunity to ask Lincoln about the strange fabric that enveloped us.

"It is made from bee propolis, tree- sap and the special fibre," she replied.

"Mmmm…right, special fibre. Strange. I've heard of *propolis* though, but what *is* it?"

Her blazing blue eyes twinkled; be it food, friendship or knowledge, Lincoln relished the chance to share.

"Propolis is the medicine of the bees. If scarred, the tree will secrete a substance to repair itself. The bees collect the healing fluid from the trees and take it to the hives. It will strengthen the hives, and when it touches the bees, they too will be protected against disease."

I nodded.

"I see. A sort of natural immunisation, I never knew that. How d'you collect it?"

She drew her long legs to her body, flattened her knees to the side near the floor and crossed her feet.

"*Pure* propolis is obtained by fooling the bees."

She waited for my question.

"Fooling?"

"We insert a small wooden box into the hive."

She parted her thumb and forefinger just so far.

"The bees see the box, but they think that it is a part of the hive that needs repairing, so they fill it with propolis," she explained enthusiastically.

"Ahh, clever!"

I looked to the entrance again and frowned.

"But there's no visible join," I continued. "Is that where the fibre plays a part?"

"When the cell is sealed," she added, "the sap, fibre and propolis join together. Watch."

She stood, walked to the doorway and pushed her hand into the surface. The framework stretched, as if made from rubber, but didn't split. She explained that it was only the application of the angled metal device- I'd compared it to a front- door key- that split the tissue.

"The propolis and fibre will remain workable unless heated by a flame. Then it would change into a liquid," she added.

She smiled again, and resumed her place on the floor. But as she did so, her foot glanced against something and I heard a light rolling sound.

"*Ohh*...what is that?"

She was staring at my torch that she had flicked across the floor.

"It's a torch. I was going to show you. Here," I answered, stretching to retrieve it. I held it up to her face, but pointed it fractionally to one side and pressed the little rubber button.

"Ohhh!" she gasped, recoiling.

"It won't hurt," I said. "Go on, you try."

She leant forward, and, as she did so, her top exposed a further sweep of her plentiful cleavage that plunged with dormant promise. Then she held out her fingers nervously and glanced them against the slender barrel. Thereon she jolted, and whizzed her hand away.

"Look, it's fine..."

She tried again.

"But...but it is not hot. Where is the flame?"

"There isn't one."

"I know it contains no blaze- beetles."

She wore a mask of defeat.

"True, nothing like that."

"I do not understand," she said, with the swift capitulation of a child.

Well, it's almost impossible to describe her wonderment as I proceeded to unscrew the plastic sheathing to show her the batteries. I did attempt to explain the basic principle. But I think that she was just content to know that it produced light, and, whilst I finished my breakfast, she spent the rest of her time in my cell simply pressing it on and off, and pointing it around the room.

"I have some things to show you," she said as I finished my food.

"Okay."

"I will bring my metal box of objects for you to see."

She split the fabric to the side, and vanished. She was back in an instant carrying a small rusty tin. She resumed her position on the floor.

"In this container I keep the things that I have found or been given. Perhaps you can tell me of their secrets."

"Well, I'll have a go. Let's see."

She opened the hinged lid and passed me a familiar object.

"It's a coin; 18...looks like '97'...yes, 1897. It's a Victorian penny."

"Ahhh…a penn…penna?"

"Penny. Currency. Money. All gone now, but this has passed through so many hands. Predates me, though."

"Yes, my grandmother found this and many others. I was told that such things bring luck; I am thinking that they have done so," she said, catching my eye fleetingly.

I rummaged through the box. It was mainly junk- an old bolt, a few ring pulls, a frosted glass beer bottle, a couple of clout nails and some washers. The coins, though, were an interesting collection and I decided to add to her curiosity.

"I've some more coins you can have, Linc."

I reached for my coat pocket and pulled out a handful of loose change. Her eyes lit up as she held one up to her face.

"You wish me to keep these, your money of old?"

"Yes."

"I will treasure them always. Ohh, I must show my father!"

Yet at the same time, I felt a pang of melancholy as if I were reintroducing a social evil into society.

It was a grand breakfast that Lincoln had put together, and I thanked her for it. Once more I remarked that she did not acknowledge my gratitude, and I wondered whether she was unaware of such a concept. Refilling her rusty tin, and quite out of the blue, she declared:

"This sun I shall show you one of the many uses for our honey. Come!"

My watch read eleven- fifty as we left the vast domestic network, and the sun, already a stirring temptress, cavorted across the tops of the town's buildings. Every now and again, a ray of sunlight would nudge a particular rooftop, and it would be bounced to another pinnacle where it would cause the burnished surface to shimmer contentedly. It was beautiful to observe, and it was as if I were watching some dazzling ballet of brilliance. Lincoln read my thoughts:

"You are seeing how the sun comes to skip across our rooftops."

"It's certainly a spectacular sight," I commented, as we headed south from the Great Hall towards an extensive vineyard.

"Come," she said, "for you have already tasted our wine. Here is where the grapes are grown."

We strolled down one of the little aisles, passing the occasional worker who was examining the crop. Columns of greenish smoke rose from large cradles that were sited at intervals of ten yards or thereabouts.

"Lincoln," I pointed to one of the receptacles that lay to our left, "what's the purpose of the smoke?"

"It prevents the insects from eating our food."

"But it smells so sweet. Surely such a smell would attract any insects."

"It *does* attract them," she explained with brio, "but once they are within a short distance, they will be confused, and then repelled, by the burning dogspaw seeds. You enjoyed the dogspaw flesh earlier, but many things of goodness can have another use. Look now!"

At that moment a wasp dived towards the smoke, hovered undecidedly, and dropped a couple of feet, as if concussed. A second later, it regained its composure, and flew off in the opposite direction.

I noticed that we were on a slight gradient, heading downhill, as we continued our saunter through the vines, sometimes taking a slight detour along a side- track to look at the many variants of grape. Even with my limited knowledge, I was certain that I recognised the Pinot Noir strain. In my Time, such a grape would ripen sufficiently in most English summers to produce sparkling Champagne; now it should be positively thriving. We walked further, and I spotted what I guessed to be the Bacchus, known for its aromatic wines. But there were many that I could not identify, and, pointing to a vine supporting grapes the size of satsumas, I asked Lincoln for help. She in turn waylaid one of the nearby workers who was busy tying the vines, introduced me to him and asked for his assistance.

"Tell me of the wine that you make from this grape," she enquired.

The leathery- headed little man, Caxton, answered proudly, "*This* grape will make a strong, dark wine."

Looping his roll of twine temporarily around the cane, he turned to me:

"We call it the 'slumber- grape'; drink a beaker and you shall see why! Ha! We do not produce much of it, for one jug will last even a man like Isaac for many moons!" His ruddy face became quite animated, a web of creases careering in every direction as he smiled, and I could tell that his work was his passion.

"Our friend might like to taste a beaker- I trust that there still remains a cask in the Great Hall." And when he laughed, it was jovial and, naturally, full- bodied!

"But the grapes are huge!" I enthused.

"We reap the benefit from a sun- blessed crop, and much rain that falls when the sun vanishes," he explained, before adding, "For every answer about grapes that I could give you, old Ike would tell you two about the finished product."

We chatted for a while before leaving him content to resume his happy trade, in a vineyard that surely would have seduced Ahab, and carried on with our stroll. It was an extraordinary world into which I had plunged, and I knew that any further irregularities that I should be shown would continue to astound me.

A soft breeze had begun to course its way through the walkways, but the sun, that constant companion and bounteous host from so long ago, sat resolute in an azure sky. I could feel the dampness on my brow, and I raised a hand to wipe it.

Lincoln looked troubled by my discomfort and took me by surprise with her next proposal.

"Come," she said in a concerned way. "You shall sample the calmness of the honey baths."

She led me to the fringe of the vineyard and gestured with her hands. I became aware of an overpowering and cloying aroma whilst being greeted by a strange sight. Spread out in a large square, each fringed by virescent gravel, was an array of oblong pools. They were all a tan shade, and divided in places by low reed screens. I saw that some of the pools were in use, their occupants reclining in the tawny liquid. More of the same receptacles that I had seen in the vineyard had been placed around the baths, and Lincoln shepherded me to an empty tub.

"These are baths of *honey*?"

"Honey is just one ingredient," she replied very placidly. "They are full of water and also herbs from the forest."

"Surely the water's cold?" I queried.

"No. Look," she said, pulling apart two wooden shutters and exposing a large convex lens. She tilted the lens towards the sun and the rays became concentrated on the strange mixture. It was then that the whole bizarreness of the situation began to envelop me, as if my blood were being pumped with some powerful sedative. I must have gone into a sort of trance for her next words cuffed me back into reality:

"The sun warms the liquid. Now touch it," she encouraged me.

I crouched down on the edge of the basin and dipped a hand into the water. I was surprised, for it was tepid and was more fluent than I had expected.

"Is this how you relax here?" I asked, looking up to her.

But Lincoln had already unfastened and kicked off her sandals, and was bending down to join me. She sat on the edge and dangled her seemingly endless legs over the side, gently lapping the mysterious liquid with her toes.

"Come," she invited me, "do as I am doing."

Without standing, I unbuckled my sandals, unlaced the ankle ties and removed them, then sat beside her and lowered my legs over the side. It was a delightful sensation as I churned the lukewarm water with my feet and felt it splash about my ankles. A group of women passed us and headed incuriously towards another pool. I dipped my hand in the water again, and, withdrawing it, wiped it over my calf.

"That is no better than a cat lick. You will feel the goodness of the water if you bathe in it, for that is why we are here," she said, her words as even as soup, and without a further utterance her hands disappeared behind her back. With a slight jerk of her right arm, she unfastened the supporting straps of her top, removed it and then cast it aside onto the gravel path. Quickly, I averted my eyes with embarrassment. But seconds later she was jabbing my shoulder in that gentle way as she said simply, "Come."

I looked back and noticed that she was now standing; her unclothed flesh was the same golden tone as the rest of her body, her unfettered modesty had left her devoid of white strap-marks. She settled her utility-belt to the ground, proceeded to unravel her loincloth, unclipped her left bracelet, and inched the lacework from her finger, did the same with the right one and, ignoring the steps on the opposite side, lowered herself unflinchingly into the pool. I hesitated at first. But I was feeling as stale as old beer, and probably smelling like a drain in a drought, so, without further ado, I stripped and removed my watch. She looked at me with an unwary openness as I slipped readily into the water to join her.

"It feels so warm!" I exclaimed, as I felt the odd concoction slop about my body. Lincoln was reclining opposite me, agitating the liquid with a wooden paddle, and I couldn't help but contemplate her loveliness; unquestionably, she was a divine girl. With her wheaten skin, she seemed to blend with the yellow-brown syrup. Entrancingly, my eyes moved from the tips of her dusky hair to her shoulders and down to her wet breasts, which were like chalices, and her attractive bronze nipples that looked like two golden medallions. I watched as the treacly mixture bobbed gently around the contour under her breasts. She was, I sensed, quite unmindful of my muted curiosity.

"The bath will cool you and relax your body," she smiled, settling the paddle on the surface of the liquid and upthrusting her arm to reach inside a small shelf for an ivory coloured tablet some three inches in length. She passed it to me. It was rougher than a regular cake of soap, and she must have anticipated my next question:

"Lavender and oatmeal," she said with atypical haste.

I don't think it was a time for discussing soap!

Her arm broke the surface of the water again.

And then, without notice:

"Tell me about your Time."

"What should I tell you?" I asked.

"Your home. Your people. Things about which I may like to hear- or...or just anything," she surged, eyes afire, and she promptly leant back against the side of the bath, cupping the water in her right hand and sloshing it over her body. I sensed that she was slightly nervous, but I knew that, for the first time since my arrival, she was genuinely interested in learning about me.

"My Time," I breathed, "was...so...different. Where do I begin?"

Where would anyone begin?

So I started by telling her my age, and, with a lump in my throat, I described my parents, and told her that I had an elder brother and a younger sister. I even listed my favourite food! Then I told her about my musical tastes, my friends and all the other important people in my life. She listened- intently, I thought- and then looked a little wistful, as if she had just rejected a thought. Then, raising her hands like swans and skating them gracefully across the water towards me, she said, "Tell me of your sister."

The strange water undulated, ferrying my emotions on an epicurean current.

"Hmmm...outgoing, chatty. Long hair- dark too."

"As mine?"

"No, shorter. Not as black. I don't think I've seen hair as dark as yours."

In acknowledgement, she touched it.

"Ahhh. Tell me of her clothes," she said, her face bedecked in fascination.

"What, *all* of them? Well...all sorts of outfits...long skirts, short ones, jeans, shoes- loads of them, dresses, vests. She often wore a black and white striped top. Or was it *blue* and white? And yellow leggings..."

Her puzzlement was evident.

"Leggings...close fitting all the way down her legs," I supplied. "A purple and green skirt too!"

She chuckled. "So many clothes! I should have no time for anything else."

I smiled. "That's how it is...*was*."

"Tell me more of your town," she said in that way that would make it hard for any man to resist.

"Well, I lived in a large town, but not a town like this one. My town was full of buildings where people lived; they were our houses- you've heard me speak of mine. But it's different here. You all live in a community, you live as one. We were individuals. We all had our own ideas; I didn't agree with many of them, but that's how we lived. Shall I continue?"

"Yes, do. I am enjoying listening to your words," she answered mellifluously and pushed her hair from her forehead.

"I did work, but not outdoors, and for that work I earned money. We didn't share like you do today. No, we traded. If I'd wanted the new clothes in my Time, I should have had to buy them. You see, money helped me to get things- remember my comment at the market?"

She gave an affirmative grin, and eased a stray drop of water from her cheek. I noticed the half- moons of her nails, as striking white as snowdrops.

"And when I wanted more, I had to wait until I was paid more money. So I'd always have lean periods where I would be waiting for pay-day. Never really budgeted properly."

I think she understood, but all this was probably too obscure for her. I changed the subject. "I haven't mentioned my old car."

She looked at me curiously.

"We travelled around in these motor- cars. They were perhaps like your magnasules, but they ran on four wheels. Very convenient, but the disadvantage was that they helped the atmosphere to decay." And I wondered what had happened to that misconceived invention. So it never really *had* a future! "But we studied the Past, and we learned from it." I

73

pondered for a moment upon the idyllic way of life that these people had achieved- and inherited- and sighed, "Maybe we didn't concentrate our studies on the right aspects of our history."

There was a menacing buzzing by my ear. I flinched. Somehow, a bee had managed to avoid the smoking dogspaw seeds and infiltrate our bathing. It flew from me and I watched then as it loitered about her breast. I looked up; her deep, patient eyes were as untroubled as the water in which we were lying.

"I'm not certain that you would have liked my world, Lincoln," I continued. She didn't ask why not, so I elaborated.

"It was a world of ever growing technology- one where, eventually, I think we would have placed more value on machines than people."

The bee continued to flit about, and then, with a brazen innocence, alighted on her wet breast.

"Obviously it all broke down one day, but I don't know whether that was as a result of the Plague."

I watched as it crawled groggily across her breast. Undauntedly, it stopped at her nipple and then proceeded to sup the tacky honey mixture from its tip.

"P'raps it was on the cards...*inevitable* that it should do so anyway. I doubt that I *shall* ever know."

She emitted a little moan, and I looked up to see her give the faintest flicker of her silken lips, like ribbons on a breeze, and a pleasurable flash- an unintentional lure- of her unfathomable sapphire eyes, whilst her cheeks flared like fanned embers. I found the experience to be oddly appealing, and it held me transfixed for several seconds; I grappled with my composure, trying to think of mundane events. After a few seconds, the bee took wing, only to be repelled, stunned and diverted by the smouldering dogspaw seeds.

"Linc..." I realised that I had shortened her name accidentally, but she didn't seem to notice, or if she did, she certainly didn't mind. "Were you not bothered by the bee, afraid that it might have stung you?"

"*Sting?*" she queried, grimacing. "The nettle will sting, as will the wasp, but the *bee* does not sting!"

"But Lincoln," I asserted, "bees- *worker* bees, the females- *do* sting, although only if you anger them, or," and I couldn't help but picture what I had just witnessed in the pool, "if they feel threatened in some way."

But still she disagreed, and I noticed that two narrow lines had formed on her brow, like scratches on teak. I realised that Lincoln truly believed in what she was alleging, so I posed the question:

"Is it really true that *all* bees can't sting, can't wound?" I asked incredulously.

"Bees cannot sting," she affirmed.

"Then what's happened here?"

I wanted to know. What strange abnormality had inflicted our popular garden visitor and left her unable to sting? My guess was that the Plague, along with all but wiping out Mankind, had attacked the animal and insect world, rendering many of them defenceless. And those that could not survive slowly died. The intelligent ones remained, and species like the bee had somehow managed to endure, albeit in a modified state.

"I cannot answer your question," she replied in her upstanding manner, "for I do not know the answer."

In the space of some four centuries, my world had altered drastically. Genetic changes surely should have taken longer to develop, and I wondered what other peculiar sights would await me in this unparalleled place. I decided upon a different tack: "What about education? Did you go to school?"

"I...do...not understand your question."

"School, a place to study and learn."

"But Mentarea is where I have gained my knowledge, and shall continue to do so. Always we learn. There is no...no...what was your word?"

"School."

"*Skoo...school,*" she stammered. "At your school, what did you learn?"

"Oh, pretty much everything. Well, it seemed that way at the time! All about the world, the people who shaped it, why the wise man built on the rocks, numbers and what you can do with them, even how an apple falls from a tree- you know, the science behind it."

She gave a semblance of a smile, but crooked with bafflement.

"The apple will fall if it is not picked; there is no need to know *how*."

No, I thought, not anymore.

"Well, that's good enough for me, too, Lincoln."

I should have realised. There was no point in my asking her such a valueless question. Lincoln had been learning ever since her mother had lowered her from her breast to the mat. She hadn't studied, say, geography. No- one went anywhere anymore; flights of wild imagination to faraway lands had been grounded ages ago. As for mathematics and physics, the descendants of these people had prevailed over all impediments to their knowledge to form a successful partnership of advanced basics and lucrative ignorance. And history? Simply consigned to oblivion, the great victories as diaphanous as the ghosts of their key players.

Our talk continued as the time seeped by.

"Do you enjoy the honey bath?" she enquired eventually.

"Mmmm, it's good. I think I'd have roasted before; it's certainly helped to cool me. I can't believe how long we've been here."

"It is good for the whole body," she suggested, and with barely a pause, she drew her breath and immersed herself completely in the water. After several seconds, she emerged, drenched entirely in the stuff. Her black hair shone, her face was glowing and, with her bare breasts gleaming in the afternoon sun, she could have passed for a glorious Nereid emerging from a Greek sea. I did the same, and, upon surfacing, I felt a sense of invigoration.

Then she stood up, stretching; the hint of her ribs, especially with the excess bath water dripping from her lithe body, made her chest look like gently rippled wet sand.

"Come," she bade me. "The rest of the herbs and honey must now be removed from your body."

She turned, walked up the treads, reached for her loincloth, drew it around her waist, picked up her utility- belt and fastened it around her once more. She then pivoted, passed me my shorts, and, disregarding the rest of her attire, started to walk to a neighbouring pool. I climbed out, donned my shorts and followed her. She positioned herself cross-legged on the edge of the second basin. She placed her hand inside the little pocket immediately left of her buckle, and withdrew a small metal instrument. Curved in shape, it was almost indistinguishable from a Roman strigil that I had viewed in a museum.

"Come. Sit by me and watch," she smiled in that rather alluring, yet still virtuous, manner that she possessed.

I joined her and watched as she dipped the flat edge of the implement into the water, and then fixed it against her shoulder. And I continued to watch as she glided it fluently down the top of her arm, but applying just enough pressure to scrape the drying honey mixture from her perfect skin. She wet the blade again and repeated the process on her forearm. She passed me another of the little utensils, and I applied the same procedure to my skin. It was a most efficient instrument, and it left my skin tingling with a pleasant smoothness. By using the finer edge, I was even able to shave at last! To say that Lincoln found it a strange sight would be an understatement; suffice to say, she looked at me in silent awe, as a child might behold a lined face, fixing her eyes on the motion of the blade! As we continued with the pleasant exfoliation, I listened as she hummed a little tune- I presumed that the words for the melody would by now be long forgotten in the mists of Time. Nevertheless, I shut my eyes to savour the moment. But everyone knows that charming moments aren't created to last, lest they should lose their magic, and all too soon her murmuring petered out and I opened them again to see her reaching into the adjacent pocket for a tiny purse and fan- tailed brush. She untied the cord, and dipped the small brush into the receptacle. Removing the brush, she then began to reapply the black substance to her eyelids, sweeping it in an upward motion until it joined her eyebrows. She smeared a band across each cheek too.

"What *is* that stuff that you're putting on?" I asked, believing it to be some sort of make-up.

"It is ash mixed with fish- oil. It protects the eyes and face from the sun. Now I am wanting to put some on your face."

Then she stretched her arm, and, her face etched with concentration, she placed the appliance against my skin and started to paint the bistre onto the same area. She also daubed a generous amount across my forehead and cheeks. Her face was so near, so near, and I inhaled very discreetly the subtle fragrance of her femininity. She didn't know my thoughts...*couldn't* know them. Could she? I felt stupidly guilty. But it didn't stop me breathing in again. That face. Those eyes. Those lips. Oh, how I could...

"It is done! The sun would be unkind to your skin without it," she said, and, looking at her face with its newly applied bistre, I began to see how she resembled the popular depiction of an ancient Egyptian.

Finally, from the third pocket on her left hip, she took out a tin, no larger than a snuff- box. She opened it, dunked in her little finger, pulled it out and proffered me a thick cream- coloured substance, resembling a blancmange. She explained to me that it comprised soap, water, honey and dried iris flower.

"You 'ub it on the 'eeth," she said, as she pasted a blob, a finger's width, across her own aesthetically beautiful teeth. She flicked her tongue over her lips, swallowed and grinned. Her teeth looked- if it were possible- even brighter. I did the same with the paste.

"Now we are ready again. Do you wish to visit the bees?"

"Of course," I replied somewhat lethargically, as I felt rather sated with sun and the soothing waters of the bath.

We returned to our belongings and I finished dressing again. From a pouch on her belt, she passed me some leaves:

"Place inside your sandals, for the leaves from the alder will help to cool your feet."

She put on her sandals, but instead of slipping on her top again, she simply pushed it into her bag. And so we continued on our way through the communal relaxation area, I dressed in the unfamiliar garb of a citizen of this Twenty- Fifth Century town, she simply sublime, bronzed, with barely a stitch on and without an apparent care in the world!

We passed several of the pools, their occupiers either paying no attention to us or merely taking a moment to address us whilst they continued in conversation. After a distance of some two hundred yards, we left this area and emerged on the crest of a grassy slope. At the bottom that verdant stretch of green, and looking like tiny sentries guarding the edge of the forest, stretching as far as the eye could see, stood several rows of grey cabinet- shaped structures. From where we were standing, I estimated that they were about four feet in height. There must have been hundreds of the strange structures, each constructed from stone setts that at one time must have had a more primary purpose.

"There!" Lincoln pointed. "There are the bees! Come...come and see how we live with them!" She seemed quite excitable as she took my hand and steered me down that slope.

My watch read several minutes after six, as an early evening sun, suspended lower against a pale cerise canvas, still burned with an unusual intensity. Because the heat was still so extraordinarily fierce, little drops of sweat had begun to prick my forehead. Every so often, I spied girls dashing between these rows, and tending to the hives. But that sound...it is difficult to describe the noise of the bees! As I walked down that slope, a low, monotonous hum met my ears, growing louder, deeper, more irritating and turning into a continuous, sonorous reverberation as I approached the base of the hillock. I likened the sound to the friction of a dozen bicycle wheels as they raced ever nearer along the tarmac.

"Still you doubt the bees, I sense?" she asked rather intuitively.

"Well, er...no. No, it's just that *sound*...I'm used to people reacting with fear to such a resonance. You see, in my Time, beekeepers protected themselves from the bees. They wore masks, gloves and other forms of safety. But now..." I was beginning to gabble, "well...now I know that bees no longer sting, then I've nothing to bother about."

I had to convince myself.

"Do not fear the sound, for it is only the noise that the wings of the bees make when they fan the air inside the hives; on one side, the wings bring in air." She crouched down at that moment and with her middle finger she drew a waving line in the grass, and continued, "On the other side, they expel it." Then she stood again, and, with her leaden concentration, flapped her hand in front of my face to cool it as if to emulate the motion of the wings. "Everything in Nature has a reason," she smiled as she gripped my hand just that little bit more tightly, and encouraged me to follow her.

We crossed from the grass onto a layer of well- trodden earth, its desiccated state suggesting to me that there had been a long, hot spell with too little rain. Our feet kicked up fine billows of dust as we headed towards the first row of hives. The bees flitted around us, hovering and shuddering in that assiduous way. They buzzed and whined and hummed and brushed against our heads and arms- brushing, but never landing- again and again as they jerked and eddied in their timeless drill with sedulous splendour. I found it a strange and unnerving experience, and it was still an instinctive reaction to attempt to wave them away. Lincoln now seemed slightly bemused by my behaviour, and I had to remind myself again that these people were not used to the aggression of an angry bee. It is difficult to convey the impression of feeling one's hot, adrenalin- fuelled fear slowly freeze to a stagnant iced torpor. But that is how I became- calm and unfazed by those omnipresent bees, for they had no quarrel with us.

Several feet from the line, she stopped, settled herself on a flat piece of granite under a maple tree and beckoned me to join her. She had an air of indifference about her. Again, I sensed that she wanted to ask me something and, as I sat with her, I made a stab at what it might have been. After all, sometimes one occasion for a particular train of discussion can be more apposite than another, and, as I sat down next to her, I deemed it a suitable moment to tell her of the conversation that I had shared with Edis in the cemetery. I had been in such a euphoric state as I lay in the bath, that, although I had wanted to, it had seemed inappropriate to broach the topic.

Her face paled slightly, and I sensed that she already knew that I would have been told of the ultimate fate of the colony.

"You know that most of the men in Mentarea are sterile. But I fear that my father did not tell you of the curse that has befallen the *females* of Mentarea, for many now die in childbirth. Some females do survive, as you have seen. There are still many children, although there exist just...ahhh...thirteen who are no more than nestlings."

She paused.

"But it is spoken of how the births will become fewer. Omas and the other Men of Medicine predict that we shall endure but eight to ten generations more. I will not live to see the end, and that is good for me. But, whilst my name will lie etched in crimson glass, what of that last generation? And what of the bees that we keep? Each hive shall fall into silence."

She stared straight ahead, her face a veneer of wistfulness, as she added, "Death is the bitterest kernel." Despite the desolation in her voice, Lincoln could still speak imaginatively. Her face grew ever softer, and adopted a sad expression as she reminded me, "I have told you that our mother is gone."

"You have. Whilst we were in the cemetery, your father showed me her grave. It's a lovely place, Lincoln."

"Ohh, I remember her. She used to tell me that she was visited one moon by a beautiful maiden who sprinkled pollen into her hair; that is how I was created."

"Now that's something I *can* believe!"

Her face crinkled as she tried to stifle a tear, before resuming:

"Her name was Linnaeus. I remember also how she had a smile wider than the sun..."

She stretched out her arms, then relaxed them again as she added, "...and hair blacker than a starless sky."

"Pretty...I don't need to look far to picture her."

Tears were welling in her eyes as she continued.

"And gone too is my friend, Melia. We were separated by but a few moons, and passed our childhood together. But, before she could bear her child by Xander, she... she died."

She sobbed. Then: "Ahhh...the sun warms *me* still, but for my poor mother and Melia there is only shade."

"Come on, Lincoln," I said, for it was heartbreaking to see her so upset, "tell me about the bees."

"I will tell you," she said, composing herself again. The cool stone was proving to be a welcome relief from the heat of the afternoon, and I prepared to hear more of Lincoln's strange world. "Look," she pointed, snuffling as she grinned. "The bees wait for me to begin."

I turned towards a cluster of unidentifiable, but beautiful, flowers, most of which were in full bloom, their delicately designed green concertina leaves with their red flame markings, spreading to expose the stamina with their wispy fronds. A dozen or so bees were darting about the flowers.

"They are the worker bees," Lincoln told me. "Watch how they collect the nectar from the flower. We both see the flower, but the bee sees more. She sees how the light travels, and can look at the pattern the nectar makes. *Ohh*, to see like the bee…," she sighed, and informed me that what I was watching was the start of the honey- making process. I could see that this was important to Lincoln and I motioned her to continue.

"Each bee has little glands in her body, and the sugar from that nectar will be changed into honey," she expounded.

One of the bees shot from the iris and flew in a straight line, albeit somewhat clumsily, back to one of the nearby hives.

"See how she returns to the hive," Lincoln continued, "for she goes to tell other workers that there is pollen nearby. Her motion will give the direction of the food source."

"How many hives do you have in your town?"

"There are many hundreds," she said quite calmly, surely not realising just how staggering an achievement it was for these people to keep bees so successfully in such vast numbers.

"Each hive contains a colony," she added, "of several thousand workers, two hundred drones- the male bees- and just one queen. The queen is rarely seen, but is known by her great length."

And, glancing to her extended limbs, I thought how pertinent were her words as I imagined the rather apt parallel between that one queen within that colony, and the almost regal quality of this pulchritudinous girl in whose company I sat now.

"The bee has such intelligence," she said, "and we too live in a colony. Our women outnumber our men, and we must do much of the work if we are to live like the bee."

Then Lincoln went on to explain how the bees are encouraged to make more honey than is needed, the surplus being used by her people in a variety of different ways. Winters were, I gathered, now so mild that there was barely any marked difference between the seasons, although she did tell me that there had been the occasional spell of cooler weather. We may have missed the threatened Nuclear Winter; here, though, was the Endless Summer but at least the aerosol and the domestic fridge had long gone! In the Twenty- Fifth Century, I conjectured that the weather and soil conditions were perfect for the bees to produce this excess of honey. Whilst on the subject of weather, I asked Lincoln if it ever snowed. However, my words were met with that childish mystified frown again. I described such weather conditions and tried to explain the basic meteorological concepts to her, but I might as well have been speaking in a foreign tongue. I told her that no two flakes were ever alike and, in total innocence, she asked me how many I had checked. I could tell her of a new snowfall on a raw winter's day, but there's no substitute for the real thing.

"All so white. *Everywhere*," she mused.

"And it's one of nature's finest temptations- a drift of virgin snow; special to gaze upon, and sacred to touch."

But, like February's frosty residue, our talk of winter soon thawed. She went on to tell me that they have been able to grow the most perfect fruit, and I recalled the grapes, which I had seen that afternoon, along with the tasty pieces that had been placed before me at the table. They had been specimens that should surely have been the envy of the fruit-growers of my own Time.

"Flawless fruit shows that pollination has worked most favourably," she went on to say.

"Flawless fruit is rare indeed, and is also pleasing on the eye," I embellished, but she didn't appear to recognise my subtle nod to her beauty.

"The honey has other uses," she said, and I enquired as to its extra advantages.

"It is used as a medicine, for it stops pains in the throat and head. It can also be put onto small cuts, and, if mixed with the good herbs from the forest, it helps the cuts to heal as it stops germs in the air from entering. It is nutritious to eat, but it must not be fed to new babies, for it contains bacteria that may do harm to them; they are weak and cannot fight any infection."

I nodded inwardly, for I already knew of the risk of botulism.

"Also," she continued, "I am certain that you will agree, it is satisfying to bathe in."

As she said that last sentence, she dipped her head ever so slightly and turned those blue eyes towards mine. I watched them dance slightly beneath her rich lashes. Perhaps it was just a trick of the light, maybe whimsical thinking and nothing more than a dewdrop from the heavens, but I was certain that, for the second time that day, I saw her blush.

"I must speak again of the propolis that the bees collect from the trees," she resumed. "That is used as a healing fluid too. It can help to protect against diseases, and, if made into a cream, can be used to treat burns. It can also enrich our food if added to it."

I touched her hand appreciatively, since I had found her talk engrossing.

It was at that moment, as if from nowhere, that a chill puff of wind scampered past us, and Lincoln said suddenly, "Come, for I think you have had another long suntime."

The time had passed all too briskly, and erelong I noticed that the sun was now slung lower in the sky, blazing against a vibrant orange backdrop. Unwelcome long shadows had inched their way towards us, like newcomers arriving to invade our privacy. She reached for her top, covered herself again and beckoned me to follow her back to the main complex. On the journey back, Lincoln pointed to the bats that jittered past, but which always kept a safe distance from us. They moved so quickly that had my companion not made me aware of their presence, I felt sure that I should have paid no heed to them.

We reached the Great Hall and seated ourselves at one of the tables. Already, the vast area was becoming rapidly depleted of its occupants. An abundance of fruit, cooked vegetables and carafes of wine lay on several of the tables, and Lincoln left me alone whilst she walked around collecting a selection of items for our supper. Across at the next table, two of the younger men were engaged in banter, a scene that should not have looked out of place in my own Time. However, as is oft the case when one is gorged on fresh air and excitement, I found that I had no appetite and, with the exception of a large apple and a tumbler of water, I resigned myself to defeat at the sight of the food that Lincoln had placed before me. Distracted, due no doubt to my weariness, I glanced up to see a young woman sliding between the tables, as silently as a widow's ghost, carrying a tinderbox and lighting the beeswax candles with a willowy taper.

"Come," Lincoln reassured me, tapping my arm caringly, "for the sleep whilst the moon is young is often the best."

So we walked once more to those strange cells, and parted company for the night. I prised off my shoes, undressed and flopped onto the mattress. I could hear Lincoln moving to my right, and I shifted my body over on to its side. By the last struggling flickers of the candlelight that seeped through the flimsy wall, I was able to see her graceful silhouette as she disrobed for the second and final time on that wonderful day, stretched, and finally settled down on her mattress. I lay awake for some time just thinking about my day and our time together, and considered what might be going through her mind. Eventually, surrendering to slumber, my composed breaths began to match the fading footsteps of the candlesnuffer and it was then that I must have melted away, fusing powerlessly with my mattress. I don't know how much later, but the cry of a baby- a nestling as Lincoln had so charmingly described- woke me. I lay still, listening to its cries ebbing as its mother pacified it. Soon the only sound was that of my own breathing. But then I also thought I heard a slight murmur, nothing more than a gentle sigh, from beyond the partition to my right. I supposed that Lincoln was dreaming, and I wondered what lucid fancies might be stimulating her thoughts as she slept.

Surely there could be no more delightfully effective sedative with which to resume my sleep and carry with me into the morning!

CHAPTER 8: *To Harvest The Sun*

From placidity- jumbled sleep I wakened to exquisite thoughts, as the day before had been one of the most splendid days that a man could wish to spend. I began to doubt that I hadn't dreamt it all, and the ensuing relief that it was indeed real sent a fleeting surge of warmth streaming through my veins. But this morning was different, since nobody had come to rouse me. All was silent, save for some distant footsteps (male or female I knew not, because I had learned that all sandalled feet sound similar) although I realised that there was sufficient light for me to read my watch. It was a little after five- thirty, and the stony light of dawn, having suffused into my sleeping area, was continuing to creep stealthily throughout the complex. For some reason, I felt that further sleep would be unlikely, and I decided to begin my day at that rude hour. I rolled off my mattress, stood, donned my clothes and stepped into my sandals. It was the first time that I had needed to leave my cell without assistance from others. Remembering Lincoln's demonstration of the procedure to open and close the strange fabric, I took my penknife from my bag and flicked the little blade from its casing. Placing it against the curious skin, I made a bold sweep with my hand and sliced cleanly down the middle of the wall. The two folds of sticky material hung limply, and, placing one hand firmly on each piece, I pulled them apart as if they were a pair of ordinary household curtains.

I peered into a corridor that was washed with a ghostly half- light. A hundred yards to my left, I could just discern a couple of figures rising from their chambers like spectres escaping from a sepulchre. I left the cell, and turned to reconnect the two flaps of material. As a novice to such a procedure, I was amazed to see that I'd completed the operation with moderate ease. The morning air felt fresh, and, as I glanced awkwardly towards the huge glass lens that lay at the apex of this boundless structure, I was conscious of the fact that the sun would soon be stirring and concentrating its bright rays upon that very feature. But a bold thought suddenly formed in my mind- *what was to stop me from waking Lincoln?* And so I walked quietly to the wall of her cell, and stood outside. My heart was racing and I felt a nervousness that I hadn't experienced since my boyhood days. I could not knock, but would my entry be considered a violation? I recalled how she had hovered about my own doorway. I spoke her name:

"Lincoln…"

No reply.

I hissed it again, louder, "*Lin*coln!"

Still nothing.

Skittishly, I reached once more for my pocket- knife, and cast the blade against the skin. With the same deftness, I separated the two pieces of material, pulled them asunder, drew my breath and glanced inside.

But Lincoln wasn't there.

Her mattress, with the barest of indentation, stood tidily against the side of her room, and a small jug lay poised on the square wicker stool. On a flimsy mat that had been placed next to it, stood a neat row of coloured glass phials and, in an orderly line in front of the containers, was arranged a selection of her utensils. To the right of me were a few items of clothing. I could smell a gentle hint of lavender in the air, and, on closer inspection, I noticed that it emanated from the foot of the mattress where there was placed a small wooden bowl filled with scented pine balls. And, aside from an oval hand- mirror, scotched from years of use, and her tin of finds, there was nothing else. But it felt wrong to be standing there, as if I were intruding, and, with discomfort replacing my curiosity, I retreated with guarded steps from the room.

I walked back down the corridor, and descended the stone stairwell. I have already attempted to describe the sheer size of the place, but to see it in the early light of dawn casts it in a different perspective. A subtle grey haze seemed to emanate from that hushed chasm, but every so often tiny glimmers of light, as the breaking daylight glanced off the bronze balustrade, would wink at me from the silent depths. Poised halfway on that stairwell, I held tightly onto the railing and contemplated the massive arrangement of individual sleeping compartments. Edis had envied the strength and resolution of the honey- bee, and Lincoln herself had compared their settlement to that of a hive. Within this complex in which I stood, in that gossamer light of dawn, dreamt the aspirations of Mankind. But this was no thriving colony, for Edis had told me of their inevitable fate. Despite that fact, each little cell would be certain to open again this morning and each worker would withdraw to face the new day. Lincoln's bees would continue to sustain themselves, but for how much longer would her township endure? Edis had spoken of several more generations, Lincoln some eight to ten. That many even? The bee may have lost its sting, but Death's barb remained. I couldn't help but admire these people, for, in the face of adversity, they remained resolute and continued to embrace each sunrise. What hopes and aspirations had they? For what did they hope in the next fifty years? There were to be no more technological advances. Now there was nothing but a slow decline, for this was the prolonged onset of Extinction. And I was here as a last-minute passenger, travelling along the shock- waves of Human obliteration, only to disembark sometime before the journey's ultimate destination. I couldn't jump ship. I couldn't run and I couldn't hide. Nor could I cower in a darkened corner, as there are no right angles in a ricochet effect.

The scantiest pattering of feet stirred me from my thoughts, and I lifted my head to see two small girls scurrying in my direction. They were both lost in amusement, but making every effort not to talk at this premature hour, and I presumed that one had woken the other with the promise of a frolic. How they resembled miniature versions of Lincoln and Gale! One girl caught my eye, and I smiled. She stopped, gave a gap-toothed grin, blushed and continued with her chase. But my main consideration was to find Lincoln, for I had whiled away such diverting hours in her company yesterday and I wished for her friendship again on this new day. The corridor wasn't lit, as there was sufficient light from the central pyramid to penetrate the route. I soon arrived at the huge dining-hall, and, although most seats were unfilled, I was still surprised to see so many already breakfasting.

"Welcome!" a forceful voice rolled dominantly across the sea of partially- filled benches; I looked over and saw Edis about to draw on a slice of melon. I walked to his table.

"Hello again," I replied.

"Sit at the table," he said, and, at his behest, I sat opposite him on the narrow wooden pew. "Lincoln will join us soon," he added, as if he had drifted inside my mind, "for she is in the kitchen preparing."

"Preparing?"

He offered me the other half of his melon.

"This sun my daughter will go to collect food from the forest behind the honey pools."

The fruit was watery and insipid, but I ate it nevertheless.

"What food will she look for?" I enquired.

"Lincoln usually returns with the finest dogspaw fruits, if they are ready to be cut, mushrooms, herbs of basil, sage and the leaves from the bay. The woods provide so much for us." He could have been talking about a loyal friend. And then, his face still deadpan, he said suddenly, "You shall go with her!"

I was taken aback by his suggestion, assuming it to be just such, but saw no reason why I should not go and help. I had been enjoying my forced internment in this placid world, and I had been treated with kindness and dignity. Now I should offer my services to these praiseworthy people. As if to sway my thoughts, Lincoln, whom I had failed to notice, as she must have walked from the kitchen, appeared at our table at that very moment. She looked fully prepared for the day's work, and I stood to greet her. That familiar loincloth was still wrapped about her waist, but she wore a couple of extra pockets that were clipped to her utility- belt; I presumed that they must have contained the various utensils that she needed for the tasks that lay ahead. But gone were the scanty tops in which I had seen her clad all week. Now she wore a sage cotton shirt, which buttoned from her neck to half- way down her chest where it became a large pouch. It was an unusual, but rather functional, garment. However, despite its queer design, it fitted her most attractively. Hung around her neck she wore a charming pendant, shaped not unlike a huge glass teardrop, and suspended on a choker of tiny pieces of polished wood. I wondered if the honey had not revitalised her in some way, for her black hair, plummeting to her shoulders where it kinked slightly as it brushed her shirt, seemed even more lustrous than the day before. She sat down, and I followed.

"It seems as if I shall never awaken before you," I said, shaking my head in mock defeat. "Couldn't you sleep?"

"Why should I sleep when the blackbird has wakened to sing its song? Already the bee is active, and the ant is busy in its tunnel. Should I rest when all else in Nature is rousing?" And she returned my smile. I have spoken already of Lincoln's charmingly simple manner of looking at life, and I found it difficult to debate any of what she said.

"Our friend will join you this sun," Edis declared. He was holding a fat candle, semi- spent from the previous evening, in his left hand, and in his right hand a knife with which he was whittling at the virgin wax around the edge.

"And I shall be happy for his company," she replied as she helped herself to a selection of fruit from the bowl and edged herself nearer to the table. She seemed reserved in her father's company, although I assumed that she just wished him to take the lead in the conversation. After a relaxing twenty minutes at the table, Lincoln said quite suddenly, "Come, for there is much to do."

She stood and flashed me that irresistible look. As we parted company with a peculiarly thoughtful- looking Edis, I heard the pot dish rattle on the wooden table- top as he inserted the newly- tapered candle.

An hour had passed already since I left my sleeping quarters, and Lincoln, who had stirred earlier than I, was obviously keen to commence her day's labour. On Lincoln's suggestion, we returned to my cell so that I could change my footwear for the walking- shoes that I had been wearing when I arrived for she deemed them more suitable for the day's labour. Then we left the building, and we were greeted by a gentle cool wind that I found most refreshing. We passed through the vineyards, and soon reached the communal bathing area again. My thoughts strayed immediately to the bath that we had shared, and I even recognised the pool in which we had lain together, now drained and awaiting a fresh mixture of water, honey and herbs.

"Lincoln," I dared to ask at last, "do you not have a man in your life?"

She looked bemused, so I elaborated, "A man who is special to you, someone with whom you share your life?"

She grinned as she answered ingenuously, "Yes, there is a man. My father is special and he has always been in my life."

"No, Lincoln, I mean a man other than your father. A man who may want to live with you, grow old with you...a...erm...boyfriend...no, wrong word...a soulmate, a lover, *somebody who will give you children?*"

Her face loosened still further, and, had I not known her better, I should have said that she had been temporising.

"I understand now of what you ask...a male with whom I can breed?"

"Er, well I...suppose so."

"No!" she answered emphatically. "When we sat on the stone and talked last suntime, I told you of the threat to the women- the mothers, the daughters, the friends- of Mentarea. Because of that risk, our father, who also carries sorrow on his strict shoulders, has forbidden Gale and me from being taken in Harmony."

Her eyes darted distractedly as she hesitated, and I thought it best to discontinue the conversation.

Having listened to Lincoln thus far with interest, in particular her unusual terminology with which I assumed she had described a marriage, I urged her to tell me more about the relationships within her society. I was intrigued, and surprised, to learn that Mankind had once more espoused a strong moral concept. Lincoln simply could not comprehend that, in my Time, a man may have left his wife, or vice versa, and sought comfort in the arms of another. Divorce, or the very notion of any form of separation, simply did not exist here- it had breathed its last with the Society of Old. The people seemed to dwell in a state of almost childish innocence and contented acceptance, but, like most of what I had witnessed so far in this incomparable place, I found it difficult to condemn such an aspect of their lifestyle. I sighed inwardly, as I knew that my people could have learned so much from the citizens of Mentarea.

We descended that grassy slope again, and I saw the rows of hives from yesterday. They were deserted because of the early hour, although Lincoln informed me that the girls would arrive later to collect the honey. As we neared them, I could hear the familiar loud droning of the bees. Lincoln led me to a sandy path some hundred yards or so from the bottom of the hill, and we walked along it into the forest.

After a distance of about a quarter of a mile, the path petered out. She then said, "Now we are near to a dogspaw crop."

She walked further, parting the foliage with an extendable, hinged scythe that she had plucked from an additional pouch on her utility- belt. I followed close behind, my hands intermittently flicking loose vegetation from my route and waving away the odd flying insect. After a few more minutes, I felt a fresh breeze tickling my face, and I was amazed to see that we had arrived at a sizeable clearing. But even more astounding was the sight that welcomed us. Oscillating in the fresh air, and making a soothing and repetitive clicking sound as they massaged each other, stood an abundance of anomalous looking cherry-coloured flora.

"What a sight!" I cried. "Those are dogspaw plants?"

"Yes," said Lincoln, "and we shall collect many seeds this suntime."

She stood back whilst I walked towards the edge of the field, and, glancing to her, I could tell that she derived genuine pleasure from my fascination.

"If only I were able to record such sights as this," I yearned. But she didn't respond. I continued, "Lincoln, I'm sure I'll enjoy helping you today. You must show me what to do."

She joined me.

"Come," she said in her usual phlegmatic way, and I walked with her to the edge of the crop where we stopped next to a weathered piece of discarded masonry. She unclasped her utility- belt, placed it on the stonework and uncoiled it to display- for my benefit- the full range of her pocket gadgets. From the third slot along on her right side she pulled a curved scimitar, the polished wooden handle of which gleamed as she placed it beside the belt. In my short time here, I had become rather fascinated with the peculiar array of appliances that Lincoln kept in her belt. That waistband was, to all intents and purposes, the handbag containing the practical accoutrements with which this girl conducted her day-to-day life. Working left around her waist from the brass buckle, I had noticed that the pockets contained the aids to her toilet- the curved strigil- shaped device, the little pack of bistre and brush, and the miniature tin of 'toothpaste'. On her right- hand side were her tools- the odd 'door- key', her versatile knife and the aforementioned scimitar. A temporary pocket, wider, held the telescopic scythe.

"Hey, Linc, I've been meaning to ask you, what's the pattern on your buckle?"

She picked up her belt and ran a slender finger over the raised design.

"I cannot answer your question, for I do not know. There are many such buckles in Mentarea, and they are very old."

That was that and she placed it down again.

"Look at the plant," she said, interrupting my thoughts, as she directed the little scimitar at the fruits that grew from the sides of the stalk. Gripping it in her right hand, she then said simply, "Watch," and, rotating the cutter in a gentle fashion, she proceeded to sever the strange fruit from the plant. "It must be cut with care," she continued, "to prevent the seeds from spilling to the floor. We will work together now. Many dogspaw plants are not ready to harvest. Perhaps two more suns, perhaps more. You must look for plants that have this blackening about the flower, for they are the ones that we shall pick this sun."

To illustrate, she pointed to a slight discolouration upon the leaves surrounding the pulpy fruit. With her scimitar in her right hand, she paused as she pointed out the components of the dogspaw. There was a thick stem, somewhat like a broom handle, fringed by wide, smooth leaves. Where the leaves grew thickest were the fleshy, bowl- shaped maroon- black fruits, each surrounded by four curved padded petals, hence the name (a five- headed flower was not unheard of, but was considered rare and even lucky, rather like the four-leaf clover). The pulp was what we had enjoyed and was clearly relished- like caviar in my own Time- due to its spirituous quality. The hard, white seeds that were set loosely in the fruit were, of course, put to a more commonsensical use.

The plant itself was either a hybrid of known species or an unidentified genus whose seeds had been cultivated deliberately or had travelled from afar to root in ancient English soil and thrive under our new sultry climes.

Lincoln donned her belt again, in anticipation of our work, and soon we were immersing ourselves in that pleasant and productive morning. I would rummage through the yard- high plants for the ripest specimens, and she would follow with her equipment. Every now and again we would exchange roles, and she would call me eagerly once she had spied a suitable bloom. I discovered that Lincoln was learned in the ancient study of mycology as, on a couple of occasions, she would probe the ground, with the determination of a redshank, in order to find the choicest mushrooms with which we could supplement our harvest. She even found some shaped like oysters and growing from a rotting tree- stump. Not long afterwards, I spotted a cluster of puffballs, some of them three or four inches in diameter, and she was happy for me to collect a few.

Across the field, some hundred yards from us, a party of three gatherers was scouting for food and I noticed that they each carried a full sack of produce. Lincoln raised a dogspaw and waved it; one fellow from the other group responded by doing the same. I assumed that this was their way of conveying to one another that the outing was proving to be a success. Just as Edis had said, she sought out herbs too and placed them carefully into the pouch on her shirt.

However, whilst this population was used to the outdoor life, I was experiencing an ever- growing discomfort in the intensifying heat. I believed that Lincoln's honey- bronzed skin was so accustomed to the sun's rays that blazed it, that I fancied it could now repel them almost like snow reflecting sunlight. She cast me a troubled look and I knew that once again she had recognised my suffering.

"Come and rest under the tree," she said, gesticulating to a large and obviously very old cordyline, with more heads than the Hydra, which was growing at the edge of the open area. I was glad of the opportunity for a break and I followed her almost without pausing.

We both sat in the shade of that tree, and then she proceeded to remove her cotton shirt, exposing her aurulent breasts. I wasn't taken aback- I believed that, as the days wore on, I would become less and less surprised by Lincoln's actions. Besides, having shared a bath already with this girl who clearly bore no bashfulness about her nakedness, I certainly had no need to feel awkward in her company. We shared water from a flask that Lincoln had packed in her bag. My sack was now brimming with dogspaw fruits, and I enquired of her as to how many more we should collect.

"The dogspaw has been good to us this sun," she replied, "and it is better that we return to this area after more suns have passed. We shall look for more herbs later, but now we rest."

Then she promptly lay on the dry earth, and, in an almost uncharacteristic way, she propped herself up companionably on one arm.

"Let us talk again," she spurred me.

I lay facing her and mirrored her posture.

"Fire away," I invited her, which caused her to frown. "What d'you wish to talk about?"

"That," she said, pointing to my wristwatch. "I have seen how you look at it. What is it?"

"That's my watch. I tell the time with it, although it doesn't seem to be of much use anymore."

"There are *times*, but how do you *tell the time*. Of what do you tell it?" And once again, as if to illustrate her wonderment, little shallow pleats appeared attractively around her eyes.

"No, Lincoln…" I began to laugh, but checked myself. "My watch tells…shows me the correct hour of the day. Now it says…" I glanced down, "twelve thirty- five."

"But it is past the point of zenith now. That is all we need to know. Then moon and stars come after sun sleeps. Sun appears when moon rests. Sometimes moon remains for a while when sun is awake, and sometimes moon does not even want to show himself fully. Why do you use strange words?"

It was quite staggering how the descendants of a people who were able to design and develop a magnasule, and maintain a lifestyle that couldn't be eclipsed, could be so primitive in their approach to the monitoring of a twenty- four hour day. Nevertheless, in the soothing shade of that hot midday, I attempted to explain the whole notion of the twenty- four hour clock to Lincoln. To illustrate, I placed suitably- sized pebbles on the ground to represent the Earth, Moon, Sun and even two or three of the planets- in the absence of anyone with superior knowledge, I could not be chastised for any I misplaced!

"I am thinking that the ow…owass…what is the word?"

"Hours."

"Yes. I am thinking that the *ho-urs* we spend together are as plentiful as the blades of grass upon which we may lie."

I smiled.

She glanced at the pebbles again.

"Tell me of the moon."

"What do you want to know?"

"It is no more than a barren rock," she said, picking up its representative pebble.

"How d'you know? Have you ever been?"

"No-o-oo!" she laughed.

"Well, it's not barren. In fact- this may surprise you- it's really made of cheese!"

Her eyes were shining.

"Have you- ahhh- ever been?"

"Nope. But others have."

I thought she was about to gasp, but she stopped halfway and her expression morphed into a grin.

"Aaaaahh! A story for a child; but it is one that I was never told!"

"No, Linc, it's *not* a fairy tale. It's true- supposedly! There *were* doubters. But I'm serious."

She giggled.

"What's so funny?"

"Travellers to the moon! They must have been sick."

"Sick? Why?"

"Because all they could eat was cheese!"

"Oh well, who needs to fly to the moon when you can fly to the Future and meet Lincoln?"

Banter aside, the trusting look from her eyes led me to believe that I achieved a partial success, although my explanation, elemental as it was, may have been better directed at Isaac who enthused over any scientific concept. Despite her agility, intelligence and stamina, Lincoln clearly saw Life as no more than a series of plain events that were linked together in an uncomplicated chain. But I couldn't blame her for that; the folk of the Twenty- Fifth Century did not need complexity in their lives. Oh no, because *that* had died with the Plague.

"Make the machine tell you again!" she implored me in the same way that a child requests a repeat of a favourite game.

"Well...here, *you* look...see where the hand lies now...it's nearly one o'clock. The minute hand- this longer one- has moved from there to here. The hour hand has moved too, but not as far."

With eyes afire, she said, "Let it tell you again later."

"I've an idea, Lincoln. We shall improve your knowledge- *you* will wear my watch. You may have been born without a birthday, but I'm confident that I can teach you how to tell the time!" I grinned as I sat up and unfastened the strap. Then I added: "There's just something that I need to do."

I carefully turned the little control, moving the minute hand backwards, the hour hand altering only fractionally. It was, of course, a totally pointless act.

"You change it. Why?"

"Well, I've just remembered that I always had my watch running fast; that's how I seemed to live my life, always ten minutes too fast! But here...*here* it's different!"

She was kneeling. I placed it around her trim left wrist, as Lincoln was right- handed, fastening the strap at its narrowest eyelet, and she looked as thrilled as any woman of my own Time might have been upon receiving a diamond necklace.

"But take it off before you wash," I added. And then I was taken aback. She leaned towards me, placed both hands on my shoulders and kissed the top of my forehead. It is difficult to describe how I felt by that sudden gesture. My heart skipped with a strange emotion as it decided to work just that little bit harder and little tremors of excitement tingled at every nerve ending. That spontaneous display of her gratitude was worth countless words.

"I will always remove the machine before I bathe," she reassured me, and she thrust her hand inside her rucksack.

But she did not have time to finish, for she had suddenly become aware of something behind me.

CHAPTER 9: *Under A Tempest Of Emotion*

The sudden expression of panic on her face shocked me, and I shot around to see what had caused it. A grey shadow had washed over the clearing, and I saw that pewter- coloured clouds were now gathering in the sky.

"Looks like we're in for a shower," I said light- heartedly, but at the same time slightly alarmed by her apparent unease.

"The rain can last. We should return now," she said.

I looked to the sky again and was amazed to see the darkening mass heading swiftly in our direction. It was incredible to see that rain- laden sky spreading towards us, and it reminded me of stop- motion photography where the movement of the clouds is increased spectacularly. But, needless to say, I still could not quite see why the threat of a badly needed shower of rain would cause such alarm, and I posed the question to Lincoln:

"Is it really of concern to us?"

"The storm can be cruel, and it is not safe to stay outside," she replied.

But the extraordinary speed at which the pending torrent was advancing would clearly leave us insufficient time to return, and the only course of action was to seek shelter and sit it out.

"Come on, Lincoln, let's see if we can find some proper cover," I suggested.

Even as we left the shelter of our cordyline, I felt a stray spot of rain on my cheek.

"I know of a cave not far from this place, through the trees," she said.

I needed no further persuasion and we snatched our sacks and ran to the woods.

The atmosphere, now clammy, had also become strangely electrified by the time we had spied a rocky crevice which penetrated the hillside by some eight feet. It was hard to comprehend such a drastic turn in the elements. Something strange had afflicted the weather, and I was witnessing conditions that had never been seen before by anybody from my Time.

And then I heard the rumble of thunder. Low, almost lethargically, it sounded, like the trundle of a weighted ball on a table- top. I stopped and looked skywards. It was a foreboding sight to see the sky so darkened. Perhaps it was the unearthly light that seemed to sit behind the cloud, but I almost felt as if that black tarpaulin were edging near enough for me to touch. I waited to count, but the roll didn't stop. It continued, changing from a gripe to an uncomfortable grumble, and then a foul- tempered, forceful roar. Swinging round towards Lincoln, I saw that our surroundings, which had been bathed in golden sunlight, had now begun to lour and that bright setting suddenly changed as it became enshrouded in an eerie half-light. Even those rocks looked angry. The entrance to the cave, contorted under that woeful sky, seemed to take on the facets of a screaming mouth. We scurried to it, and I saw the last vestiges of sunlight slip from her face.

"Come," said Lincoln when a series of rapid flashes suddenly lit up the sky, as if the stars themselves were being hurled across the heavens. She ran inside the shelter, and I stood outside to watch as the sky itself appeared to be ablaze; it was fascinating to observe the phenomenon. The flares glimmered with varying degrees of brilliance until finally, as abruptly as they had started, they ceased. For some seconds I held my breath with anticipation. I could hear nothing, not even Lincoln whom, by this time, had withdrawn from the cave to join me as I watched the dazzling spectacle.

There was simply no sound at all.

I breathed again.

All was placid.

Just my slow, steady breathing.

It was an almost unworldly serenity.

I blinked.

An eggshell silence.

But the portentous crack that followed, a savage and doom- laden roll, could well- nigh have been the stratosphere itself being wrenched apart. Seconds later, another stillness; nothing more than a whimper of calm but barely enough time for me to catch my breath before I heard the familiar sound of rain tickling the trees.

The storm had started.

The sound magnified, like tacks tipping on tin, and no words could do justice to the downpour that ensued, for it were as if the some of the mightiest lakes and rivers of the world had been transported from below to sit atop the perforated fabric of cloud above. It was time for us to take refuge.

"Well Lincoln, I fear we're here for the duration. How long do you think it will last?" I asked somewhat glumly as I moved to a dry spot at the rear of the crevice.

"I cannot tell. Some of the storms have lasted from one sun, through moontime, until the next sun," she replied dejectedly.

"A whole day and night!" I exclaimed. "Well at least we have plenty to eat," I said, gingering up our spirits and nodding towards the two sacks of freshly- picked dogspaw fruits.

"And we have enough to drink too," said Lincoln, her face breaking into a cheerful grin. Her next move amazed me, as, like a magician with a rabbit, she pulled a miniature flask from her bag. The flask was followed by two metal beakers, no larger than cotton- reels.

"What is it…more water?" I asked.

"You recall the words of Caxton in the vineyard?" she prompted me.

"The wine…the wine from the huge grapes," I replied.

"The wine from the *slumber- grape*," she said, stifling a grin.

"Ah! Of course."

"We shall eat like you say, but not *just* dogspaws," she said, producing a selection of fruit from her little rucksack. She carefully unfolded a square piece of cloth and spread out the items on top of it. Lincoln's culinary skills could fashion the most ordinary selection of fruit into a mouth- watering presentation, and I watched as she cut the food with an almost artistic precision. She sliced the apples into perfect quarters, and removed the peel teasingly from the large orange, taking care not to tear it, in one neatly whorled shape. Next, she split a couple of dogspaws, and gently scooped the pulp from them; the grapes, of which there were two or three varieties, she pulled from their bunches and rolled them gently onto the mat. We ate, and then I poured two beakers of wine and passed one to her.

"Lincoln, in my Time we would raise our glasses," I said as I held out my drink towards her. Glancing to the rain that slaughtered the ground outside, I thought how singular was my situation at that moment. She clearly misunderstood, and took the beaker from my hand.

"Now I have *your* drink also?" she queried.

"No, pass it back to me and I'll explain," I smiled. With the beaker back in my hand again, I raised it once more and called on her to do the same. Now totally intrigued, she mimicked my action and I clacked my beaker against hers.

"Cheers!" I beamed. "Many compliments to you on your preparation of our fine picnic. It's just a shame that the weather's not on our side."

She thought about that last comment, but she obviously decided not to query it, for her eyes then shone with a happy fascination, and I realised that in the space of less than an hour, I had introduced two Twenty-First Century customs into her unconventional world.

"What is its purpose?" she asked, and then sipped from her beaker.

"It's a sign of friendship, a social gesture. People do it when they're together; it shows that they like each other," I explained.

There was a hesitancy.

"Do you like *me*?" she asked, her head bowed slightly.

I was startled by her question, and I know I reddened as I thought of her sitting there naked but for a loincloth, belt and ankle- boots. I drank some wine.

"Yes…yes of course I do…you're my friend…you and the others are all my friends here."

She looked up at me for a second, lowered her eyes in a coy way and then lifted them again. In that moment, I fancied that they had metamorphosed into deep blue pools. I didn't just want to create a ripple in those waters; into those depths I wanted to plunge. If I hesitated, I knew that I should draw back lest the water splash my feet. I leaned over and kissed her on the lips. I was startled, for she didn't respond and I pulled away. But I was unperturbed and tried again, opening my mouth over hers. She did the same and, her nerve cropped, returned my affection. I paused after a moment, and, as I moved away, a thin strand of saliva left her lips. Her whole countenance was alive, vibrant now. We kissed again and I stroked my tongue against hers. I was aware of the rhythm of her senses as my own pulse began to galvanise me into readiness. She placed her hand on my hair, gently caressing it, and as she pressed herself against me, I could feel the peaks of her breasts nudging me through my top. I reached around her neck and gripped her thick tresses, massaging them between my fingers. Almost too soon I moved my hand from her hair, gliding it gently from her shoulder down the slope of her silken breast whilst she tautened in expectancy.

But then I stopped.

There followed a gasp of wind, a lament from the elements. It could, I fancied, have been the cave itself groaning.

"Lincoln," I sighed as I elaborated on my last answer, "I know now that I am in *love* with you. I've tried to resist it, but can't. I've seen many fine things in this Garden of the Future, but to cut the most beautiful rose from its stem in a moment of folly would be wrong."

I wasn't here to blight these waters and I don't even know whether she understood my analogy. But there was a more important reason: reminding myself of the deaths in childbirth, I clearly did not dare risk the consequences of any amorous advances. Tact was paramount and I was careful not to add that, once cut, the finest bloom will wither and die. In a matter of seconds, her face ranged in emotion from trepidation through disenchantment to sadness. I watched as a solitary tear ran from her right eye and down her cheek, from where it dropped to the sand.

She sniffed, before replying, "I know that in my heart there is a warmth that I have never experienced before, and there is something else too; there is an aching that comes when I am near to you. It is an aching *inside* me, wherein lie the intricacies of my womanhood. Oh how my thoughts are wilful, as I thirst to be stripped of the pith of my...my girlhood!"

"Oh, dearest Lincoln," I said as I gazed at her beautiful feminine form, "they weren't wrong. Such poetic words could never be wrong. *I* was forgetting myself. Would that I could whisk you from this Time and..."

For the first time, and with a troubled voice, she interrupted me:

"Isaac calls you the Storm- Traveller. If you *are* a traveller, it means that you must return when the elements find favour for you to do so. Am I not right?" She began to drain her heavy heart, and now the tears formed as little plashes of dejection in those misty eyes. I pulled her to me and embraced her, stroking my fingers along her naked back.

"Lincoln," I whispered into her ear, "I just don't know if there *will* be a way back for me. Not ever. After all, there's a storm raging now- not *just* out there, either- and I'm still here! Somewhere, not too far from here, a long time ago, people are missing me. They're still out there...*back* there. They didn't all cease to exist for my convenience just so I could be entertained here and now. I hope they never forgot me."

I leaned back, but still held her.

"If you left here, I should never forget you," she snuffled, "and those you left behind would remember always."

"I know, I know. Sometime between then and now, maybe I became a brass plaque on a bench somewhere!"

Outside the rain continued to fall, causing little spouts as it pounded the earth. A shower of water was cascading over the edge of our cave, and draining away in small rivulets as it lashed the ground. The noise was unabating.

I pulled her to me again. For several minutes I held her tightly to me, and I felt her heart throb steadily against my chest. How I wanted to seize this girl, but I fought against such an instinct for I knew that it would be an improper act. I let her go, and sat apart from her in contemplation. I could see that she was upset, but I could do nothing at that moment to lessen her emotion. So we sat at the rear of the cave, for what seemed like an age, but in reality lasted perhaps a half- hour and the inches of dry earth that separated us became spread like a ravine of flooded sentiment. Despite such potent wine, I could think of nothing to say for I had already expressed my feelings with wanton abandon. She merely sat motionless, like a hindered acrobat, running her fingertips dejectedly through the dirty sand and with tears in her eyes. And the glass pendant around her neck, which I had likened prophetically to a teardrop, no longer sparkled for now it had absorbed the refrained mood of that moment.

There are some things that happen in life when the moment is at its most problematic, and I have always liked to imagine that they present themselves for a specific reason. Our silence was broken by the most menacing but, perversely, welcoming sound I have ever known. It was a wild and unkind noise, and it shattered our muteness like the ear-hammering din of a jet on an idle afternoon. Nature was switching a gear, stepping up her onslaught. The rain continued to pelt the earth, but its thrashing then became superseded by an intimidating howl, the scream of an almost ungodly wind. Lincoln broke our silence as she stirred with alarm:

"Now… there is wind," she said quite suddenly, sniffing whilst making a concerted effort to wipe the moistness from her reddened eyes.

I was just relieved to hear her speak again.

"This is quite a storm. Are you still thinking that we should return?" I asked, sensing her concern.

"We should go back, yes. This storm could do much damage," she replied knowingly.

I looked towards the entrance of our cosy shelter. The thought of returning in such conditions didn't appeal to me. Nevertheless, if Lincoln wanted to make her way back to the Great Hall, I would obviously go with her.

"I'll go back if you want, but we're going to get a pounding from the conditions out there," I said. As if to vindicate my concern, a flash of lightning lit the cave and the rain had become so intense that slender runnels were now skulking stealthily to the rear of our little abode.

"Come on then," I urged her.

She picked up her shirt and slung it through the cords of her sack of fruit, and moved herself nearer to the edge of the cavern. She cast me a daring look, and then turned her gaze to the outside again.

"Well, I'm ready if you are, Lincoln," I said as I grabbed my bag too.

There was no need to say anything else, for at that moment we both darted in unison from that place across the open sward to the trees beyond. It was only a distance of some thirty yards or so, but by the time we reached the fringe of the forest, we were both drenched. Lincoln was so fleet- footed that she cleared that space in barely any time at all. But as she reached the first trees, she stumbled and went headlong into the undergrowth. I was close behind her, but too late to catch her.

"Lincoln...are you all right?" I asked as I crouched down to assist her.

"Sometimes even the bee, although clever, follows the path that is unsafe," she said, mocking herself as she pushed her hair from her forehead and tightened her brows in a rather stunned way.

But she was bleeding.

"You've cut yourself," I said.

She obviously felt it because she placed her fingers to her left shoulder before she even bothered to look.

"I am cut...*tsskkk*...I have no honey for the wound!" she bemoaned.

"Lincoln, no... it's only a cut...*I'll* doctor it for you," I said, taken aback by her reaction.

The trickle of blood ran from her shoulder in one continuous line down towards her bare breast. I ripped a piece of fabric from the bottom of my sopping vest to help to mop the blood. The dribble was now running down the slope of her wet chest. I folded my cloth and skimmed it gingerly over the droplet that was hanging tentatively from her opulent breast. I then poured a few drops of water onto my cloth and pressed it against the scratch.

"Well, my prognosis- for what it's worth- is that you'll live!" I exclaimed genially.

"Ohh...but I do not think you will like to see me bleed," she continued in a cramped tone. Had I not seen the expression on her face, I should have thought that she were joking.

"I don't want to see you hurt, of course I don't. But it's only a small cut, deep though. It should start to heal whilst we're talking. I've seen worse, but I hope it doesn't scar!"

After several minutes, I released my pressure on the swab.

"See…it's not bleeding now. It will scab over soon. Just a scratch, nothing more," I told her reassuringly, retrieving her shirt from her bag and passing it to her.

"Put it back on, you'll probably feel more comfortable," I suggested, and assisted her. I pushed the torn and blooded cloth into my pocket, then looked at her shirt again as a silly thought struck me.

"Lincoln green!" I was unable to resist the pun, but she just rouged, like a child who hears an adult joke, smiled and looked down innocently at her tunic.

We listened to the rain as it bombarded the canopy above, but fortunately the cover provided by the trees was dense enough to prevent all but the occasional wet splinter from penetrating. We took the opportunity to rest for a few moments, our predicament made worse as the agonised wailing of a brutish wind crept closer with every heartbeat.

"Come," said my unyielding companion, "we must move quickly, for the wind grows stronger and angrier."

As if to illustrate her point, a loud crack sounded from somewhere to our rear. There followed a fearsome splitting noise and I knew that a substantial part of a nearby tree had been torn by the gale.

"There…there it is!" I pointed.

Some yards from us, behind a group of smaller trees, suspended by the thinnest of joins, was a large bough. It hung from the trunk precariously. Then it rocked, grating like a shovel- head on rutted concrete.

It stopped, almost in defiance of that foul wind. But not for long.

There followed a twitch.

Next, a shudder.

The sound of a groan.

Finally, reminding us of the constant danger, it ripped, coughed and plummeted to the ground below.

"Let's go!" I shouted.

We made our way hurriedly, but watchfully, through the wood and emerged at the rear of the hives. There was no sign of activity from the hives, for those intelligent insects had sought the shelter inside. We ran along the waterlogged path, battered by the elements now, that we had walked only that morning in a cheerful sunlight. The gale continued to howl relentlessly as it hounded us from that track. But soon I saw an ominous sight in front of us.

"Help me. Oh help me!" the man hollered, his voice tapering in the wind.

I was horrified by what I saw. I was witnessing a scene that, on first account, appeared to have all the makings of a catastrophe. Lying motionless under a pine that had been wrenched from the earth was a small child. Lincoln emitted a little gasp of shock, but ran with me to the aid of the desperate couple.

"It will not move! It will not...*move!*" he puffed, as he tried to shift the solid piece of wood.

The child, a small boy no older than nine or ten, was still alive, but was obviously in a state of shock. The tree had dropped across his mud-splattered legs. The man, whom I took to be his father, was beside himself.

"Quick, Linc, grab that end with him. We need to move quickly," I told her, positioning myself near the lad.

Lincoln placed her hands near the roots of the pine, and, battered by the wind and the punishing rain, we all three pulled when I gave the command. The needles scratched my hands and arms as I gripped the tree, which was greasily leaden from the unremitting torrent. And the rain- that *rain*- it ran from my sopping hair into my eyes, prickling them.

But Lincoln's wet hands slipped from the trunk and she cried out before teetering backwards and all but tumbling in the churned mire left by the roots as, simultaneously, the man stooped with the weight. He groaned as Lincoln huffed. Then she composed herself, and wrapped her arms more firmly around the wood. We struggled in the unkind conditions, but with our combined strength we did manage to shift it. We lifted the little lad out and I could see that his left leg was undoubtedly broken. But he was able to bend his right one.

"Frank...Frank, my son, you live...you have been saved this sun!" his father shouted emotionally.

"Come on, let's get him back," I urged.

His father scooped him gently from the mud, and I helped him to carry the tearful boy as we walked back as quickly as we could in those torturous conditions. Lincoln carried our sacks, and on the way back, her unflappable tones thwarting the bellowing confusion, she made my acquaintance with the poor fellow, whose name was Olst.

Once back in the Great Hall, we took him to a small ante- room whilst Lincoln ran to look for Omas or another person with suitable medical knowledge. She returned after ten minutes or so with Omas himself and a middle- aged woman with attractively greying hair. The father, smiling broadly, but still sweating from the shock, walked over to us and placed one hand against my shoulder, the other on Lincoln's. He said simply, "My son lives. I shall never forget your help in this time of rain." Few words, but spoken fervently.

Omas, obviously experienced, studied the boy for several minutes. His brow was knitted in deep concentration as he checked him over. He recognised the fracture and proceeded to devise a splint from a case of accessories that lay on top of a nearby wooden cabinet. Lincoln looked at little Frank with concern as if she were witnessing a fatal injury.

"He'll be fine, Lincoln," I told her. I had thought that nothing could go wrong in this well- balanced society, but I had been party to a dramatic change in events in just a short space of time. The elder woman spoke:

"Frank is the son of my own son, and you two have helped to save his life this storm. No words can express my deep joy at such an act. Lincoln I know already, but *you*..." she said as she wrought her ferrous eyes on mine, "...you are the Stranger they talk about."

Lincoln introduced me to this humble woman; her name was Monet. I calculated that she was somewhere around fifty in years, but, even with that silver tint to her hair, she could have passed for a decade younger.

"We are just glad that we were in the right place at the right time," I responded. There was not really anything else I could think of to add.

She smiled, and little dimples formed in her cheeks as she said, "We will all be in your debt." And then she turned to see to the little invalid, who had put on a brave face.

Outside the storm still raged, and Lincoln led me to an unpretentious square room on an upper storey from where we could watch. In damp clothes, we stood in awe for a while as we gazed at the mighty squall belching havoc in this peaceful place.

"There will be other times when we can harvest our food," she said confidently.

I nodded, and watched as the tall tree I had had in my sights finally gave way to the pressure of the elements and tumbled majestically to the ground. We spent the rest of the afternoon indoors with the crowds from Mentarea. Mealtime was not the usual relaxed affair, and I told Lincoln that I should like to go outside, now the tempest had all but subsided, and see if I could help to repair any damage. Along with other folk, like ants we scuttled from that place, all eager to clear up after the foul conditions. The sun, banished some hours earlier, had now reappeared as a flimsy orb, peering nervously from behind gun- metal fingers of cloud. Together, we worked for three hours or more clearing the debris. There was no structural damage to the pools or the hives, but several handsome trees had been felled. We stacked the severed timbers in a large pile, and a muscle- bound worker informed me that, once it was dry, we would have "a grand fire under the next sun." It had been a long day, and beaten by exhaustion and a fresh fall of summer rain, the gang began to drift back towards the complex as they retired for the night.

We could assist no further, so we left and went back to our cells where we changed out of our muddied clothes. And having seeped into the fabric of my shorts, where it had spread along and impregnated the creases, was Lincoln's blood from the sodden piece of vest that I had scrunched into my pocket, now staining my pocket in the shape of a beautiful coral tea- rose. I removed the rag and pulled apart the ends; it was still damp, and smelled sweetly salty. I placed it by the end of my bed just as Lincoln appeared by the entrance to my cell.

"Come on in, Linc."

She stepped inside.

"Been quite a day," I said. "I'm not as tired as I should be though."

She looked revitalised. She had changed into a short towelling skirt, from which vertical straps of the same material, some three inches wide, ran from two clips on the hem up to, and over, her shoulders.

She squeezed my arm.

"Come," she said. "We shall relax before moontime, for, although my body is ready for sleep, my mind is unprepared. There is a place where we can go."

"I know what you mean. My mind's buzzing too,"

She pondered. Surely I knew what should follow.

"I hope it is not buzzing like the bee."

"Nope, just active," I laughed. "Where's the place?"

"Come."

As she turned, I saw how the straps clipped neatly to the rear hem of her skirt. Down another corridor she led me, narrower than usual, and without a door, to a room the size of a school- hall. Its walls were painted in an emerald green that coalesced with a sky- blue about half- way up. And on the walls was painted an array of images- bright daisies from which flew a ladybird to a mushroom growing beneath a rose around which hovered a bee. Some depictions were superb, others rudimentary, and the whole scene wouldn't have looked out of place in a children's hospital ward. There were no openings in the walls, but near to places on the mural where natural light should be emphasised- such as a raindrop on a petal, or the tip of a dragonfly's wing- there was fastened to the wall a sconce from which protruded a candle, its flame dancing on the mural.

"What's this room for?" I asked her.

"It is the room of music, wine and peace."

"Okay. Sounds good."

Scattered around the room were huge cushions, and in the corner on an even larger cushion sat a man with a harp...or something resembling a harp. A man and woman were playing with some wooden blocks, an old woman was talking to another- younger- whilst an elderly man was flirting with his drink. A girl of sixteen or seventeen was pouring from a jug: as soon as she spied us, she trotted over and placed two full beakers on the floor by the cushion- a nightcap, and much needed!

"Thanks," I said.

She smiled as she said, "Enjoy your drink." Then she walked to see if the elderly man wanted a refill.

"What's she given us, Linc?"

"Wine from the elderberry."

"Oh, right."

She sat. Her flesh against the fabric as she sat was like syrup on flour.

"Will you sit?"

"Of course."

I was sitting on a bean- bag supping at elderberry wine!

"Do you like the wine?"

"I do."

I sipped again. Then I swigged.

The girl reappeared and the harpist began to play.

"It's good- the wine, this music. Everything here is just so...good."

My second beaker didn't last much longer. She eyed the speed with which I drank, the glow from the candles seducing her cheek. I longed to explain to her about the time in the cave and my behaviour, which I deemed inappropriate. I couldn't bring myself to say it. Then:

"Do you have any desires for the next sun?"

"Tomorrow? Er…not really."

I was being given a choice and I didn't know how to answer.

"Too..*toomow*?" attempting to repeat.

"Tomorrow…the next day…I mean the next sun or new sunshine."

"Aaahhh…if you have no wishes, *I* have an idea."

"Oh. Will I like it?"

She paused, and moved on her cushion. There was a slight sough as the filling shifted causing her cushion to tumefy on one side.

"I would not show you something that you would not like. Shall we bathe again? After the events of this sun, I am ready to do so."

I'd accept. Here, anything seemed right.

"Sounds fine."

"Do you wish for more wine?"

"Are you having more?"

"I will do so."

"One for the road. I mean *another*…why not!"

"You must place your beaker by your feet."

"She'll just *come*…if she sees it on the floor?"

"Watch."

A moment later I was nursing a second refill.

I shuffled further down my cushion and gazed at a point on the mural opposite, feeling my limbs relax but still mindful of the beaker in my hand, and imbibed the mellowy notes. The harpist never looked at anyone; he just teased the strings.

"Lincoln, what are they playing?" I nodded towards the couple with the wooden blocks.

"They play the game of Old Tower Tumble. They say that it is how the Old Times ended once the people had died or left."

"I know the game- I've played something similar."

I yawned.

"Time to go, I think."

"Moontime beckons. Now we are relaxed."

I expected her to glance at my watch, which she still sported proudly on her left wrist.

"*Moontime beckons*- I rather like that phrase."

*

"Lincoln," I spoke as we walked once again into that huge Chapel, "...about today, when we took shelter...if I did anything to...well, if I was wrong in any way, I...I..."

I knew what I wanted to say, but I couldn't form the words. I wasn't going to go to bed without...what? Setting the record straight? Apologising? Telling her again how I loved her?

"I am wishing that you will not say anything that may spoil any dreams that I may have during moontime," she said in a very gracious way. "There is no wrong between us, and I have feelings inside me that I cannot explain...it is a love unlike any other; and what I do now will give me comfort as I sleep," she added, as we reached the bottom of our staircase. Flashing me a demure look, she kissed me gently on the lips, although I didn't respond in case anyone saw. We walked up and stopped outside her cell where she split the fabric and held aloft the left hand side. With her free hand, she swept her hair lightly from her forehead and said, "I have your watch...what do we 'tell the time'?"

"No, Linc, not *what*, but *how*. It's now...let's see...ten- to- eleven," I told her, "remember the big hand...look...then the smaller one- see how they're nearly touching; they'll touch for but a short time, and then they'll be apart once more..." and I looked into those now dark as midnight eyes- a trace of bloodshot- as I added, "but only apart until they touch again."

"I shall keep it safe with me as I dream," she said, fluttering her lustrous lashes, and stepping into her cell.

And then, like a petal on the wind, she was gone.

CHAPTER 10: *And To Propose The Moon*

And so the days passed with Lincoln and the rest of her fine people in that well- adjusted community. On one particularly delightful morning, I was lying on a grassy hillock next to her, chewing a piece of yellowed grass between my teeth, as most men like to do on such occasions, and doing nothing more than just thinking. She was leaning on one arm, and was dressed in an attractive v- shaped cream sash that covered both breasts and ran to a point just below her utility- belt. It had been nearly two weeks since my strange arrival, and I had been not only welcomed, but also assimilated, into the society. I had become- without choice- a Mentarean. But what a society! Despite its simple, established concepts, which in my Time should have been nothing more than a communal experiment for the purpose of gracing the pages of the weekend papers, some beliefs remained time- honoured. They included the women's inclination to "shop" and to look desirable, the family relationships, productive farming methods, a perfect cycle of work and relaxation, the burial of the dead (albeit lacking any detailed epitaphs) and- naturally- a liking of fine wine. I had been treated as more than just a guest, enjoying a staple diet of fresh fruit, fish, cereal, wine and, of course, honey. I had relished my time here, be it harvesting, bathing or simply just relaxing in the peaceful, childishly- decorated music room where Lincoln had taken me the other day and where we had imbibed our elderberry wine to the soothing chords of the harp. In return, I had helped with tasks whenever I had been able. But it was not my world, and, although I had grown to like the place, I knew that the remnants from my Time must lie beyond this locale. I was homesick and I was restless. There lay my dilemma, for my feelings for Lincoln had grown stronger with each passing day, and it had been- how long had it been? - a week since the day of the rainstorm when I had told her that I loved her. But I did love her. I loved her more than I could ever have imagined I could love a woman. I am certain that my heart must have jumped the moment that I first cast eyes on her. Although I had never attempted any further contact, my body ached with the desire to touch that virtuous golden flesh. I know my distancing myself from Lincoln upset her as her feelings towards me were just as strong, and I truly believe that she felt I had rejected her.

"Of what are you wondering?" she asked softly, breaking my reverie.

"Oh, just things, all sorts of things really," I replied nonchalantly, as I removed the grass from my mouth and threw it away.

"Will you tell?"

"Well, if you must know, I was thinking of a paper bag."

"Aaaahh…the one in which you kept your sweets?"

"No. Similar, though. You know…no, sorry…the one on the ground on a blustery day, the one that never moves when everything else is blowing about. D'you know, Linc, it used to fascinate me? It's true, really. It would stir, but not really *move*. Then eventually it would be whisked away, gone forever."

"Do you wish to discuss the unmoving bag?"

"No," I said, grinning. "I was just thinking. You asked!"

Then she looked somewhat anxious. A question was coming.

"Since our time in the cave, have you had thoughts of me?" she asked hopefully, glancing shyly towards the sallow grass as she spoke.

"Of course I have. I think of you nearly all the time, Lincoln." I sighed then. "But I also think of people and places I knew and loved, things I remember."

"Do you miss them?" She hadn't changed position all this time.

"Yes, I miss them. I yearn for the people with whom I travelled through life, the places that were known to me…even my ridiculous day-to- day routine." Because, compared to the uncomplicated world in which I now dwelled, my lifestyle did seem ludicrous and prosaic.

Promptly, and apropos of nothing at all, she said:

"I have been wanting to ask you a question; there was a better moment to ask, but our talk had turned to sadness and I think that my chance passed like the song of a bird."

I wondered what should follow.

"What is it?"

She stiffened.

"Was there a Lincoln of your Time?" she fished, dropping her eyes again.

"No Linc, there was no- one like you. Had I promenaded with you on my arm, I should have been the envy of many a man." I shook my head, but smiled nevertheless.

"What would you have shown me in your Time when the sun shines as it does now?" she enquired.

"Ohh…on a day like today…let me think…I'd have taken you to the finest shops in the morning and then to the local park for the afternoon. We'd have lain on the grass just like we're doing now, had an ice- cream by the river, and then fed the ducks with a few slices of stale bread. For our meal, we'd have eaten at my favourite restaurant- I'd have bought you everything on the menu- and seen a film at the cinema. But you'd have had to have dressed in a more conservative way!" I laughed, but then I stopped and exhaled a long, slow breath. I had spoken to her in riddles, but I hadn't cared because, selfishly perhaps, I wanted to remind myself awhile of those precious lost amusements. "But we'll *never* go the cinema together or do any of those other things, Linc," I lamented.

"Tell me of the…the *sin..sinnema*" she urged.

"The cinema? Oh, you'd have enjoyed that too…a big room…perhaps like your Hall, where we would sit and face a screen. By combining light with sound and images, you could watch moving pictures of men and women. Those men and women were actors- they pretended to be *other* people and in so doing told a story. For a while- the time it takes for, say…for the movement of a shadow across the ground, you could escape and forget your problems. You became involved in *their* dramas. Do I explain it well?"

"Perhaps."

She seemed to be staring beyond me and I liked to imagine that she could see what I described. I wished I could see her depiction of it.

"I think I shall try to dream of all the things you tell me."

Her face was scrunched now, but her pretty blue eyes showed understanding.

"I suppose that's all you *can* do, dream. I've no pictures to show you, but your mind is resourceful enough," I said rather sadly, and proceeded to explain in detail about fine restaurants, summers in the park and many other favourite pastimes. Every so often, little flickers of response darted across her face. But soon I began to ramble:

"Where are all the great buildings, the bridges, the monuments? Generations of humans had left their mark on the planet by my Time. There's no proof to contradict the thought that all I remember is nothing more than pure fantasy; with the exception of your Elysian world, there's nothing to suggest that anyone ever achieved *anything*. All that remains here are the copper plates, now stored in a gloomy and sterile twilight, along with the valueless fruits of Mankind's aptitude. As for the landscape that I knew…I don't even know *where* I am. The cities, the towns, the rivers…I'd love to see them again, walk through those places, cross the bridges- just go and visit them …or whatever's left of them."

"Do you want to *look* for those places you remember? Perhaps they still exist outside of Mentarea," she suggested, fingering her utility- belt nervously with her left hand.

"I know now that I *do* want to leave and look for my memories. I have to. You have to understand that. I need to see what's become of them. I need to *leave* this perfect place and search for something-*anything*...perhaps the 'Eternal Nothing'," I answered.

Her hand stopped dead, and she looked down. At that moment, a shadow spread over the grass as, unusually, an isolated cloud drifted across the sun. I eased her chin gently with my hand and saw that she had tears welling in her eyes.

"But I burn with a fever for you," she began to sob, "and if you go...I will...I will go with you!"

That stunned me into silence, and I could think of nothing to say at first. But, deep inside, I knew- had known instinctively- what I wanted to say. I added boldly, "If we leave this place on a journey together, we go as a married couple- I should like us to attend a Ceremony of Harmony- *our own*! Will you marry me? Please, Lincoln...I am asking if you will attend the Ceremony with me."

There was a pause.

It was a porcelain hesitation, and a dormant regret was waiting for my approval to rise from my stomach.

"You wish for the Ceremony of Harmony with... *me*?" she questioned in weeping disbelief.

"Why, yes...I've told you already of my feelings for you, and I shall not take you from this place unless you go as...well, as my *wife*! Lincoln," I said, "I should love to marry you."

She was clearly stunned and stared at me in a perplexed way. My remorse had begun to germinate now and I feared that our beautiful friendship had slipped through my fingers and shattered into a thousand shards. What was I doing here anyway, and why should I feel bold enough to presume that this unblemished fledgling would be prepared to take flight on my behalf?

And then, like an early mist dispersing furtively as it concedes to the new morn, her face brightened and she said calmly, but with a passion:

"My flame has been kindled. If you stay, I know nothing shall extinguish it. I will be as one with you, and I will fly further than the bird and work harder than the bee to help you in your search. To attend the Ceremony of Harmony with you would give meaning to my dreams. For ever since we met, I have thought of you and even when the moon appears you have visited me in my sleep where...ahhh...I should not tell but...my dreams have been of unfamiliar diversions."

She flushed as she spoke those last words.

Then I shut my eyes and kissed her briefly, but tenderly, on her lips, and, as I opened my eyes, that little cloud stole away from the sun.

"Oh Lincoln, you'll join me…really? And the Ceremony? I shall ask your father; I don't know how far we've travelled with our traditions and our etiquette, but I will ask him for your hand in…I mean that I shall ask him for you to attend the Ceremony with me!"

"He will agree. Oh, *will* he agree? Yes, he will…I am sure. I know that my father respects and likes you. Do not forget that he lost his own son."

"I hope you're right, I really do."

I put my hand to her cheek to wipe away the bistre that had been streaked only moments earlier with a teary dejection, and I noticed how a tear had dropped onto her sash causing a tiny grey smear.

"Come," she sang. "We shall tell him now."

It was stirring to see her in fine spirits again, and I swear that there could never have been a happier woman than she at that moment.

"No Lincoln…I will *ask* your father, not *tell* him," I waved a careful finger at her as if to chastise her.

"It is good to go now. Look," and she pointed to my wristwatch that she wore faithfully about her wrist, "watch tells…watch tells…Noon! Both hands meet…I am right?"

"Let me see…yep, you're correct- a few seconds past Midday. Let's go and find your father."

I had always believed Edis to be profound in his thoughts and sincere in his intentions. I too had grown to admire the man, the father of my cherished Lincoln. But now I was to add another quality to his character. Lincoln and I found him in the Great Hall, sitting in one of the old metal chairs alone at a small table with a look of intensity etched into his features, as if he were trying to dissect some unwanted conundrum.

"Afternoon, Edis!"

"Hola, Father!"

He looked up, glanced at Lincoln then stared at me.

"Edis," I began as we sat down, "I have something to ask you."

"I know what you have come to ask of me," he replied.

He lifted his hands from the table and steepled his fingertips.

"You…you know?" I was taken aback.

"You have come to ask that I make my daughter available to you and that you become as one in a Ceremony of Harmony."

"But...but how did you know?" I asked, still flabbergasted by his perception.

Lincoln sat there not knowing how to react, for her father looked angry.

"I have seen you together. I saw you earlier this sun as you lay on the grass; my eyes are not *old* yet! There are many feelings that the face of a man may not disguise; love and desire are but two. Even when I have pretended not to see you in companionship, I still have not been able to ignore the new jewellery that my firstborn has started to wear!"

I nicked my lower lip between my teeth.

"Edis, sir, it is my desire to leave this place. Whether my decision will be foolhardy remains to be seen, but there are many sights that I miss, perhaps answers that may need questioning, and I will not rest until I've undertaken such a venture. But I cannot leave Lincoln. It's obvious that I don't need to tell you of the depths of my feelings for her. Edis, I'd like to take your daughter Lincoln as my wife...my own."

I put forward my explanation as nobly as I could.

Then his cheeks flushed with a scarlet choler, and his eyebrows jolted like lightning bolts. Fellow diners appeared to dissolve into their surroundings, their voices muffled as they fused into one indeterminable murmur. It seemed as if we three only occupied the vast Hall at that moment, closeted in our own glass tunnel.

With a resonant tone, he spoke:

"You have been here but a few moons.

You come from a Past that despoiled the Good Earth.

You are trapped in a Time where you do not belong.

I have asked myself if you do not come here to pillage and wear the crown of a ruler, with Lincoln as your...your *queen of old!*"

I swallowed. Yet I sensed there was more to come. I leant back as he slammed his hand on the table.

"Now my greatest fear has been realised. I hoped that, by their avoiding the fate of carrying and delivering a child, my daughters would outlive me."

He pressed his palm on the table- top, his face a mask of pained resignation.

"How I have wished that whatever brought you to us- the freak storm that carried you to us, to Lincoln- would take you back again. Back and be gone forever. Back to your Time of greed, governance and irresponsibility. But I know that you will never go back, and I have had to watch your feelings for each other grow. I know that your love is as real as your presence here."

He sat quite still.

"If I do not give you Lincoln, what is there for you here?"

I remained silent, easing forward again.

"I will give her to you. Of *course* I will give her to you, for my daughter blossoms in your company. You are not cursed either, and I knew that one sun I would have to concede."

Then his face relaxed again, as a balloon softens when the excess air is eased from it.

"But I should like you as a son. Take her. Become one with her. And keep her by your side on your journey."

Lincoln gasped.

"Ohh, Father! I have heard your words, and they have made greater the happiness that I am feeling!"

She hugged Edis as only a daughter could, and then turned to me again.

"If…if," she was almost breathless with excitement, "if only we could do it…do it…*this minute!*"

I grinned as she used a new phrase, and, her face beaming with euphoria, she flung out her arms and embosomed me.

And then we all drank to the future from a carafe of red wine.

CHAPTER 11: *A Budding In The Garden*

The events of the previous day, coupled with the copious amount of wine I had imbibed, had left me in a state of languidness, and, still tired, I woke almost reluctantly in the next morning light as a flower might make a resistant effort to bloom in the dying throes of the summer. But I had Lincoln to think of, and I hoped that she would long remain a good reason to start each new day. I dressed and gently prised a tear in the wall of my cell- I had become quite proficient in entering and exiting those little bedchambers. I had overslept, but Lincoln, ever leal, had waited patiently for me in the Great Hall.

"Good morning to you," I said, as I saw her there at the table, a pile of fruit placed neatly in the centre. She was dressed in a fetching one-piece costume that comprised row upon row of tassels suspended from horizontal bands of the same material. It was a very appealing outfit, and it revealed tantalising glimpses of her bare flesh underneath.

"Good...*morning*," she replied.

She had lost none of her buoyancy from the day before.

"Watch tells me that it is... thirty past the ten hand. I am thinking that you may have been in a happy dream somewhere."

I smiled as I watched the childlike expression on her face. Her eyes, even at that early hour, were enticing me into that magical world again.

"Come," she continued. "Sit, and we shall eat together. The sun will not notice that we are not outside."

Over breakfast, it was only natural that we should talk of our forthcoming Ceremony.

"Will there be much to organise, to prepare?" I asked.

"There will not be much to do. The Ceremony is quick. I have attended two such Ceremonies with Gale."

She seemed quite proud of that achievement.

"And what will you wear?" I asked.

She dropped her head coyly.

"I shall wear a band of the most beautiful flowers around my waist and a ring of plucked petals about my head," she replied, and, desirous of pleasing me, she continued, "I shall be adorned in many fine ornaments, but my upper body will be bare for I shall be decorated with the image of my choosing."

"An image?"

"Yes, here that is the way of a girl- in- Harmony. Gale and I shall decorate each other. I too have been a decorating maid at one of the Ceremonies I attended."

"And what image will you choose?"

"What would *you* like me to choose?" she rebounded the question.

"Oh, I don't mind really…in fact I think you'll look resplendent with anything painted on your body."

"I shall look…*resp*…?" she repeated.

"Resplendent…good, fine," I explained.

"I *think*…I think I have decided already," she said.

"Oh? Let me guess…a bird?"

"*No-o-o-o*…" she began to sketch an invisible shape on the table.

I paused for a few seconds and then:

"A leaf?" I cried, looking at her moving finger.

"*No-o-o-o*…you must think of something different," she teased.

"Well…hmmm…I think I'd like to just wait and see. I don't want to spoil the surprise!" I said positively.

And then she did a rather light- hearted thing. She pretended, quite vigorously, to erase her imaginary drawing, adding, "Then a surprise it shall be, and I will leave no clue on this table." That was my preface to Lincoln's puckish sense of humour and she became like an uncorked champagne when I reacted by grinning.

"So Gale will choose something different?" I asked.

"Yes…a Maid must *never* wear the same design! She will always find another design from Nature," she chirruped, although I couldn't help thinking that I had asked a plainly obvious question.

"And who will come to our Ceremony?"

"Those who *wish* to come," she fizzed.

"Will it be in this place?"

"No, we will be looked on by the sun," she replied, absolutely relishing my interest. I couldn't really think of anything further on which to quiz her. Lincoln had advised me that the Ceremony itself was a brief affair, and from my short time with these people, I had already assumed that the wine would flow freely. I even found myself wondering whether Isaac wouldn't become drunk! It wasn't long before Gale joined us at our table. Her eyes were positively burning with expectancy as she told Lincoln that she would be proud to paint her.

"Tell me how you shall be decorated. What have you chosen? I know what *I* shall be! Ohh, *do* tell me Lincoln!" she jabbered at her sister.

Lincoln smiled mysteriously at those words and leant towards Gale. She eased her sister's hair from her ear and spoke in veiled tones to her. A tide of glee gushed across Gale's face, then Lincoln pulled away to allow her sibling to respond. As she whispered into Lincoln's ear, the latter's head bobbed up and down, and her blue eyes widened with placid anticipation. In another Time, another Place, it would have been of no interest to me to see two girls engaged in such discussion, but somehow the sisters gripped me in entrancement as they murmured to each other in that clandestine, yet strangely childlike, way. Finally, after a few more caresses and exchanges, Lincoln put her fingers to her sister's lips to seal their secret and kissed her lightly on her forehead.

I spent most of that afternoon apart from Lincoln, as Gale had asked if she could take her to pick the flowers for both her Ceremony Ring, which she would wear around her slender waist the next day, and the crown for her head. But I wasn't bored, as I strengthened my bond with Leo who seized the opportunity to ask about the culinary delights of my Time. I liked Leo, and in many ways he reminded me of an old acquaintance from early in my life.

"But why should one choose to devour the flesh of the beast when there are so many other delights?" he queried, smoothing his bony finger over his creased forehead as he continued a conversation he had started.

"Well Leo, most people- but not all by any means- thought that the animal's meat was very tasty. I would relish a good roast dinner," I told him. I had never mentioned the eating of meat to anybody in this vegetarian society until now, but Leo seemed fascinated by the cooking methods and restaurants of my Time.

"Tastier than a pineapple? More flavour than the *fin*- est apple? And you *never* ate it with honey? Ha! I think you have eaten poorly throughout life's journey my friend! Perhaps you now dine in a…what did you call it…a *howt*…ho-o…?" he asked loudly.

"Hotel," I assisted.

"Had I spent many suns eating the wild beasts, I should have ended up built as one of the bulls in the field!" he exclaimed and waved his spindly arms in front of me as he laughed.

"No, Leo, it didn't necessarily make people large. It was good for you…it was the bad food that piled the weight on people," I corrected him.

"When the next sun appears, you will eat the best fruit, including ball mushrooms that you picked!"

Gradually, our talk turned to other topics.

"Leo, did you ever have a Ceremony of Harmony?" I ventured.

"Yes...but she died as the woman of Edis died...and the child was our first," he sighed.

"I...I'm sorry Leo...I had no idea...this vile bequest has scarred everybody it seems."

"Do not be sad...I have my friends and my food, and I help to satisfy the hunger of Mentarea. Here we all have a purpose as you know. But you are not affected...and Lincoln could give hope for the Future," he insinuated. And I felt my cheeks flush, but not through drink.

The afternoon passed quickly in Leo's company. At teatime- or the time of day that I knew to be such- wanting of some fresh air, I excused myself and went for a stroll to the market. I avoided using the magnasule, for I felt that the exercise would do me good after my somewhat sluggish day. I had decided that I too would try to look my best for the next day. I entered the clothing shop where Lincoln had taken me on that first tour of the town and, after some deliberation, chose a rather smart cream-coloured tunic. The man who was busy tidying the place told me that he thought it was a good choice and that it should last me "for many suns and moons." As it did not cost me anything, I thought that it wouldn't really matter how long it lasted- but I didn't say that, for it seemed rather flippant!

There was no opportunity in which to meet with Lincoln again that day, and I climbed up the steps disappointedly to my cell. However, by the finger of moonlight that lingered protectively outside her chamber, I could just see that she was already curled up on her mattress, perhaps lost in the aspirations of a thousand tomorrows.

I had strange dreams that night. The first involved my arriving at my workplace, but not only was it deserted; it was also in a state of ruin. Not just temporary disarray. I mean devastation. However, as is often the way with dreams, I did not seem bothered by all this; instead, I was quite relaxed about the whole affair, simply pleased that I should have no work to do that day! The second dream was more disturbing, for I had become an unwitting guest at some bizarre and nightmarish party. All the other invitees were huge insects. The creatures devoured all the cakes and other sickly treats, and began to talk amongst themselves (strangely, I was not shocked by their ability to speak) about the identity of the lone human being, wondering who had invited me. Understandably, I wasn't at all comfortable at that gathering, and I sensed that I was to become the next meal for one of those foul creatures! I woke in a sweat, and for a few seconds, I couldn't think where I was.

I donned my new tunic, and wore the shorts that Lincoln had chosen for me. With my sandals fastened, I felt ready for the day. And what a day it was to be! I met with Edis in the Great Hall, and he greeted me warmly.

"You will not want to eat much now, for there will be food and drink at the Ceremony. Leo will not spare the fruit, and Ike will bring the finest wines," he advised me.

"I'll look forward to it all," I said, but then added, "When shall I see Lincoln?"

"My daughters rose before the sun," he laughed, as if I should have realised, "and Lincoln will join you once you are at the Place of Harmony."

"When shall we go?" I hoped that I didn't sound too impatient.

"We will go when you say that you wish to go," he smiled.

"Well...I...I'm ready now really...I...er...see no reason to wait," I stammered.

And he stood, saying simply, "Then we *shall* go now."

Edis asked Leo to spread the word that I was ready, and beckoned me to follow him outside.

It was a wondrous morning. The sun sat dependably in an unblemished firmament, and birds sang lyrically from their perches aloft the trees. On what turned out to be a lengthy walk, we skirted around the complex, past the buildings, through a bountiful orchard, and arrived at a charming little garden area at the northernmost perimeter of the town.

"Edis," I cried, "this is lovely. I had no idea it existed."

"It is where the Ceremonies take place- we call it the Garden of Harmony," he explained, as we walked along a central path of loose chippings.

I estimated that the area was about ninety feet in length by some twenty feet wide. It was encompassed all sides by six- foot high hedges, and strewn with an array of delightful pink and white lilac shrubs, exotic slipper- shaped salmon- coloured orchids, peculiar purple crocus type flowers, blooded tissue- leaved oriental poppies, implausibly sized umbrella- cupped fuchsias and other fantastic blooms. A small circular pond lay roughly in the centre of the area, and half a dozen lofty pines grew steadfastly at the top end. Most of the grass had long since conceded to the severe dry conditions, but odd patches had survived and grew from a mixture of loam and gravel. An extemporary large granite table lay to one side, and old tree stumps had been deposited randomly about the place. No sooner had we reached the end and turned around, than Leo, Ike and another man walked in bearing platters of fruit. Another four or five younger men followed carrying an assortment of overflowing bowls of edibles, beakers and large jugs of what I presumed to be wine. The various receptacles were deposited on the table, and the men, with the exception of Leo and Ike, left. I spent some time marvelling at the banquet before me, for there were sliced apples, perfect pears, burgundy grapes, peeled bananas, hunks of pineapple, cubed dogspaws, orange pulp, a load of raisins, blushing peaches, glossy cherries and various other fruits. There were also tomatoes, cucumbers and the largest lettuce leaves that I have ever seen. There was bread. There was cake too. There was red wine, white wine and a rather dubious looking punch. And, of course, there was a huge basin of honey, with a small and contained flame burning brightly beneath it. But the voices faded, as if controlled from elsewhere, and then stopped altogether, and my attention was soon distracted from the sight of the spread before me as I looked to see what had caused such a change in mood. It was a moment that I shall remember forever:

Lincoln had entered the Garden.

I hadn't really known exactly what to expect. I had known that she would be semi- naked of course, and I'd tried to envisage a crude-looking design adorning her body. But nothing could have prepared me for the spectacle that I saw. Lincoln led the little group of people that walked into the Garden, and she looked absolutely divine. She wore a pretty array of flowers around her waist and coiled beneath her groin; a crown of corresponding curling petals bedecked her head. On her left wrist she wore my watch, and on her right one jangled three or four copper bracelets. A chain of polished buglets was hung around her fine neck. However, apart from those items and the delicate sandals that she wore, she was almost naked. But perhaps the word 'naked' does her an injustice, for she was painted about her upper body in the image of a queen- bee! And it was truly a fantastic sight. It had been done as meticulously as Gale's skills would allow and in the most realistic colours. Its body stretched from just below her navel up to the beginning of her neck, and its bottom legs had been painted so that they followed the line of her lower ribs, disappearing somewhere around her back. Its middle legs, shorter, followed a similar trajectory and stopped on the sides of her chest wall. Two small front legs ran up towards her shoulders, whilst the little antennae curved up the underside of her chin stopping just short of her face. Its wings had been painted from a glistening substance, and they ran from half- way down her bare breasts, causing her nipples to gleam, where they followed the curve to continue down her chest. From under her chaplet of petals, her dark tresses spilled evenly to her shoulders. The natural shadow on her face had been highlighted with the same bee-yellow tone, and her bottomless eyes flattered me from beneath crisp black lashes. She was a feast for the eyes, a goddess of Nature standing majestically before me. As for Gale, she completely naked from the waist up and had chosen a beautiful twin- headed sunflower with which to adorn her splendid body, bright orange- yellow petals coiling around her breasts, which curved like treble clefs, and emanating from black and white seed heads painted onto her generous nipples.

"I didn't guess," I smiled at Lincoln, flicking my eyes up and down her delightful body as she stood there in front of me, "and you look…you look absolutely lovely."

"Do you like it?" she asked.

It was almost difficult to respond to such a simple question.

"Lincoln…it's beautiful. Did Gale…d- do it all…herself?" My voice was wavering, as I was aware that all those gathered were listening.

She smiled enthusiastically, "Yes, Gale painted me as soon as sun rose. And *I* painted *her* sunflower."

"You're so clever, both of you…you really are," I praised them in earnest.

Lincoln and Gale were accompanied by Monet, who was painted with the image of a rather unusual bird on her unclothed chest, Olst, who wore a strange sackcloth type of outfit, and, still sporting a splint on his leg and reclining self- consciously in a rough cart, young Frank. Omas and Isaac had also come, and I was overjoyed that all these people thought it important enough to attend this joyous occasion. There were about twenty other people, obviously friends of the family, including two girls whom I recognised from that first mealtime and who brought up the rear of that small, but happy, cortege. Many of the women were bare-breasted and painted in some way, with the exception of the two girls who wore sashes across one breast, presumably implying that they were attending in a catering capacity.

"Come and stand before me," Edis suddenly instructed Lincoln and me in his characteristically firm way.

We edged towards him, and he placed his left hand on Lincoln's shoulder and his right one on mine, the second time someone had done such an act. Without being told, everyone else, including Gale, walked serenely, but purposefully, to stand behind him.

"You have a journey to make," he said, looking only at me, "and you wish for companionship on that journey."

I didn't know whether he wanted me to reciprocate, but I decided that I should remain quiet for the time being.

Then he directed his stare at his daughter, looking her squarely in the eye. He said, "And you wish to be the companion on that journey."

Lincoln said nothing, but blinked those still untroubled eyes once or twice. I realised then that he was making a statement, reaffirming a fact, and certainly not wanting an answer.

"You wish to be together...as one. And it is for that reason that you both wish for the Ceremony of Harmony."

Lincoln turned to me and smiled with such depth that I knew I could wish for nothing more than her constant companionship. How my heart burned for her more than ever at that moment.

"I do not know of a reason why the Ceremony should not be celebrated, and I know that the people here have come for such a celebration."

I was almost expecting him to ask if there was anybody present who could give a reason why we should not be wed...

Then, depressing his hand more vigorously, he said simply, "Be in Harmony together!"

And, in unison, the assemblage behind him repeated his words: *"Be in Harmony together!"*

And that was it, as he then released his hands from our shoulders; it had lasted but a moment. Straight away, Lincoln faced me with a teardrop in her eye; but this time it was a tear of euphoria.

I kissed her.

We spent an hour or so in celebration and the wine flowed freely. Isaac drank several beakers, and I knew that his day would end prematurely. Edis and Lincoln introduced me to the various strangers who all seemed happy to be at that wonderful occasion. I took the time to talk with young Frank and his family. The last time that I had seen the lad, he was caked in mud and crying in pain.

"You're looking a lot brighter, Frank," I said encouragingly, as I stooped to his improvised wheelchair.

"In just a few moons, I will be running again and climbing the tallest trees!" he said confidently.

"I don't doubt it...but don't go climbing in a storm," I quipped, patting his glabrous head.

"You are a man of good fortune," a voice said suddenly.

I looked up to see a pair of intelligent eyes fixing themselves on mine.

"Oh, I know that Monet. Truly the luckiest man in Mentarea at this moment," and I placed my arm confidently around Lincoln's waist.

"I know of your plans, and I hope that Predestination will guard you both on your journey," she continued, and smiled placidly.

The little gathering soon followed the time- honoured tradition of party guests as they began to disperse at regular intervals. Eventually, just Edis, Gale, Lincoln and I remained. The girls' father spoke: "Live healthily and live long together. But tell me of your plan to leave, be it by sun or moon." He placed each hand on our heads, smiled and turned to leave.

Gale seemed reluctant to go, and then said a rather surprising thing. "If you require a maid on your journey, ask it of me," she volunteered.

We hugged her in turn, and watched as she walked out of that Place of Ceremony, her bronzed body with its elaborate and heart- shaped leaves sweeping up her back giving her the look of a dryad in some sublime Garden of Enchantment.

Lincoln waited until she had disappeared from view, and then, with elation in her eyes, said, "I have a gift for you."

"A gift...to mark the occasion? But I've nothing for you," I said.

"You have given me the watch, and I am learning to...'tell time' with it. It is not the way to give a gift, but I wanted to do such a thing...for you," she reassured me, and walked to the rear of the table whence she retrieved a small cloth bag. She came back to join me at the pond.

"Look," she said, untying two delicate strings.

From the bag, she removed a curious object and passed it gingerly to me. It was roughly the size of a house- brick, made from a single block of polished wood and, oddly, perforated at both ends with a set of holes of varying sizes. A piece of cord had been fastened to the top with two small cotter pins, and three delicate metal triangles hung from the underside. I didn't want to insult her, but I couldn't even hazard a guess as to its purpose.

"Lincoln...it's a lovely gift, but I've never seen anything like it before," I told her as tactfully as I could.

"It plays music," she clarified, "but only when the wind blows."

I was relieved that she didn't appear affronted. "Music...but how?"

She took it from me again.

"The wind will pass through these holes," she expounded as she pointed her slender finger to the series of bores on one edge, "and leave through these." She flipped it around to illustrate, and then gave it back to me.

I turned it over a couple of times in my palm and inspected it. It really was a handsome device.

"Lincoln, thank you...I shall treasure it always. Did you make it yourself?"

"I did."

I placed it down gently onto its cloth bag on the ground as I sat down. Then I said, "Sit with me."

She sat beside me, her long limbs outstretched, and looked at me with those captivating and hopeful eyes. I leaned towards her and kissed her for the second time that day, but this time I didn't stop. I opened my lips over hers, placed my arm around her and reclined her softly onto the patchy ground. She responded by running her hand over the back of my neck, gripping it with desire. I pulled away to remove my tunic, and then continued. I snapped the narrow band of flowers, glided my hand down her breast and found her nipple. I rubbed it gently under my thumb, and felt it spring into life. And I continued to kiss her, moving from her mouth to her chin, from her chin to her breast, and continued kissing her breast until my lips reached her other nipple. I flicked it with my tongue, and heard her emit little murmurs of satisfaction. I looked to her face, her eyelashes fluttering like a raven's wings, and then I stopped briefly to disleaf her beautiful flower garland before I carried on kissing her glorious body. Her sensuism unyoked, she began to moan with a volatile ardour, clutching at the strands of grass that were growing, pulling and twisting and wrenching them until they snapped. And then I made love to her.

And when it ended, and she sighed in her delirium, I knew that caution had not been thrown, but positively launched, at the wind and that a caged bird had been released into its rightful territory.

CHAPTER 12: *Germination And Planning*

"Four point six billion years...that's *very* old," I said in response to her question.

It had been a balmy night, and we had lain outside for its duration, not moving from that wonderful Garden wherein we had celebrated, and consummated, our love for each other. I had slept well under the stars, waking just once to the scurrying of a small creature. Under the light of the full moon, I had looked to see what was making the noise. I could not see the animal, but its gentle scuttling suggested that it was probably nothing more than a timid field mouse. It vanished, and then the only sounds were Lincoln's breathing and a soft intermittent soughing of the pines. Turning upwards to face the stars again, I could discern the familiar shape of the Plough in the northern sky, and I reminded myself that I should draw Lincoln's attention to it on another occasion. At that moment, for some pointlessly ambitious reason, I had started to count the stars that lay within my field of vision. It was never going to be a task that I would finish as the next thing I knew I had woken to the sight of Lincoln cutting an apple, the strikingly illustrated bee still regal and vibrant upon her unclothed chest. When she offered me half, my mind flashed back to that first weird day when I had likened the emptiness to the Biblical Fifth Day; consequently, there was I in the Garden of Eden ready to accept a slice of fruit. I didn't need tempting! Fed, we lay down again on that inspiriting earth, and looking at the clear early morning sky, we began to ponder the fantastic eternal tapestry that was woven around us.

"Will it live forever?" was her next question about the sun.

"Oh no, like other stars it'll die one day. It might last, say, another five billion years, and then start to swell. As it grows bigger, it'll become redder too, and, after several more million years, it will shrink and cool. Compare it to a person, Linc- you could say that it's now reached adulthood! So it definitely won't last forever, but *we* don't need to worry about it," I smiled.

"What of the other planets? I have heard our Men of Science talk of them, but little is known."

"Oh...*w-e-ll*...Pluto's very, very cold." I tried to remember. "Mercury's *nearest* to the sun, but it's not as hot as...er...Venus!"

"A planet nearer to the sun would be hotter than one further away. Surely you are not right?"

"I know it sounds strange, but I'm right...there are thick clouds of gas, carbon- dioxide, I'm certain, covering Venus, so they trap the heat from the sun. That's why it's so hot- even too hot for you, Linc! And Mars...that was always the next big thing- I wonder if we ever got there. No, obviously we didn't because too much knowledge has been forgotten already."

"Is there life on the other planets?" she asked.

"Could be, I suppose, but they won't look like us. They may be hideous monsters with green skin and blood- sucking tentacles," I said, laughing.

"Ugggh," she shuddered. "I am glad I live here."

"*I'm* glad you do too. Now I've a question for you," I said as I adopted a mock- serious expression.

"I cannot answer you if you ask about the planets, for you have more knowledge than anyone in Mentarea," she said quite candidly.

"Well...I think you'll be able to answer *this* question," I said.

"Ask it of me."

"Are you ready?"

"Ye-e-ss," she chirred, beginning to giggle, for she had my measure, "I am prepared for your question."

"What time is it?" I laughed, for my wristwatch very rarely left her arm.

She flicked her wrist from her side, and tightened her brows in concentration: "Watch tells...it tells...fifteen from...eight, yes...fifteen from eight," she said as she raised its dome towards me.

"Nearly, it's eight fifteen- quarter past eight...and I'm hungry! Shall we go back and eat?"

"And I am hungry also. But first, love me again. For solitude such as now is uncommon in Mentarea!"

Lincoln donned a rather functional, but nevertheless attractive, white frock that she had brought with her to wear after the Ceremony, and we strolled back, holding hands, to the Great Hall. It was emptying as we arrived back, and we breakfasted on bread, cooked fish and fresh fruit. Having the table to ourselves, we seized the chance to talk of our pending journey.

"We'll be covering a lot of ground, Linc- I'm going to wear my walking shoes that I wore when I...I..." it seemed strange to say it,

"...arrived. I'll take my sandals with me, too. But I could do with some protection- where can I find a hat?"

"A... ha...*hat*?"

"Hat...for my head, to keep the sun from my brow," I explained, pointing to the top of my head whilst attempting to circle an invisible shape with my other hand. It had not ceased to astound me how some basic words had disappeared inexplicably from the language.

Her eyes lit up.

"Like a tree gives shade! We shall go to see Horat, Weaver of Grass. He may be able to fashion what you describe. I will need another pair of boots. I will also need more tools for my belt, and more clothes."

"I'm going to travel as lightly as possible. I've got my rucksack, but I don't really want to fill it. And then there's food to think of. We'll need to take some with us."

"We shall ask Leo. He will provide for our journey," she spoke in her usual reassuring manner.

"Perhaps some wine too?" I suggested hopefully.

"Of course. Come," she bade me in her charming way. "Let us find my father and sister, and ask them to help us in our readiness."

We left the Hall in search of Edis and Gale with the intention of making the necessary preparation for our journey. Catching sight of my watch on Lincoln's wrist, I saw that it had just turned nine- thirty as we crossed the busy plaza outside that prevalent communal Hall. The sun, having now discarded its early morning disguise, was beginning to emerge in all its blossoming and unperturbed finery. It was going to be another sultry day.

"Come on, Linc, let's take the magnasule- it's too hot to walk," I said, rather inertly, as I spied a couple of the gleaming capsules lying dormant on the ground.

"Do *you* wish to make the magnasule travel?"

My guts flipped. Of all the things to suggest, why *that*?

"Well...I'll have a go. With you as my co- pilot, I feel that I can't possibly go wrong."

I hoped that the next moments would not cause me to rue my optimism. Lincoln tilted the craft onto its side and pointed to the small panel of controls, indicating which lever I should need to pull in order to lower the machine once airborne (for, as I have recorded, although low in height, the vehicles did indeed fly). Flicking the switch on its underside, she levelled the vehicle again and it moved vertically to a point about four feet above the rail where it just hovered and twitched occasionally like a bee on a bloom. I did manage to climb in, although I was not as smooth in my movement as she and tumbled on my first attempt. Seeing that I was unhurt, Lincoln gave a wary glimmer of a smile. I was embarrassed, but I put on a brave face and was successful with my second effort. And once again we were coasting towards the bustling market place.

"You are thinking that we shall journey for many suns?" she asked, taking care not to avert her concentration from the route.

"Yes, many."

"What will we see?"

"Oh…remnants. Things I've never seen before, things I recognise…*places I remember*," I answered hopefully.

"You have seen many new things here…now I may see new things too," she said.

"True. What would *you* like to see?" The machine jerked a little as she dropped a 'gear'. I hadn't been concentrating properly.

She smiled, and without looking at me, said, "A *sinne*mar…and a fish."

"A fish?"

"A fish of *gold*!" she braved and turned to me, her eyes shining like trinkets.

At that light- hearted moment, the vehicle stopped and we dropped effortlessly to the ground.

"Come."

She reached for my hand, and it felt good as she touched it. "First we shall find more clothes."

Inside the clothing outlet, I met with the same man who had provided me with the stylish tunic only two days earlier. Like an idling workman, he jumped to his feet when we entered and placed both hands on my shoulders.

"I had not known that you came for clothing for the Ceremony of Harmony when I met with you!" he cried quite joyously. His eyes seemed to be burning with sincerity. "If you had told me such, then I could have given you a necklace for your Companion in Harmony!" Chuckling, he swept his right hand towards a brilliant arrangement of bijouterie and bangles, not unlike a carousel display of jewellery in a shop from my Time.

"My good thoughts will stay with you," he continued, and removed his left hand from my body. Then he turned to Lincoln and, extending a similar felicitation, he repeated the gesture.

"We have come for clothes, for we leave on a journey soon," she told him, and we proceeded to look around the small, but extensively stocked, shop. Lincoln, with her innate efficiency, knew exactly what she sought, and in a matter of minutes had selected, amongst other items, two small cloth coverings for her waist (as I had observed on the occasion of the honey- bathing, these functional cloth wrappings excluded the need for underwear), a spare singlet, a very attractive tasselled band for her upper body and a thicker top, almost akin to a familiar sweatshirt, except for its pleated edges. I selected several garments including a further pair of shorts and a similar heavier top, but lacking the pleats.

We strolled to an adjacent outlet, roughly the same in size as its neighbour, and each found a pair of the practical ankle- boots. Next, we visited a store providing utensils and Lincoln procured a few tools for her multi- functional utility- belt, one of which was a small lens dome which was, I learned later, for the purpose of starting a flame in that primitive, but effectual way, by harnessing the sun's rays. She also collected a small metal cooking- pot, whilst I acquired a blade of some six inches in length and therefore superior to the small one on my penknife. It was an attractive piece of metal- working and came complete with its own scabbard that clipped tidily onto a matching belt. The next place could almost be described as a boutique, and it was there that Lincoln collected some bars of soap, a supply of the sun- block, or bistre, and a peculiar linen sheet, which sparkled like a frozen pond.

"What are those? Beads of some sort?"

She held aloft the folded sheet.

"They are solar crystals. They absorb the rays from the sun and the sheet will stay hot throughout moontime."

"Unusual," was all I said as I had a feeling that my request for an explanation would be non- productive.

Having placed the items into a cloth sack, there remained just one more item to acquire- my hat.

"*Who* will we see about my hat, Linc…Horra…?"

"*Horat* will make what you wish. Come!"

She led me to another of those all- encompassing storerooms and introduced me to a man who looked as if he had been fashioned from the very materials with which he worked. Horat's whole complexion was of a mottled brownish yellow. He seemed to be double- jointed, a feature that could only assist him in his trade, and had a slight stoop to his posture. His fingers looked very delicate, almost flimsy, yet they must have been fine and adept digits, for they had transformed masses of osiers and an abundance of straw into various everyday items such as stools like the one that I had seen in Lincoln's cell, little tables, containers, baskets and even the large screens that shielded the honey- pools. Towards the rear were stacked three or four wicker boxes, which, although I didn't ask as to their purpose, I guessed to be coffins!

Even when the man spoke, it was with a wavering and reedy voice: "What...do you...*seek*?" he rustled.

"I'd like a ha...I'd like something to cover my head," I explained, adding that I wanted to shield it from the sun.

"It should give...shade...like the *tree*?" he asked, ever so softly.

"Yes...yes, that's right, nothing too big," I answered.

Eager to help, and recalling my own description, Lincoln grinned as she traced the shape in the air around her own head. Horat understood and instructed us simply:

"Return before moontime...it will be ready, but I will use...*straw*...strong straw," he said, overcoming his shyness by smiling for the first time.

"If we cannot come, I shall ask my sister to collect it," Lincoln said, and we left Horat to his work.

We occupied the rest of that morning, our first full day "in Harmony", just ambling around the thronging central piazza, and doing no more than chatting and watching the folk go about their daily routine. It was amusing to see two girls, several years younger than Lincoln, sitting cross-legged in the sand and playing a curious looking board game.

"What are they playing?" I asked.

"It is the game of redwhick," said Lincoln.

"I'm intrigued. What's the purpose of the game?" She motioned me to sit beside the two girls; they glanced at me and then looked to each other, and I sensed that they felt quite pleased that someone had come to observe them at play.

"Watch," Lincoln said, flashing her white teeth.

They were playing on a wooden board on which were etched one hundred and forty- four squares. One player had a number of white counters and her opponent possessed the same number of black ones. On the board, placed randomly, was a number of red pieces. Watching the girls, it seemed that the object of the game was to flick the individual counters with the aim of snaring the 'rogue' reds. Lincoln explained to me that the first to seize all the red counters was the winner. There were of course various rules:

"But if a counter lands on the sand surrounding the board, that piece will belong to the other player. If a piece lands within the edges of a square, a player may have another try."

"*Tsssk!*" one of the girls uttered suddenly. She looked thoughtful for a moment, as if attempting a mental calculation, and then, to my surprise, removed her chain of wooden daisies and offered it to her contender.

"A player may give the other a piece of jewellery or clothing to forego losing a counter, if he or she wishes it that way," Lincoln explained, "and the game can last from the wakening of the sun until the coming of the moon. Maybe longer! You do not wish to play?" she asked, arching her dark brows, as she perceived that I did not relish the thought of spending a day engrossed in such pursuit.

"Well...I think...I think I'd grow bored after a while."

"But you would like me to trade my clothing for my counters?" she asked, jigging the low neck of her pretty white dress.

I nodded and smiled as I conceded to her intuitive nature.

We left the two girls to continue their game, and Lincoln led me to a cluster of stone chairs, placed haphazardly near the marketplace and which I had not noticed on my previous visits.

"Let us sit and await my father and sister," she said, adjusting her dress for comfort as she took her place on one and patted the neighbouring seat.

The worn slab was cool against my bare legs, and too hard to lean against in any comfort. I bent forward slightly.

"Linc, do you ever just watch people and try to work out what they're doing and where they're going?" I asked.

"But I can ask where they go."

"True, but sometimes it's fun to guess," I said. "Look at that man over there by those two orange trees. What do you think he's doing?"

"He is standing between two trees," she affirmed.

"Ah...but is he *waiting* for someone? Or is he just resting?"

"I think...I think he waits for a friend," she replied.

"And why's that?"

"He looks around. He expects someone."

"I think you're probably right. You try."

She looked embarrassed as her eyes darted around the milling crowd, trying to find a possible subject for our little game.

"There is a girl...look," she pointed her elegant finger after a few moments in the direction of a girl of about eight years.

"Hmmm...I think she's waiting for a friend too," I surmised.

"You are not right."

"*Ohh*...perhaps her mother is in the market and she waits for her instead."

"You are not right." She was trying to keep a straight face.

"Well...maybe she's lost her dog!"

"*No-o-o-o*..."

"Okay...I'm beaten...tell me," I admitted.

"In her hand she holds her packet of bistre."

"So...?"

"She holds it because her belt is gone," she continued.

"Hmmm..." I was running my tongue along the back of my lower teeth as I waited for the denouement.

"Her belt is gone because it needed mending. She waits for her belt!" She looked pleased with herself as a large man suddenly left the nearby store with a child's belt in his hand.

"Now that's called deduction, and I'm impressed, Linc!" And I really meant it.

We continued with our game for another hour or so, Lincoln having the advantage for she possessed an intricate knowledge of the customs and quirks of her people, our diversion only ending, with her the victor, upon the arrival of Edis and Gale.

"Hello again Edis. Hi Gale." I stood to greet them.

"Leo has prepared food for your journey, and he waits to give it to you. Come!" And the four of us meandered back through the bustling town to the Great Hall.

In the Hall, Lincoln and I were led to a table near to the entrance on which had been placed two large plates of fresh fruit and a rather heftily sized malt loaf. As we sat down, Leo himself returned to the table with two empty beakers and a jug.

"I have prepared food for the start of your journey, but you will need to find more once these items have been eaten," he said, almost apologetically.

"If you find nothing else on your journey, my friend," Edis spoke, "you will learn the skill from Lincoln of finding food from nature."

I wondered whether Edis did not think our journey futile, but Lincoln looked quite proud at her father's words.

There were no more preparations to make. Gale, perhaps to make the most of her sister's company that afternoon, sat in conversation with Lincoln. I spent time with Edis and Isaac. I made a promise to Edis that I would return his daughter safely to him, and I gave my word to Isaac that I would tell him of everything I discovered. Over a drink, of course! It was odd that Isaac did not suggest accompanying us, but I had gathered that the people of Mentarea had an almost apathetic attitude to the outside world. The only comparison I can make- and this may be a poor analogy- is our conditioning not to dwell on our own death. We have an inherent mechanism that enables us to keep our thoughts in check. I think quite honestly that these people, with their prosperously outworn lifestyle, showed no interest in the countryside beyond the immediate surroundings of their town. Mentarea *was* their world. Everything they needed, and wanted, lay within its confines. Otherland was just another place, perhaps like a far continent to Twenty- First Century Man; it existed- there was no doubt of that- but they knew they would never travel far beyond that old wall nor would they even have any desire to do so. If the population of the world- and my guess that the Plague had spread all over the planet seemed almost certain- had been decimated and more latterly almost annihilated, then why leave the safety of the womb that feeds them?

"Return do, but do not bring illness with you Storm- Traveller," Isaac said sourly.

"Like Noah's dove, I shall come back, Isaac. But instead of a sprig of olive, I shall just return Lincoln safely!"

Then he reached to the carafe and carelessly poured another beaker of wine.

Over the remnants of the afternoon, word of our imminent departure spread, and all of the folk whom I had met- plus many others- called to say goodbye. We said final farewells to Edis, Gale and a very inebriated Isaac. Our plan was to leave in the coolness of the dawn's first light, and Lincoln distracted me from my companions later in the afternoon.

"Come," she said, placing her fingertips softly on my shoulder, "for our journey nears, and I will sleep for long. Moon is not here yet, but my eyes tell me that it will soon be time to dream." She rubbed her eyes, and, something I had not seen her do before, yawned. Gale confirmed that she would return to Horat to fetch my hat, and we excused ourselves from the company to retire for the evening. I went towards my cell, but Lincoln looked distressed.

"Don't worry...I'm coming now, but there's one thing I need to do," I reassured her.

I ripped the adjoining fabric and shoved my mattress into her cell. She understood and began to move very carefully her pretty glass phials, repositioning them next to her wooden scent bowl. When she had finished, I placed my mattress alongside her own.

"Now we're in the bridal suite; five- star at its best, and the honeymoon's just beginning," I affirmed.

She strove to smile at such cryptic words. There would be so much more to tell Lincoln on our travels, but that could wait as I was already pulling her arms above her head and removing her dress, once more exposing that tantalising golden flesh and the painted queen bee. We kissed as we lay on our mattresses and then we made love again, but softly and slowly. And afterwards, with the cell drenched in a rapturous brume, I just held her in my arms.

"The queen is in her hive, and all is right with the world. I love you, Linc," I whispered after a while.

But she never heard me.

PART TWO:

With each hour there should exist a new enchantment.

CHAPTER 13: *The Journey Unfurls*

"This is where it all began, or at least as far as our relationship's concerned," I said to Lincoln as I stood by the very tree from which I had descended just over two weeks earlier; I wondered whether I should have possessed the hardihood to have ventured into Mentarea had our paths not crossed that day. It was still early in the morning, and we had sloped from our cell into the Great Hall whence we had collected our rucksacks for our trek. I was wearing my new shorts, my old shoes, one of my new vests covered by a threadbare pullover that I had carried with me on my journey across the centuries, plus, of course, my hat; she was dressed in her loincloth, the skimpiest of vests, the latter fastened teasingly with a single bow across her cleavage, and her ankle- boots. The first tentative light of the new day had greeted us as we emerged from the Hall into the deserted town, and now, as we stood together by that trunk, the pale blue- grey veil of morn was already beginning to distil into that perennial and encouraging azure sky, cauterising the breaking day's greyness from the colourful and scented flora.

"You were as the rabbit when not warned by the gatherer of berries," she reminded me risibly.

"Ha! An apt comparison! You certainly startled me. You really were the last sight I expected to see...had it been Isaac who greeted me that day, I think I might've been too drunk to even reach your town!"

"And under this tree both of you would have enjoyed the sleep induced by wine!"

Then she wavered before continuing:

"If Gale had greeted you, would you have been as happy?"

Now that was a typically devious female question, and I didn't want to be caught out. After a tactical pause:

"Hmmm...only...*only* if she'd told me she had an elder sister called Lincoln," I answered.

"Ohh...that answer is good!" she cried, colouring slightly.

"Come on, Linc, let's press...let's continue. There's an old saying that the journey of a thousand miles begins with the first step," I said.

She thought about that for a second. Then she looked at me enquiringly, and I knew that a question was imminent.

"That is correct, but which part of the journey is the most difficult?"

"Hmmm...the last bit, those final steps."

"You are not right."

Although I could tell when Lincoln was playing with me, I never knew quite what would follow.

"Ahhh, okay…the first part. Yes, the first step- making the decision, the initial effort- that must surely be the most difficult part," I said, nodding with satisfaction.

"You are not right," she smiled.

"Not the last and not the first?"

"Not the last and not the first."

"I know, the middle part…that bit when you've gone too far to turn back, but you've still too far to go?"

"No. You have not found the answer."

Her eyes were sparkling.

"*Tkkk…tkkk*," I clicked my tongue against the roof of my mouth, "…go on then, tell me."

"It is the part when the pebble lies in the shoe!"

Back up that slope we trawled. We walked with a happy purpose, retracing the route that I had taken on that first day, as it was my intention to try to reach that little ruin where I had passed that first lonely night in this place. Then we marched forward for more or less seven hours. We drank regularly from our plastic flasks, but took just two very short but well- earned rests, until we arrived at our destination.

"Linc, we're here! Look- it's just as I told you."

Like a trusted friend, the small brick structure stood across our path.

"Your first moontime! You were here?"

"I was here…and I saw the glow from Mentarea- of course, I didn't know then that it was caused by a host of candles. I was right here, at this very spot. God, I remember thinking that I was in the middle of some frightful nightmare. Not a nightmare now, but I *still* can't believe it!"

"It is real, and I am glad!" she gleamed.

We refilled our flasks from the stream behind the building, and sat together as we rested:

"Linc, what time is it?" It seemed strange asking her such a question, as it was my watch that she wore.

"Watch tells…eleven…eleven and the *thir*ty!"

She was improving, and had needed but a negligible pause this time.

"Well, it was good enough for me on my first night, and I'm just about all in. Let's rest here for the afternoon and night, then carry on at sunrise," I suggested.

She had seated herself on the flat edge of a large rock, the body of which was protruding at a rather painful angle from the ground, and her flawless legs lolled as her now unshod feet fidgeted with the undergrowth. She seemed to be quite pleased at my suggestion.

"I must let you decide, for I know nothing of Otherland," she answered. Excluding us as players in this outlandish pantomime, I was certain that our surroundings would have remained unaltered for centuries; even the attrition of the very rock on which she sat must have been infinitesimal over the years. Once again it pitched those thoughts into my head that all this was illusory. It *should* have been, but it wasn't. This was real; *she* was real- how I adored her very existence. I unfastened my bag from my shoulders, and sat down on some packed earth opposite her.

I let out a long sigh.

"Are you hungry?"

"I am hungry. And the thought of food has given me an idea," she answered, as she leaned forward to peer at the ground.

"What are you looking at?"

"The ants. There are so many. I am thinking…ahhh…the stone just there," she said.

She moved from the rock and crouched by a flat stone the size of a turkey platter. Without delay she lifted it, let it drop backwards and exclaimed:

"A nest. The eggs are many. Look!"

I went and looked with her. The ants were teeming and already trying to protect the eggs by carrying them into tiny holes in the ground.

"Oh no, no way, Linc, I'm not eating those!" I cried as she scooped up a handful of the tiny eggs and ran to fetch our dish.

Food always tastes better in the open air- or so it seems to- and we devoured a veritable feast of pear, apple and blackcurrant pie and sliced fish. And yes, I ate my words too as I had to admit to Lincoln that the ant pupae, fried lightly with a touch of syrup, were rather good. Then we drank most of our water and each had a beaker of dark and very rich red wine. Afterwards, she handed me a few little cubes of an orange- hued article, seemingly not unlike celery in its texture.

"What are they?" I asked.

"Crasticks," she said.

"*Crasticks?*"

"Watch me," she instructed as she placed one in her mouth, and began to champ at it. After wrestling with it for a few seconds, she removed the gnarled morsel from between her teeth, and tossed it to the ground.

"They are good for the hair and nails, but do not swallow them for they are hard to digest," she said, and held one in her pristine palm.

"Like vitamin pills really...Mmmm...not bad," I said as I rolled it around my mouth. "What's in them?"

"They are made from royal jelly and the skins of the finest mushrooms. I packed many for our journey. I am to care for you in every way on our journey," she replied, those sincere eyes burnishing with contentment, as she tipped the rim of my straw hat with affection.

"I'm to care for you too, Linc- you're my wife now! Besides, I promised your father that I'd bring you back safely. Wouldn't want to anger him!" I joked.

"And I will return you safely also," she concurred.

Then I pulled her forcefully from her perch, and I held her as she tumbled to the ground with me. I turned over, placing her onto her back. She was laughing now, enjoying our tussle. I kissed her gently on her lips, my fingers fumbling for the little knot on her vest. Success. I undid the string of her top, and opened it. There was the bee, smudged now with the sweat from the morning's walk. I planted little kisses on her breast, still shining with the varnish where the bee's wing had been, and she began to twitch her body with satisfaction and desire, every so often emitting sweet moans of appeasement. And, away from the confines of Mentarea, with just a chirping bird and a gurgling brook for company, we made beautiful love.

Gorged on fresh air, exercise and our love for each other, we slept that night for ten hours, and any idea of repeating our early start was soon forgotten come the morn.

"To quote the words of a lady '*why should I sleep when the blackbird has wakened to sing his song*?'" Her words had stayed with me from the morning of that dramatic day of the storm. She stirred, and I eased the still- warm solar sheet from her.

"You...you have woken before me. I- I was in a dream..." she uttered.

"Tell me of your dream," I prompted her. She was sitting upright now, her breasts exposed. Her lustrous hair hung smoothly and perfectly to her shoulders. As I had remarked already, I imagined that Lincoln could surface from her sleep looking as pristine as she did on the previous evening.

"I will tell of it before the mind fails me."

She rumpled her hair and shirred her brow as she attempted to put the events in order.

"There was a bee- a queen bee like the one that Gale painted." She skimmed her fingertips over the mass of smeared colours upon her naked chest.

"It was not a good dream, and it was not a bad dream," she said, composing herself.

I nodded. "Go on."

"The bee was eating much food- food that a bee would not enjoy! The drones brought her fruit from the trees and fish from the stream, and she ate everything. Now you will laugh- they carried the food on plates because they were walking like we do!"

"I'm not laughing. Dreams are usually strange. Most of mine I never remember- the rest are just daft!"

"But there is more," she said.

"Oh…"

"Perhaps *now* you will laugh: the queen was holding a beaker of red wine and shouting."

"Sounds fine to me. Perhaps she was thirsty."

But it was Lincoln who giggled.

"There is…there is more still," she said as she tried to regain her composure.

"O *ka-a-y.*"

"A blue butterfly appeared from nowhere and everyone- I am to say every *bee*- was happy. But I do not think a butterfly would like to be in a hive; and the bees would not like it, would they?"

"I doubt it. If you have that dream again, tell it to keep away!" I smiled. "Is that how it ends?"

"No-o-o!"

"How then?"

"I cannot answer your question."

"Why not?"

"Because I do not know the end," she gushed.

"But why not?"

"Because you caused me to wake from my sleep!"

After we had breakfasted, we went outside, sweetly- scented lavender and oatmeal soap in hand, to the brook to bathe. The water was cool, and we spent no more than fifteen minutes at our ablutions. How I longed for the warm and palliative waters of the honey pool! The last remnants of Gale's artwork had now gone from Lincoln's body, and I should have loved to have recorded that image for posterity. Then we sat on the edge of the stream, completely naked, with our feet dipping in and out of the water. Lincoln applied, delicately above my eyes but more liberally on my cheeks, the strange black mixture that would shield the skin on my face from the harshness of the sun. She even seemed to breathe with a deep concentration as she focused all her attention on the task at hand. Her face had inched closer to mine and I made her giggle as I peered into her beguiling blue eyes.

"Tsssk! Now I have smudged it."

"Oh well, I don't think anyone will notice," I chuckled.

Then she asked me to paint it carefully on the corresponding parts of her own face, an act that, up until then, she had always done herself.

A task to test the greatest of painters- how can one enhance the Mona Lisa?

When we had finished applying the protection, we dressed for the day. Lincoln wore her sturdy ankle- boots, and around her waist she wrapped one of her little cloth- pieces. The trusted utility- belt was restored to its rightful position, and she donned the tasselled band that she folded around her breasts, the shreds of material dangling towards her navel. I wore my walking- shoes, shorts and t-shirt. The shirt was the same one that I had been wearing when I arrived, a dark blue one with a small and now poignantly irrelevant manufacturer's logo in the middle.

"So," I said blithely, "we're ready!"

"This sun we walk as before?" she asked.

"Well, we need to get some distance behind us again. I think we should aim to cover as much ground as yesterday," I answered.

"That is good. Let us walk."

"Which way?"

She faltered for a moment, pointed and then said simply:

"That way."

And so, like a pair of primitive pioneers, we embarked on the second leg of our journey.

"*Owww!*"

"You are with pain?"

"I've just caught my leg on that bush…that was sharp."

We had been walking for a couple of hours, and were attempting to wind our way through the more accessible parts of some fairly dense undergrowth.

She placed her hand firmly on my thigh and bent down.

"It bleeds," she said. "Now I can help you." She smiled, and I knew that she really wanted to minister to that little scratch for me.

"Now sit," she ordered me, and I could just discern a glimmer of elation in her eyes. Perhaps Lincoln had never had the opportunity to tend to anybody before. She sat on the ground beside me, and grabbed my leg to extend it. Then she removed her sack and began to rummage for something.

"I have it now!" she cried, and withdrew a small pot of cream. Then she reached inside her belt and took out a small device with an attenuated cup shaped scoop at one end, similar in design to the cosmetic ligula used by the Romans. She jerked the pot lid, plunged the instrument into the stuff and spooned out a shining globule of the cream from the container. She was able to translate the expression on my face.

"Honey, lavender and crushed dock leaves; Nature and the bees help us always," she said, as she smeared it across the cut and began to rub it with the tips of two fingers.

"Wow…I could get used to that. In my Time, Linc, you'd have made a great nurse. I might even have come back for more."

She looked rather flushed, then wistful as she asked an interesting question:

"*Could* I live in your Time?"

"Er…I suppose so, I mean…why not?"

"But if I had travelled to your Time, everything would have been strange to me."

"But everything here was, and still is, strange to me. It's a totally different world here."

"But easier for you here…. am I not right?"

"Easier in many ways, definitely."

"But here it is not new, not strange, only different. It would not…it would not be easier for me in your world." She didn't really *ask* it, just said it somewhat reticently.

"Well…that's true." I could see what she was trying to say. I could adapt to her world because, compared to my own environment, this was a paradise. A paradise that was dying, true- but still a nirvana. What did I really miss from my own Time? But she, a gentle and trusting soul from an age beyond mine- a peculiar age governed by neither person nor clock- couldn't possibly hope to survive in my Time. What outlet existed in the Twenty- First Century by which Lincoln could channel her soul? A glamour model? No, for she was unexampled, as if Nature had commissioned her, designed her and finally moulded her from the very earth itself, and with such sublime beauty she would surmount those around her. Perhaps she would have ended up roaming the woods, unclad, a mysterious enchantress, famed for her natural skills, and thus become renowned as a keeper of bees, gatherer of mushrooms and saviour of lame dogs. No! No, there would be nowhere for her to blossom in that old century, and, had the situation been as she suggested, I fear that she should have wilted as a flower in darkness, being incarcerated in such a vile suburbia. On the morning that I 'proposed' to Lincoln, I'd had those fanciful notions of romancing her in the old-fashioned way, and I'd talked of the cinema, the park, the restaurant and other delights. Well, it could have worked, and would have done. But what of her daily life in my world? Working and paying bills? Shopping and planning? Noise- God, the noise- and pollution? No, this was Lincoln's Time and this was her world. Right here.

"I am thinking that you like to tell me only of *good* things from your Time. Am I not right?"

"You *are* right, Linc. There are many things that you wouldn't like and just as many that you wouldn't even understand. You belong here. No-one moves the brightest and choicest bloom from the border and plants it on a compost heap."

She just smiled at that comparison, but I wondered if she wouldn't give further thought to the scenario from time to time.

I looked at my leg. The blood was beginning to congeal, and I kissed her in gratitude. We shared some water, and each munched at an apple. Then I stood up and stretched my arms in anticipation of the next leg of our journey.

"Onwards and upwards then?"

"Onwards is correct…but upwards is the sun," she replied, her brow crooked.

And that was just another reason why I loved her.

CHAPTER 14: *Reflection In The Landscape*

It was Lincoln who spotted it first. She had been chasing an unusual bird that we had seen hopping from one branch to another on the trees that fringed much of our walk on that second day. It was the length of a starling, but more slender in its build, and, oddly, its feathers were a shade of silver- blue. I had owned a pocket- sized book on tropical birds, and I believed Lincoln's bird to be a tanager; like the dogspaw plant, it had crossed the globe to make a new home here in this strange Britain. It had been a tiring afternoon and I had become footsore. Her cry startled me, as my mind along with my body had begun to fade.

"There is water!"

She was standing by a rowan with her left hand pressed against its smooth grey trunk, the tassels on her top stirring in the faint breeze. I had assumed that she meant another stream, and I paced sloth- like up the small ridge to join her, stepping over a crevice into which the rowan's roots stretched. However, I was to be pleasantly surprised.

It was a welcome sight. Down a slope, through a mass of cream and purple heathers, across a fern- clad plain that was strewn intermittently with hunks of molded green- white limestone, littered with dropwort and wild flowers, and fringed in parts by weeping willows, lay a beautiful lake. Its waters were tranquil and doing nothing more than reflecting the peace of a hot blue summer's afternoon.

"What a beautiful scene!" I uttered after several seconds, perhaps more to myself than to my reliable bride because sometimes appreciation of Nature's wonders is a personal joy.

Turning to me:

"Let us stay there for moontime."

"Well…it certainly looks good enough. And look," pointing, "there's even a sort of natural shelter between those two trees…see it, just over by that tall rock…"

She followed my outstretched finger, and needed no more encouragement.

"Come," she said, and already she was tripping down the hill, skirring over the rocks and weaving in and out of the aged heathers.

I had been right about the potential shelter created by the tangled arms of the willows, which stood in front of a massive outcrop of the weathered rock, and we flopped onto the shaded ground beneath. We didn't eat. We didn't drink. We just lay there and dozed for about half an hour.

"Were you dreaming again?" I asked her, hoping that I had not intruded a second time on her mind's wanderings.

"No, I did not dream. Or if I did, I do not remember," she replied.

She sat up and pulled her legs to her, clasping her hands together around her knees.

"I am sad for you," she said quite unexpectedly.

"Sad? Why?" I lay there, almost too lethargic to sit up.

"Because we have travelled for a sun, a moon and much of another sun, but still we do not find that which you seek," she said dejectedly, and shuffled her body to face me.

"You mean you're disappointed? Well, we've only come about twelve miles. We'll find it. We'll find *something*, we've *got* to- otherwise I'll end up doubting my own existence!" I joked. "After all, Old Father Time can't change everything!"

Thankfully, her expression altered on hearing those last words, and her mouth broke into a little grin. Then she frowned, and finally chuckled.

"What's so funny?" I asked.

"You have spoken of an *old father*."

"Yes...Old Father Time...Time itself; it's just another of those silly things people say...*used* to say," I tried to explain.

"I understand what you say, but he cannot be very old," she laughed, rocking her body.

"And why not?" I knew Lincoln well enough to know that she had duped me again with her simple logic.

She took her hands from her legs, and, moving her right palm rapidly across the sand, said, "Because, since I have known you, each moon comes faster than the one before. So I am thinking that 'Father Time' is not old because he walks with long legs and with wide strides."

I could not think of anything to add to that, but Lincoln could:

"I am hoping that we have many moons in which to live in Harmony."

"Don't forget the suns too!"

She lay down beside me and that's all I can remember of the afternoon, for it had turned five o'clock when we woke. Then we attempted to reinforce our humble abode for the coming night. I moved a few of the more manageable boulders and built a very rough dry- stone wall across the 'front' of the area, and I snapped off a few of the lighter branches from the neighbouring trees, pushing them upright into the sand to form a buffer of sorts. It was unnecessary, of course, but it just felt like a good thing to do. Behind us, as I have described already, we were blocked by a chiselled wedge of that gnarled stone.

We dined that evening on chunks of bread, on which we spread a splendid rowan- berry jam, fresh fruit, water and, of course, red wine. "With the new sun, I will catch fish for us," Lincoln told me as we lay together. It was another warm night, and we lay naked, our only cover being the sheet, laced with the strange crystals, that Lincoln had packed to keep us warm (and which also shielded us from any annoying insects).

"Are you hopeful of a good catch?"

"I am thinking that we will catch many fish like we did last time."

"Just a thought- d'you bring a net?"

"I have a net."

"Mmmm…okay, good…" I was fighting to keep awake, and knew that I should succumb to sleep at any moment.

"But the big net will not be needed here."

"Right…Mmm, why…why not…?"

"Here the water is still. It does not flow. I will tie a small net to a fallen branch."

"Okay."

"When I wake I will look for a branch."

"Mmmm…"

"I am sure…"

And those were the last words I heard from her as those wonderful encompassing and anaesthetising surges of colour- the type that come only when physically, and perhaps mentally, sapped- stormed my mind.

It was the prating of a bird that woke me, and for a second I believed myself to be back on that first morning again in this strange world (it was only some time later that I realised my mind hadn't returned first and foremost to my old bedroom). I had woken so suddenly that all I wanted to do was to turn over and try to go back to sleep. I reached for Lincoln's bare flesh, but my hand scrabbled at empty earth. I flung the coverlet from me, donned my shorts and walked out from under the trees' cover.

Lincoln was standing patiently about ten feet out into the lake, the water snug against her bare thighs, and hadn't seen me. I noticed that she had positioned her utility- belt neatly upon a boulder a yard from the water's edge. I sat down with my back to the stone, watched her briefly and then stared down at that hypnotic motion of the water as it lapped in little wavelets some six inches from my toes, trickling back and forth over the same pebbles, but never gaining any ground. Had that been like my life thus far- well, up until my arrival in Lincoln's time anyway? Forward it continued to seep, never staining the stones that it failed to reach and always retreating at the same point just as I never touched the lives of those that lay beyond my remit. Or was I more like one of the thousands of pebbles that lay along the shingled fringe of that lagoon; forever washed over and suffocated by the tide of life, not free like those that were scattered further up the shore? My life had been dull before. I had always felt that there must be something better, something else. But now...well, now there were words that could only begin to describe it. Now it was unprecedented...strange...surreal, and in Lincoln I had found Life's 'More'. I had been drawn to her like a dandelion clock to a lawn. And it was good now. Yes, it was good. And there was something very right about it too. That paper bag had blown away.

Back and forth and on and on the water dribbled. I glanced up to see her looking at me.

"I was thinking that you had fallen into sleep where you sit!" she shouted.

"Well I reckon it's about time I was up and about," I replied, with more than a touch of humour in my voice. Lincoln, who could always extract a smile from me, was grinning cheerfully.

She waded back towards me, holding aloft a net that contained at least three fish. She had obviously fished with preoccupied gusto, splashing herself, for her hair and naked body glistened wetly in the morning sun.

"A good catch as promised?"

"I am happy. We will eat fish," she said and, placing her homemade rod on the ground, she knelt down beside me and gave a little shiver. I pulled her to me, and felt her still wet flesh cool against my bare chest.

"Linc...thank you. I bet you're cold now. Is the water warm?"

"It has enough warmth. Now we ask the sun to help us to cook our fish," she said and reached for her utility- belt, removing the lens from one of her pouches.

"I'll fetch some wood," I said eagerly. The thought of freshly cooked fish was tempting indeed.

I walked around the area of our little encampment, ferreting for pieces of dry heather and old branches that had fallen from the trees: the boughs had lain where they had fallen on the rocky plain and many were so aged that they had become brittle and bleached throughout countless suns. It was as I bent down to collect some twigs that lay in a pile by a small rock that I felt it. Coloured like the wood that I was gathering, it was hard and rough in my fingers. I brushed the tinder from my hands to isolate the object, wiping the excess dirt on my shorts. It was about two inches in length and undefined in its shape. But it wasn't made from wood and was too light to be metal. It was something from another era: it was plastic.

"Hey, Linc! I've found something here," I cried. She was busy preparing the fish, and on hearing me, she placed them carefully by her belt and dashed to my side. She knelt down and looked at the object that I was holding in my palm.

"I do not know what you have," she said in her puzzled way. Lincoln did not like to be defeated and I knew that the find would become *her* challenge as well.

"I'm not sure either. I think it needs cleaning up a bit more. Have you got anything that I can use?"

She ran back to retrieve her belt, and I heard her humming as she swung it in her hand when she returned.

"These will help I am thinking."

She had passed me a metal ring that held three slim pins (I was to discover later that she used the devices, in turn, as a toothpick, nail cleaner and file).

"Thanks."

I scraped away at the object using the finest of the three implements, delicately gouging out the soil from any areas in which it had accumulated.

Recognition was simultaneous, although it was she that said it for I was still turning it over and over in my hands.

"It is a man!" she gasped.

"You're right, it's easy to see what it is now. It *is* a man. More to the point, it's a *soldier*- a child's toy soldier. We're near to...near to somewhere that I may recognise."

I passed the figure to her, and she poised it on the palm of her hand. Her face was bathed in a guileless delight, and, for an instant, the scene reminded me of one of those old faked sepia photographs of the girl with the fairy.

I fashioned a crude but effective spit from five stout twigs, then I asked Lincoln to pass me her lens- dome whilst she finished preparing the fish. I was satisfied that I had already arranged the dried wood into an appropriately shaped pile, and I proceeded to tilt the convex glass towards the sun. It was easy enough to channel the rays from the sun, but success in starting a fire took a little longer and she struggled to stifle her amusement as I tutted impatiently at my first few failed attempts. On about the fourth or fifth try, and having blown gently onto the dry tinder, the flame caught. I skewered her three fish, and turned them slowly at a distance of about a foot above the flames. They were soon cooked and tasted as exquisite as I had expected. She looked at me expectantly as we ate, glancing towards the rock on which lay our fresh fruit, and then darting her eyes to my face.

"You look like you've got something to ask me," I said.

She dropped her eyes again.

I tapped her sleek black hair: "Go on…I know there's a question in there somewhere."

She looked up again.

"I have no question."

"Ohh…?"

"I was thinking of the time when we fished with Gale."

"What about it?"

"*You* asked a question of Gale and me."

"Did I? I don't remember."

She was silent, chary I thought, wanting me to continue.

"*Ohh*, I know… the fish that we caught; I asked what type they were."

She touched her hair.

"I think I was not right with my answer."

"Why not?"

"Because I said that fish are fish, and are without names."

"Well, that's okay."

"No. It…was…not right." She spoke those last words with dispassion.

"But why *not?*"

"Because I sounded as if you had asked a question that had no answer. But in your Time there would have been an answer, and I think that I stopped you from asking more of me. I too must learn that here is new for you, for in your Time I would ask questions from one sun to the next without stopping!"

"And I'd answer anything you wanted. I know what you're saying. You weren't 'not right' though. Forget about it."

My response seemed to placate her.

"Now I am in Otherland, so here is new to me also. I think *I* will ask things of *you* on our journey."

"And if I have the answers, I'll share them with you," I reassured her. "But first I'm going to enjoy this fish!"

We occupied our afternoon just fooling around in the lake and generally relaxing. I was a contented man that night as I lay down, for I had passed another insouciant day with the girl I loved. I looked at her in the semi- darkness, but, as I knew already, she was fast asleep. Then I glanced to the 'entrance', and the last thing I saw was that silhouetted little plastic soldier, my first find, standing resolutely on top of my stone wall, his conflict now as silent as that of the two dead Tommies who lay at rest back in Mentarea. Come the new day, we would be tracing the footprints of long- vanished ghosts; but still souls that had once lived and breathed the very air that we now shared. I shut my eyes then, but before I too yielded to sleep, I am almost certain that I heard once more the sloshing of the water and the spirited cries of Lincoln's laughter echoing in my ears.

We spent another whole day and night at that spot, a place that, much to Lincoln's amusement, I had christened "No Man's Land," for two reasons; firstly, it lay between Mentarea and the unexplored reaches of Otherland, and secondly, on account of my finding a two inch plastic straggler which, like me, was a survivor. 'He' had dared to leave the safety of his battlefield trench, just as I had ventured forth from Mentarea!

Our sleep was unbroken and with the arrival of the new morning, we prepared for our departure.

"I'll miss this place, Linc, I really will," I said as we set off once more. It was a Wednesday, although I alone knew it, and it was going to be another torrid day. I had ripped the sleeves from my t- shirt for comfort whilst Lincoln wore one of her trim singlets along with her loincloth, having washed her tasselled band in the lake. My shorts were still marked with the grimy handprint from two days earlier, and I reminded myself to wash them at the next suitable location.

"I will miss it also. Perhaps we shall find another place like it," she said optimistically. Off we walked; Lincoln was concentrating as she tried to leap from one stone to another across the verdant ferns, a feat which she accomplished with much ease on account of her long legs. We skirted around the lake until we reached more woodland and enjoyed a shaded and manageable walk through the area that consisted mainly of spaciously positioned eucalyptus trees. Then we reached open land and continued on our way, trekking over undulating terrain for the rest of the day. We spent that night in a patch of murmuring soft grass.

As we walked through a forest the next day, we chatted about birds, fish, the limited animal life that I had seen since I arrived and even our childhood games. I was particularly intrigued to hear of an amusement called 'Waiter by the Wall' that Lincoln used to play with her friends, Abeth and Reagan- whom I had met- and the ill- fated Melia. Derived from the immediate aftermath of the Plague days, and consistent with Edis's words on my first day in Mentarea, it was similar to the playground 'tig'. The last to arrive at the designated 'den', wherein dwelt the 'Keeper of the Gate', was denominated the 'Waiter'. As our feet trampled the crowded forest mantle, I responded by telling her about various games, such as five- a- side and 'British Bulldogs', most of which entrenched her curiosity, although, as I should have expected, she failed to see the rationality in 'Hide and Seek'. Suffice to say, we were in good spirits and I decided to try an old joke on Lincoln:

"I have a question for you."

"Ask it of me."

"When we've passed through these woods and they are empty once again, a branch may drop from a tree. But if we are not in the woods to hear it, will it make a noise?"

A pause.

"Your question is good and I am going to think of an answer. But if I am late with my answer, do not think it is because I have forgotten."

"I won't. It's a question that's as old as the Earth itself, and I think you'll enjoy mulling it over!"

As we continued on our route, Lincoln changed the subject as she asked me more of the strangeness of my Time:

"Did you ever go a journey such as this?"

"Ha! I've never been on a journey like this one before. After all, I don't even know where I'm going...and with such a perfect travelling companion too! Seriously though, I did like walking- you remember that I told Isaac that on my first meeting with him? And I've been to some exciting places."

"Tell me of the places you have seen," she asked as we walked, slower now, her blue eyes wide with interest.

"Once I went to America and I saw thirteen different States. I went and…"

No, wrong approach; what the hell was I saying to her?

"You don't know *what* America is, do you?" I hoped that I had not belittled her in any way.

"I know only of Mentarea…and, now I am with you, parts of Otherland," she answered.

"I know. You wanted me to tell you *about* the places, not tell you their names and where they are…or even where they *were*. Maybe such places don't exist anymore- that's a possibility, I suppose."

I sighed before I said, "Okay, I'll start again. I went once to an unknown land- well, unknown to me anyway- and had a happy time there. The people were like me but they all spoke with a different accent- in a different way, just as your voice is not like mine."

"Ahhh…" She understood, and her eyes smiled back at me.

"I ate food that I'd never tasted before and saw many exciting things such as huge glass buildings that were taller than any I had ever seen- taller than those in Mentarea too. I saw the scariest animals in the grandest zoo imaginable." I lunged forward, bearing my teeth like an alligator. I will never know how Lincoln imagined such a reptile to look, but my impression certainly caused her to wince.

"And here's the part even I never understood- I *flew* there, Linc. I flew in an aeroplane- like your magnasule but much, much bigger- and with metal wings too. I journeyed over a vast distance. Up there…higher than the greatest mountain!" I thrust out my arm vertically. Squinting, she looked above the leaves to that unmarred blue canvas, and I wondered what my thin description must have evoked in her mind.

"Tell me of…*aaaagghh!*" She didn't finish, and cast her eyes to the ground rather huffily.

"What's up? What's happened?"

"I have struck my toe on that," she said.

"Tree- root. You all right? Let me see." I knelt down in the earth, and examined her slender toe.

"It seems fine…can you bend it?"

"I can bend it. Watch."

"Still life in it…not broken at all. Only a true lady could react like you did, Linc."

"I do not understand."

"Well if I'd just stubbed *my* toe, I think I might've said something…hey, it's not a root. What…"

She sat down with me as I rubbed the soil from the surface. I noticed that it was rust- coloured and it felt grainy in its texture. Recognition jostled with disbelief as I rammed fingers, trembling now, into the earth in an attempt to grasp the object.

"It's…it's a brick…it's a house- brick. It's still got the maker's mark on it!" I was excited now as I continued, "That's a more significant find than our friend here." I stretched my arm into my open bag to retrieve the little figure. "It's so important. You know what it means? You do, don't you? Tell me you do!"

"I do; *now* it has caused *more* pain to my toe than a tree- root would have done!"

CHAPTER 15: *The Shifting Sands*

There must have been hundreds, if not thousands, of them. We had unearthed eleven that lay just beneath the surface. All were intact too, which surprised me.

"Why do you think many more are buried?" Lincoln asked.

"Because we've stumbled upon the ruins of something here. This is much, much older than that first building I saw." I reminded her of the structure, still in reasonable condition, its purpose unknown, that I'd chanced upon during that first harrowing day.

"What do you think was here?"

Now my inventiveness could soar, fuelled like a rocket, as I answered:

"Ohh…I should say a large detached house set in its own grounds. Over there…" I pointed to a gap in the trees, "…would have been a garage- no, make that a *double* garage. And some great big wrought- iron gates just about…there! These people had money, so let's give them their own pool- you'd have loved that!"

"A pool of honey?"

"No, no, just a normal swimming- pool. In my Time, you'd made it if you had your own pool!" I laughed. I imagined suddenly an asinine scenario of Lincoln and a group of her people being cast into the Twenty- First Century and helping themselves, quite innocently as were their beliefs, to everybody else's possessions. The house's owners would return home to this spot and find my trusting companion basking naked in their pool.

"Or maybe it was just an old factory!" I added, defacing that hypothetical scene. "Whatever it was, we're close to what was once civilisation."

We were sitting on the ground still, our hands grimy from our scrabbling at the soil.

"But one brick is like another, and I'm not here to rebuild. Besides, we haven't *time*, have we?"

"Ahhh…the watch!"

I liked to ask her whenever I could, as she enjoyed answering me.

She turned her wrist, and, without pausing, said, "Watch tells two- fifteen. I am right?"

"You're accurate to a millisecond! Don't reckon I'll catch you out with that question from now on!"

"You are wishing for food?"

"No…bit too soon after all that fish. Did *you* want something to eat now?"

"No. I am without hunger."

"What about that toe? Are you going to be able to walk?"

"I shall be glad to walk again. I am not in pain now. That is good for you."

"Well it's good for *you* really, Linc…good that it's not hurting you."

"*No-o-o*…it is good for *you*."

She was making every effort to keep her face straight.

"Go on then, why?"

"Because now you will not have to carry me!"

We walked for three more hours, a distance of perhaps eight miles at our pace, but saw nothing. As I have described already, the woodland in which we journeyed consisted of fairly sparingly- spaced trees. Most of them were silver- birch, and they had grown to a considerable, almost unnatural, height. However, as we walked, the forest became more devoid of growth, and it was not long before we were trekking across a vast area of scrubland, populated only fleetingly by the odd tree- elms, mainly, although I spotted yews and sycamores. In the distance lay a steep rise. It was covered in ferns of varying tinges of green, and dotted in confetti of rust and amber heathers, with white tracks of scree intersecting the display like jet vapour trails scarring a bright summer's sky. To our left, and, slightly further, to our right, lay still more forest, and it was my intention to tackle the verdant prominence that stood before us before finding a spot to rest for the night.

She knew what I was thinking:

"Hmmm…" I ran my hand through my dishevelled sweaty hair. "Ready for a climb?"

"I am ready."

I went first, attempting to walk on the rocky path by meandering my way through the ferns and heathers, whilst at the same time holding tightly on to Lincoln's left hand. For those initial few steps, I found it to be a sobering thought as I realised that I was dislodging loose stones that may have lain undisturbed for centuries. I looked for any natural mantels as I went, leading Lincoln upwards in the most direct, and hopefully safest, way possible.

*

After a rather nerve- wracking fifteen minutes, I spied a small plateau under a crooked juniper shrub and made a sideways detour towards it.

"Now you'd think they'd have...*pheewwww*... stuck a bench here: '*Rest Awhile*'...or something similar!" I gasped.

"Nobody has come here. There is... no- one to... make a bench."

Some things didn't need to be explained to my delightful bride- she would just have to accept them as quirks in my character should she ever ponder over such phrases. She sat down next to me, and stretched her neck upwards. She shut her eyes in appreciation of the feeble breeze that dusted her face, and smoothed back a few loose hairs from her temples.

"No, Linc, there *is* no- one- there's no- one but us. Mentarea is a long way back there now."

She opened her eyes and lowered her head again. I pointed vaguely in the general direction of her town.

"Thirsty?"

"I have a thirst."

We shared a whole flask of water on that strange little ledge on the side of the rise. After that, I put my arm around her and pulled her close to me. She buried the side of her face in my shirt.

"I'm so glad I met you. Where would I be now, I wonder, without you? What a *strange* Future this is!"

"After I saw you during that first suntime, I hoped that we would not part when we returned to Mentarea," she said, continuing my train of thought. She caressed my arm with her fingers.

"Well, I have to admit that everyone in Mentarea made me welcome, but I thought about *you* often."

"When did you desire me?"

"*When*...?" She had taken me surprise with *that* one. "I have to admit that I thought you were very...er...well, you know...er...very attractive the first moment I saw you. It's just that I was still in a state of awe; it was as if everything were still a dream."

I kissed her head.

There was a movement in the ferns at that moment, and we looked for its source.

"Sssshh!" I whispered.

She leant forward and tried to peer into the undergrowth. As soon as she stopped, a tiny vole darted from the foliage, shot past our feet, paused, froze, and retreated whence it came.

"It is a furleaf! There are few in Mentarea."

"A what? A furleaf? That's another new word for me to learn. It's really called a…"

I was going to correct her, but stopped myself. Why should I attempt to alter her words? What right had I to change anything she said and believed? I was Here now, no longer back There in my own town more than four hundred years ago. Those elusive centuries had seen a reworking not just of customs, biology and climate, but also certain words. I was not here to change anything; indeed I had no purpose here at all. I was just lucky to be accepted. Not just that, I was fortunate to be *alive*. Had it not been for her, would I have survived? Physically, of that there was no doubt; but *emotionally*? Who else in this world could have cushioned the wrench from all that I held dear to me?

"I am not right?" she wondered.

"Yes…yes of course…you're right. It's a little…furleaf."

She smiled as she said, "Ohh, to move through the undergrowth with the cunning of the furleaf!"

We left a piece of apple for the vole, and set off to conquer the remainder of the slope.

"Six with the twenty! I am wanting to say just six- twenty!" she exclaimed gleefully in answer to my question, and beamed broadly.

We were just approaching the top and the walk had become less demanding now as the slope diminished in gradient.

"I don't even need to check. Six- twenty will be right," I nodded.

We clambered up the last few yards, side by side now, through bright purple bell- heather, paler ling and wild thyme, and I could feel myself twitching with anticipation of what we might find over the rim.

"We're here, Linc. We've done it, love."

I put my hand to my mouth and blew, channelling the cool air to my forehead.

The first thought that struck me was one of comfort and familiarity, as it could have been one of those views that one always appreciates after climbing a mountain. Down below us lay the elegiac, but no longer chequered, greens and tans of the ancient English countryside, and, as a backdrop to the fantastic scene, plum- blue hills brooded with dignity as they defended its gate like weather- beaten old guards. To the right lay the ocean, wisps of white flickering at the edge of an endless shimmering blue. And to our left lingered the bleak smoke- grey and brick- red monuments that once housed both life and arrogance, now tilting, twisted and ruined, lying like discarded packages with their contents devoured. And far, far behind them, looking rather like an ineffective scarecrow, stood a solitary electricity pylon waiting patiently for an energy surge that would never come.

"I see so much before my eyes. Even in dream I have not seen these sights." She was frowning, but in awe. The sight that had greeted us was more than she ever could have contemplated.

"I didn't think I'd ever see the sea again. There's a bit of everything down there for us," I said, moving my head in one direction and then the other. "But first of all, I'd love to take *you* to the seaside."

She looked to where I was pointing.

"So much water. Shall we fish forever?" she spumed.

"Oh, we'll fish all right. Come on, Linc. We're going to have a villa by the sea for a while!"

And at that moment, a reassuring trace of brine, carried on the soft breeze, just caught my nostrils, ever so fleetingly, before it vanished again.

By the time we had scrambled to the foot of the hill, it was turning seven o'clock and the sun, positioned beyond the barren structures that lay to our left, cast an assortment of intimidating shadows that warped and lurked upon the sweeping landscape.

"I know what you're thinking, but there'll be plenty of time to explore; it's not a place we want to be in at night," I said, as she stared westwards towards those hollow edifices.

"It is not like Mentarea. It is not a happy place." And, despite the early evening warmth that bathed us as we stood there, she gave a little shudder.

"It *would* have been a happy place once, Linc; but it's the people who bring life to a place, and they went a long time ago."

My own words had prompted a memory to pop into my mind, a recollection from a late summertime of my boyhood, of an empty birds' nest that had dropped from a tree and lain, ragged and brittle, on the lawn. I remember picking it up and wondering why it had been abandoned, as well as remarking on the proud effort that had been spent in its construction, and, with a childish zest and time on my hands, I had even wanted to repair it.

So on we marched for another half- mile or so, across those still recognisable pastures, until we reached a field the far edge of which morphed tidily into a shingled foreshore. We sat down together on a grassy knoll some feet from the beach, and threw our bags from our shoulders.

"Like it?"

"I do. It is a sight I never should have seen had I not met with you," she replied indebtedly.

"Come on, let's go and paddle!"

We walked over the shingle and onto the sand, which was still damp for the tide had only recently begun to ebb. She reached down promptly to ease off her footwear, and then took my watch from her wrist and, like millions before her, tucked it carefully inside one boot. Then she peeled off her singlet. I removed my shoes and my torn t- shirt, and we just left everything right there on that unexplored shore. The cool sogginess felt kind against my bare feet. I dug my heels into the sand, then straddled sideways and watched as the water squelched to the surface to fill the little pockmarks that I had left. She copied me, and giggled as she walked in a peculiarly stiff way whilst trying to make her imprints as deep as possible. When we reached the first wavelets, we did not stop- we waded into that gentle and enticing swell where we whipped up little billows of sand in the crystalline water. We didn't venture further out to swim- that could wait until tomorrow. Instead, we sat down in that invigorating sea, scanning an ocean that no ships would ever sail again, and let the bountiful waters lap against our bodies. The minutest fish darted back and forth, stopping and spurting away at the slightest movement from us. In a move that caused me to start, and with her lightning- quick reflexes, Lincoln splashed her hand vehemently below the surface, and raised it again. Once the water had drained through her fingers, she unclasped her palm to reveal a solitary writhing minnow.

"Even *I* do not wish to fish for those, for I should spend from one moon to the next for just one meal!" she groused, and lowered it gently back into the water.

I have already commented on the extraordinary hotness of our old sun. The evening temperature, although dropping, was still so unusually warm that we were able to spend longer in the sea than I expected, chatting and splashing and laughing and edging out further to keep up with the slowly retreating tide. It was only after a while that Lincoln said suddenly:

"I am thinking that time is... *flying*."

Her acquisition of my newly- antiquated phrase delighted me, and she in turn grinned with accomplishment. But she was right. The air had become a windless drape, the water a creeping chill, whilst the reddening sun, its intensity fading, was tinting the ocean with a pink patina and sedating the sand with a delicate tangerine- grey. The whole scene could have been eternised as oil on canvas. But there would be other evenings, many others. For now, we still needed to find a suitable place in which to spend the night.

"It is. It certainly is," I agreed.

I wanted to reciprocate her words, for they had been spoken with a warm- heartedness. I thought for a moment, before deciding on the appropriate words:

"And the moon...will follow soon."

She smiled again; my choice was good.

Back on the beach, I saw our footprints, not as defined, but still there like little ruffles on a bedspread; just as the hand smoothes out the creases, so too would the tide flow over our prints and wipe them away. We stopped to put on our footwear and tops again. For some pointless reason, I brushed the caked sand from my shoes with my fingers.

"See a good spot?" I asked her as we reached the field again.

"I am thinking that over there, beyond the gorse bushes, will be a good place to pass moontime," she suggested, pointing beyond the cluster of gorse, distorted, but still resilient, by years of easterly winds sweeping across from the ocean.

"Hmmm...not quite as pleasant as old No- Man's Land," I said.

She smiled on hearing the name of our previous encampment again.

"But it looks okay. The bushes are flowering too. You won't have heard the saying 'the gorse is in blossom and kissing's in season'."

"I have not heard that before. What is its meaning?"

"I'll tell you later. Let's see what we can find."

We found the ideal place to set up camp- well, ideal in such strange circumstances anyway- because the gorses shielded a row of pines. But it was one pine in particular that drew my eye; the one that had been uprooted. Where the roots had begun their winding descent was a hollow, and it had given me the idea to construct a shelter. My survival skills had been left in abeyance many years before, but the hollow had roused my inner determination. I described to Lincoln the type of branch that we would need for our main support, as I had decided that we should construct a covered shelter in which to sleep. She, in turn, responded with a simple touch of her hair and a subtle widening of her azure eyes, and sprang lightly over the pine needles to begin her search. I cut the roots from the tree base, and she reappeared just as I finished scooping the detritus and collected sand from the hollow. Her branch was about six feet long, and, once I had sliced off the arterial twigs, was as good a pole as one could expect to find, notwithstanding a kink near the top. We needed to find a rock, and, our first choices rejected, we managed to shift a sizeable boulder to the edge of the hollow. Thereon, we rested the pole on the rock, found a suitable place on the trunk where the branch met at a forty- five-degree angle, and stood back to survey the beginnings of our shelter.

"I am thinking that we should add the sides."

"Right...shorter branches, varying in size, for the sides. They're the ribs."

"Aaahh...," she said, as she traced her fine index finger over her own exposed lower ribs. So we carried on and laid tree branches, varying in size, in an upside down "v" pattern on both sides of the pole. Then we threw grass, needles and leaves on the top, the last we sloped downwards so any rain- *should* there be a downpour- would drain away.

Our minds may have been content on finishing, but our bellies were aggrieved, so whilst Lincoln prepared the remnants of our food, I made several journeys to and from the adjoining area of beach to bring back suitably sized chunks of stone with the intention of building another small boundary wall. Lincoln helped me once she had cut the fruit, and, after a further hour or so, we enjoyed a welcome evening meal washed down with a flask of red wine.

It is difficult to describe those last fading minutes of twilight. The sea, a new joy for Lincoln and one that would thrill her always, continued in its repetitive and timeless motion. To the west stood the buildings of the long- forgotten town, now etched darkly against a claret- red sun in a blazing sky. To the south stood the slope from which we had descended that day; and, opposite it, stretching to the north, the overlapping hills that were now washed with a charcoal grey.

I woke just briefly in the night, and all I heard was the gentle motion of the sea as it respired with an almost subdued consideration coupled with the faintest of chimes from my beautiful music box that hung from a nearby tree. Before I fell asleep under that hushed moon, now in its waning last quarter, I heard a flapping- an owl presumably- as it swooped from a nearby tree, its wings causing but a ripple in the stillness of the night- sky. And on and on the waves continued to curl, on and on to greet the next breaking day.

CHAPTER 16: *Withered Echoes*

It had been a long time since I had woken to the screeching of gulls. Lincoln had arisen before me- I felt certain that I had heard her stir, but I must have dozed off again before I gave any thought to joining her. I eased the cover from me, yanked the nearest branch and propped myself up on one arm. I could see that she was sitting naked on top of the grassy mound, her legs stretched, crossing her feet over each other repetitively, and looking above her head, following the motion of the impatient birds. I left our bivouac and went to join her.

"They are huge. They fly, but they are not sparrows. They make much noise, but they are not crows. They are *screaming*; what are they?"

"They're gulls, Linc, *sea*gulls," I answered her.

"I do not think that the fish will escape the sea...sea- *gulls*," she said.

"True, they know where to look." Lincoln was right; they *were* big birds, although she had not seen a seagull before so they were just naturally large to her eyes. But to me, they were positively freakish.

I inhaled briskly.

"Wow...smell that salt!"

"Sea has been to meet us," she said. "And I am thinking that I shall bathe before I do anything else for my relaxation in the water with you last suntime brought even more happiness to me."

"Sounds like a great idea."

It was a splendid sunny morning, and I needed no invitation from my bride to join her in the tempting water. I took off my clothes, in which I had slept for fear of cold. I noticed that she had placed her used clothes in a neat pile by the side of the hillock, near to the purplish flower of a bloody cranesbill. She saw me look, and said intuitively:

"I will wash my clothes after I have bathed."

"I'll do the same."

"Let us not wait. Come."

It was glorious in that water. We had only needed to walk a few yards before we reached the flowing tide, and I had waded out with Lincoln up to my abdomen, before I had let go of her hand and we had both swum out deeper into that refreshing sea. We stopped at a point where the water was snug about my shoulders, and just glancing her neck. Then we submerged ourselves before reappearing, completely invigorated. We frolicked for a while, and then swam to shallower water from where we splashed back to the little waves that patted the sandy foreshore a few feet from our clothing. Without leaving the water, she motioned me to lie down in the gentle surf. She sloshed onto her side, the water slopping over her body again, and embraced me. The water was splashing our faces as we kissed, snatching our gasps of breath and washing them away; her lips tasted salty now, and some stray hairs had flopped across her cheek, their sodden tips catching like seaweed in my mouth. But the salt had consumed me with a raging thirst for her and I clutched at her naked wet body. I forced my hand behind her back, my knuckles grinding into the shale beneath her. I could feel the toes on my right foot penetrating the wetness of the sand, pummeling it mercilessly. Her body began to writhe like a landed fish, her limbs enveloping me like tentacles, and we made love with a fiery passion that not even the deepest ocean could begin to dampen. And afterwards, with the sand clinging patchily to our bodies, we lay on the moist foreshore, limp and wet, like flotsam left behind by the tide.

We breakfasted later that morning on the remnants of our fruit and loaf, our clothes draped quaintly over branches so that they would dry in the sun.

"Now we are without food," said Lincoln rather dejectedly.

"There's plenty in there," I said, jerking my thumb behind me in the direction of the sea, "and there'll be mussels galore in and around those pools that we haven't explored yet." It was a certainty, for the mussels could tolerate the dry periods between tides. But I didn't fancy another session in the water that day, for I was itching to investigate the town that lay to the west.

"Let us walk to that strange place now," she decided, "for I am certain that there will be much to see. And I will find us food, for, as you have seen, the land provides for those that ask."

"I'd say it's a couple of miles away- maybe three- shouldn't take us more than an hour or so to get there."

And without further delay, we both dressed in fresh clothes from our bags. I donned my clean pair of shorts and a new vest. Lincoln wore a slender band, made from the same cotton as her loincloth, which wrapped around her waist and stretched up the centre of her chest, across her breasts, over her shoulders and down her back; she looked, for all the world, like a cave maiden. We applied carefully the fresh bistre to our faces, put on our shoes and then she fastened her utility- belt around her waist. I put on my straw hat and picked up my knife- belt, clipping it around my waist.

"Ready?"

"My legs are stronger than they were last sun. I am glad that we have rested. Yes, I am ready."

Off we marched once more, but on this occasion our gloomy destination lay within our sights all the time. Those abandoned buildings began to loom ever larger in front of us. They had not been obliterated. They had not been restored. They were neither one thing nor the other; they rose grimly from the earth like tortured souls that had been doomed to linger for eternity at the gates of purgatory. Now they just stood there, decaying, the very life- blood drained from their arteries.

"Berries!"

She made me start as I must have been lost in melancholy thoughts.

"Where?"

"Over there!"

I stopped to look, turning away from that flinty mausoleum that stood about a mile away.

"Oh, I can see what you're looking at now."

"You remember that my eyes are...*sharp?*"

"I do. They certainly are."

We walked over to the dense undergrowth that lay across the field to our right. Even before we reached the plants, I recognised the familiar and delightful sight of wild raspberries and blackberries, growing in giant tangled knots. Without saying another word, Lincoln broke in to a trot.

"Hey-y-y...wait for me!" I cried.

She had reached the matted stems, and was now holding one aloft, pinching the vine gently between her finger and thumb of her right hand.

"Now we have food for many suns!" she said triumphantly.

I walked over to where she was standing to inspect the fruit.

"They're certainly big," I marvelled.

Most of the raspberries and blackberries had grown to a ludicrous size, rambling to an abnormal perfection in the ideal conditions of that sun- drenched plain close to the lower level of the escarpment.

She tweaked one of the raspberries, easing it delicately from its vine. Then she held it to her mouth and placed the flavoursome looking fruit between her lips, drawing on it and severing it messily with her perfect teeth. Her eyes reamed, like a summer's sky breaking through the cloud, as she moved the other half away from her again, a vivid crimson driblet catching on her lower lip, and she said:

"Our first fruit on our walk of suns- you should taste half." She smiled again in that alluring way that made it hard for me to resist anything she suggested.

How you elapse with ease, self- control!

I opened my mouth and she positioned it gingerly on my tongue. Then I bit into it. It was sweet and succulent: pure ambrosia.

"Mmmm...as good as it looked," I said, as she wiped the red stickiness from her mouth, and then skimmed the back of her hand across her covered breast, staining the material fractionally with the juice. And so we spent another half- hour or so at those wild berry bushes, picking a mixed selection of the fruit and placing it into my bag. Afterwards, we drank from a cackling stream to the rear of the bushes, filling our flasks once more. Fed and watered, I left my bag at that spot with the intention of collecting it on our return journey, and we set off to walk the short distance to the town's perimeter. Strewn with the rubble of many centuries, much of it covered by weeds- some recognisable, others truly weird- as Nature had been victorious in many of its attempts to reclaim its rightful place, our route became rockier, more dangerous now. Hidden craters lurked perilously between the misshapen hillocks.

I touched Lincoln's arm to warn her of the potential danger that lay with each step as she would be totally unused to such an environment. Although so would I be too. Furthermore, it would become worse once we entered the main environs of the old town.

"Watch where you're walking now," I said. No sooner had I finished speaking than she dived towards my right leg and grabbed it forcefully, suspending it in mid- air as I wobbled on my left one.

"You warn me of danger, but who shall warn you? Look!" She was still holding my leg. I peered down and noticed that I had been a split-second from snaring, and almost certainly gouging my ankle on a warped, rusted and useless piece of metal that was protruding from the ground like a hunter's gin, waiting to incapacitate an unsuspecting victim.

"*Who-o-a*...that was close. Could've been nasty! Thanks, Linc!"

She smiled again, pleased with herself for having saved me from injury, and a look of satisfaction shone from her eyes. She released my leg and I placed my foot onto safe ground.

We carried on walking, more carefully now, until we reached the first structure. It rose some twelve to fifteen feet in height, and was built from granite blocks. Apart from a large split that had rendered it in two from the top to the middle, it stood largely intact. I placed my hands onto its surface, feeling the smoothness, as a visitor to an ancient stone circle might touch the structure hoping to experience mysterious energy surges. Lincoln just watched me. Then I walked around to the other side and was astonished by what I saw. In an arched cavity that had been built into the feature sat a bronze sculpture of a man. He was no ordinary man, as, had he been upright, he would have been nothing short of ten feet, and his sheer size contrasted with the modest carved stool on which he was seated. Like all statues and monuments, his giant size must have reflected the fact that he had performed some notable achievement during his lifetime. The sculptor had immortalised him as a thinker, but not like the one Rodin carved, and he looked as if were still suspended in the same deep thoughts like a person that stares at a window whilst pondering over a perplexing crossword clue. A great man obviously, but his talent would remain forevermore hidden. I grasped at the weeds that grew about the entry, pulling them and snapping them and twisting them.

"You look for a plate of letters, like the ones that Isaac showed us in the dark room in Mentarea!" Lincoln sang intuitively as she realised what I was doing, and helped me in my search.

Finally, we found it. It was still secured to the plinth, and, apart from the familiar smears of verdigris that had stained its surface, like the sad tears on the face of an old soldier, it was remarkably well preserved, the copper square having been protected from further erosion by being cloaked in wild choking undergrowth for hundreds of years. It said unpretentiously:

> # ROBERT RICHARD JOHNSON, 2053 – 2115 AD:
> ## Benefactor
> ## Loved By His People

That was all. Apart from being a benefactor, I should never know if old R.R.J. had done anything else, but the people- *his* people- revered him for it and did not want anyone to forget it.

"Who *was* he?" Lincoln asked, her eyes igniting with fascination.

"A man whose most notable characteristic was his generosity of spirit to his town and the people within it. He's long gone now, but his image remains. I wish he could speak though!"

She stared at the carved strands of hair on his head, and then she turned back to me.

"He is like you," she said, in that charming way of hers, as she tugged at a wayward length of hair behind my ear.

"He's got less hair though...besides, he's *much* older than I am. Quieter too!" I quipped.

For some pointless reason, I pushed the flattened weeds back against the plaque. No- one else would ever see it, but it might as well stay covered so that it would last longer.

We walked on to the next ruin. It had lost its roof long ago, but three of the four walls remained in a good state of preservation. The glass had gone too, and masses of lime- green chickweed choked the bottom of the walls, whilst glorious buddleia grew from the inside ground floor of the edifice, throwing out their straggly arms from the vacant apertures and over the tops of the walls like inquisitive sightseers. Bees sat engrossed, and butterflies rested motionless upon the purple and white flowers. I counted four or five varieties of butterfly, including the petite Adonis Blue, the gold and indigo Swallowtail and, of course, the Cabbage White; but there were at least two, tropical again for certain, the names of which I couldn't even begin to guess. We walked inside the old structure, but our path was blocked by dense vegetation, and I decided that it was pointless to spend time and energy hacking away at it for no reason. There was nothing to see, so we left again.

"Won't be getting any squatters in there. I can't even guess what that place was used for. Let's move on," I said to my eager companion.

"Skwatt...ers?"

I'd done it again- it still came as second nature to use everyday words and terminology.

"Squatters- those who occupy a place without permission, make it their own."

"Like my ancestors in the place they would one sun call 'Mentarea'?" she suggested.

"I suppose so...never really thought of it like that. At least the owners never came back," I said, grinning.

And so we entered the main body of the dead town, now like a massive corpse strewn on the ground where it had fallen and never recovered. We meandered for what seemed an endless amount of time but in reality was just over an hour, until we came to an overgrown boulevard that stretched ahead of us, which at one time would have been a bottleneck of traffic; to either side soared huge constructions, now soulless, blackened, empty, tired, many tilting through decades of neglect. Prime locations in the town centre would remain worthless barren plots throughout Eternity. To say that it is difficult to describe the experience of a town centre devoid of human activity is an understatement. How could one begin to relate the episode to another? It is something that modern Man cannot begin to imagine, as noise had polluted the environment and permeated every crack of sanity by the Twenty- First Century. But now there were no cars and no music. There were no crowds and no garish colours. There were no flashing lights and no church- bells. There were just we two. Only two newcomers walked that once- thriving thoroughfare. We were as tourists who travelled strangely along that street and we carried with us our two cheap day return tickets, their expiry dates inexhaustible, to weary old towers, depleted department stores and exhausted offices. Just we two travelled along that empty road, a trip to nowhere except perhaps to the End of Time itself.

"Of what do you think?" she asked me, and touched my arm lightly.

"Oh-h-h...just how it used to be...how I should have thought, before I came to your Time, how it *would* be still. This is the nearest that you'll ever get to it. I wonder what you'd have thought...just shut your eyes, Linc, only for a moment and try to imagine all the people from Mentarea here. And these buildings...picture them as they were. Can you do that? *Can* you?"

She faltered.

And then:

"I can picture such scenes without closing my eyes," she spoke quite absorbedly.

"What do you see? Tell me what you see, what you imagine."

"I see Gale standing at this place. She has travelled on a magnasule to come to the market because she looks to replace her old shoes. That is what Gale does often. Aaahh...there is the market."

She pointed to a grimy, ruined terrace that, unbeknownst to Lincoln, at one time probably *would* have housed a row of shops.

"Tell me more...go on." I wanted her to visualise it.

"Gale waits for...*me*...yes, she waits for me."

The Silent Hive

She had drawn my attention to the concrete stump of an old streetlight, or some other similar obsolete appliance.

"I am in another chamber; I am looking for a belt, but I look out from that place. People walk past Gale- they are busy- they walk everywhere. The two girls that we saw...do you remember? They are here too...they continue with their game of redwhick."

She grinned from ear to ear as she joked, "Did I not tell you that it is often a long game?"

Two ruined brick piles stood across the road.

"And Isaac...Isaac drinks his wine...always he drinks wine...just..."

She put her finger edgily to her lips as she scanned our surroundings for another convenient location, and stretched her arm towards a straggly old sycamore.

"...just there."

"Don't stop. My mind fails me already. Please Lincoln, put some players on this empty stage for me. Turn up the music at this dull party."

She dismissed my analogies, and her face was animated now.

"My father comes...he sits on a bench. He sits on...aahhh...*that* bench over there."

She pointed to a mound, from the top of which protruded a large hunk of masonry.

"Keep going..."

"Horat! I see Horat, and he carries a...a hat in his hands- another hat for you!"

"More..."

"People everywhere. The noise of Mentarea is everywhere."

"And the buildings...what about the buildings?"

"I...I cannot answer your question."

"Why not? Why not, Linc?"

"Because you ask me to imagine places that *you* knew. We have crossed the boundary into Otherland together, but *my* mind has walls that cannot be climbed."

"Damn it!"

She watched me nervously as I tightened my fingers into fists.

"You are...angry?"

I inhaled deeply through my nose.

"No...no, I'm not angry. Not with you anyway. It's just me. I'm being stupid. I'm expecting you to humour me."

I sighed.

175

"It's just that ever since I arrived here, I've relied on you to make things…make things right. But they're *not* right- they're never going to be right. I ask too much of you; *I'm* the one who needs to shut his eyes and dream!"

"I try to think of people in the places they know. That is something I can do because I am thinking of people that I know…but buildings are different; I cannot picture such rooms from another Time."

"No…no, I know that. It's okay, forget about it. Just…just come and explore this loneliness with me."

We continued to pick our way along that emptiness, and all the while, increasingly, I became aware of little prickles of moisture dancing across the back of my neck as if a hundred shadows were groping their way blindly in our very footsteps. I shivered, because, despite the damp patches on my vest, it felt as if icy pearls were trickling down my spine on that hot afternoon.

"S- so cold here. Cold…and dead."

She stopped in her tracks, and stared at me deliberately. Her eyes were wide, but this time with the reluctance that she now appeared to be carrying.

"Your thoughts are as mine?" she asked instinctively.

"I…I don't know. I don't know what you're thinking, do I? It's bleak here, desolate. I'm almost beginning to wish that we hadn't come. Everything was alive before we came here."

"You are wanting to return?"

That is what she wanted too, and she seemed to grow an inch in height having dared to speak those words.

"Yeah…yes, I'd like to go back."

However, to save face, I added:

"But there's more to see. It won't be our last visit. And you?"

She sat down amongst the parched weeds, and forced the palms of her hands nervously along her bare thighs towards her knees. Then she spoke, but with an atypical calmness, lifting her right hand from her leg and sweeping her arm in a circle to include all that stood around us: "Since I awoke at this time of sun, I have walked from light into darkness. Even people from two Times far apart know that fruit grows only in the light and that in darkness everything dies!"

I sat with her. She looked perversely comical, an object of beauty amongst thriving weeds in a perished town.

"Shall we return?"

"I have answered your question; to return is right, for once sadness has visited, it is good to end an activity even *before* sun says so."

I conceded to Lincoln's wishes- call it her logical reasoning, even her intuition- for we had seen enough for one day, and she had not liked the strange territory into which I had led her. We walked back to retrieve my bag of raspberries and blackberries, and continued on our way back. It was nearly four in the afternoon by the time we arrived at our coastal encampment.

We flopped onto the pine needles and dry earth at our little base, where we just lay and thought about what we had seen that day. For our evening meal, we devoured the magnificent berries that we had picked on our way into the old town. We drank water from our flasks that we had refilled from the stream on the way back, and I poured a last beaker of wine for each of us. It had just turned seven- thirty.

"Cheers Lincoln."

"*Chee*- yers!" she beamed as, remembering the time in the cave, she nudged her beaker against mine, before she added amusingly, "one for the...ahhh...road, sir!"

We took our dry clothes from the branches, and settled down for the night.

I cannot recall which one of us fell asleep first, but I was gripped by sudden panic and confusion when Lincoln jerked my shoulder during the small hours.

"What...mmmm...wha...!"

"I am awake."

"Mmmm...okay...what's wrong...?"

"I have been thinking."

"What about...? Oh, go back to sleep..."

"I must tell you."

"What?"

"I am thinking of your question."

"Which *one*?"

"The branch and the empty forest."

"*Lin*coln!...what- what's your answer?"

"I do not have one. I said I have been thinking only. An answer will be found, but now is not right. But it is lonely being awake without you."

"Okay...let's discuss...it...tomorrow."

I pulled her to me and held her tightly, and I can say quite honestly that I do not know what she said in response, because I fell asleep again.

I woke to a peculiar scraping sound, regular but scratchy.

"What are you doing, Linc?"

"I am making supports for the net. Look." With both hands she flipped the slightly arched branch around, and pointed to the finely whittled protrusions that formed a y-shape at the end.

"The net will fasten on here," she expounded, "and also on here when I have finished." Bare- footed, she was wearing just the v- shaped sash that I had seen her wearing on the morning that I 'proposed' to her.

"A vast ocean...won't be like our previous sessions..."

"That is why we have a better net. You will hold one end and I shall hold the other. It is a bigger net now and we will catch more fish."

"Hmmm...you're pretty good at all this. I knew we wouldn't starve!"

She squatted then, and, placing her net on the ground, she changed her tone.

"During sleep I woke."

"I know...I know, you woke me too."

"No, not at that time- the answer to your riddle answer evades me still, although I have given much thought to it. I woke later, but I did not tell you."

"Oh?"

"I had been dreaming," she spoke as if her mind were elsewhere, and she positioned herself more comfortably on the ground.

"Silly or sensible? Good or bad? I think I can guess."

"It was the dream of the queen bee once more."

"Oh, *that* one- a *recurring* dream, eh?"

She was fingering the band of cream material over her left breast, moving it back and forth exposing her bare flesh.

"The butterfly was there again. But in this dream there was another one."

"Two of them? Together in the hive?"

"Yes. There were two. They were taken out of the hive once they left their chrysalis."

"Makes sense- didn't you say last time that a butterfly wouldn't be too happy living in a hive?"

"I did. But they had red wine on their bodies because the queen had spilled it on them."

"And?"

"She licked it from their bodies." She grimaced as she said, "*Ugggh*! A queen bee drinking red wine!"

"Doesn't sound very likely; perhaps it was a rare vintage and she didn't want to waste it!"

She frowned.

"What next, anything?"

"Then it moved forward in time."

"*Forward?* How?"

"The two butterflies grew bigger and were liked by every bee. They were different...I am thinking that they were different because they were...*beautiful* and of such bright colours."

"No, they were different because they were butterflies. That's obvious!"

"No. It was not like that; the bees did not seem to notice that they were *other* insects, just that they were...different."

"Any more?"

"Yes. The bees gave them more honey to eat," she added, and then said, "That is strange too- butterflies that eat honey!"

Then she chuckled as she went on to say:

"A voice spoke from behind me."

"Male or female?"

"I *think*...I think- no, I do not know. It was just a dream voice."

"Mmmm, know what you mean. What did it say?"

She knitted her brows as she attempted to recall the precise words.

"It said, '*There fly...there fly the prettiest butterflies in the land.*' Yes, those were the words. It must have been a bee speaking, but it is strange for a bee to say such a thing."

"Strange for a bee to say anything at all," I laughed.

"You are right," she smiled.

"Anyway, I know another reason why that's a nonsensical dream."

"Tell it to me."

"I don't think you can have *two* butterflies emerging from *one* chrysalis!"

"So now we fish?" she asked, a short time later.

"Why not?" I said, as I stretched and threw the sheet from me.

"This suntime we will...*look!*"

Her eyes were like marbles and I turned to see what had distracted her.

"Where...what is it?"

"On top of the hill. There!" she pointed.

It must have just come into her hawk- eyed field of vision, and I was as surprised as she when I saw it. Like the stroke of a pencil moving across an empty page, the solitary figure was making its way tentatively down the side of the hill, etched wraith- like against a crowded landscape, as it appeared to be following a similar route to the one that we had taken.

"I cannot...yes, yes I see now. It...it is Gale!"

I was taken aback.

"Gale! What brings her here?"

And every now and them, a smaller shape would reveal itself, popping up from the foliage like a wooden marionette.

"She brings the dog too!" Lincoln cried. "I do not understand why my sister should follow us," she continued in a rather serious voice.

"I don't either, but we'll know soon enough."

CHAPTER 17: *Time And Tide*

I dressed and, forgetting all thoughts of fishing, we set off to meet Gale. Friday bounded to us, panting thirstily and trying to yelp in excitement. Ecstatic at seeing us, Gale threw her bag to the ground, and as soon as I was close enough to her, I realised that she had undertaken a far more strenuous journey than we. Whilst the sisters embraced, I took off my shirt and scrunched it up. Then I poured some water onto it, and urged Gale to sit down at that very spot for she looked shattered. Her cheeks were glowing, and, like beacons in a fog, they penetrated the lines of grime that streaked her face. Lincoln smoothed her sister's hair lightly from her forehead, and I proceeded to dab the wet shirt on her brow. The single white garment that she was wearing comprised a bikini- style top that connected, by a double diagonal x-band, to similarly brief bottoms, and was marked with all manner of stains from her time spent outdoors.

"I had thought that I would await your return," she said after some moments, perhaps slightly nervously. Although she was clearly fatigued from her journey, I still wondered whether she might not think that she was intruding. Thinking about it, we were still on our 'honeymoon' after all. But no, I was thinking conventionally: no place for that anymore! "And I thought that I *could* await your return," she gasped.

Lincoln looked perturbed.

"Our father- what did he say?"

"He said I should go as he did not want me to be sad. I passed just one moon in Mentarea without you, Lincoln."

"But surely your father wouldn't let you travel on your own?" I queried suspiciously.

"I was not alone," she replied, quite innocently, as she tousled Friday's fur. And anyway, our father came with me for one sun and one moon. Then he returned. He made me promise that if I did not see you, I should go back."

"And did you see us?" I continued.

"I saw you. Always you have been far away, but I have seen you. The dog had your scent, until you bathed."

"You could have shouted our names," Lincoln suggested.

"My shout would not have been heard," Gale sighed with a hint of despair. "Once I fell and hurt my arm, and I shouted with panic until my throat ached. No- one came. There *was* no- one. It was at that time that I wanted to return. I will tell you now- do not tell father- that I cried. But I did not go back, for you were nearer to me than Mentarea."

Her arm was littered with little scratches, and a large black bruise had spread over her elbow like oil on sand.

"If we had known that you followed, we would have waited for you," Lincoln reasoned.

"It was not hard to follow your trail- the ashes from your fire, the red blocks that you dug from the earth…most times I followed in your steps, but I am thinking that sometimes I went the wrong way!" she said satirically, and pointed to the congealed blood on her chin.

"I'm just wondering why your father didn't come all this way too." I had begun reluctantly to doubt Gale's story.

She dropped her eyes at my words, and replied sheepishly, "My father wanted you to…to, aahhh…be alone…be with each other and no- one else. He does not laugh often, but he did smile when I asked if he would come. He said that he did not want to risk your anger at his intrusion. He said that I could 'meet with you', but warned that I 'might not be wanted' here. He left me to make that decision."

"Okay…you're here now. You've found us, and we're not angry. Well, I'm not. Are you, Linc?"

"I have no anger. I have missed my younger sister."

"So, why not come and see our little place?"

And then, to Lincoln:

"Think she'll like it?"

"It is all we can offer."

I grabbed her bag, and as we began the walk back to our encampment, I said, "Two things though: you're on the mattress on the dining- room floor, and you work for your keep!"

Gale blinked innocently at my first words, but took my last comment seriously as she added, "After your Ceremony, I offered to be a maid for you and that is what I shall be."

As we ambled our way back to the seaside camp, Lincoln asked Gale for any news from Mentarea.

"There *is* something to tell you," trilled Gale.

"Tell it to me," Lincoln urged her, running the fingers of her left hand gently through her sibling's hair as they walked.

"Isaac drank so much wine one time of early moon that he fell from his bench," she giggled.

"Ohh…was he hurt?"

"No- one knows because he did not say. He was like a dizzy crow and had to be helped up again by Leo and another man, whose name I do not recall. He was angry though, for his wine fell with him!"

"He probably just hurt his pride," I contributed.

"Ohhh…his *pride* was injured! That is funny," Lincoln laughed.

"And I have more to tell you," Gale continued.

"Of Isaac?"

"*N-o-o-o*, not Isaac! Do you remember Jose?" she asked, rouging.

"I remember him. I saw you together from one of the towers."

Gale looked surprised.

"When?"

"One sun…" Lincoln answered, glancing at me with those deep eyes, "…one sun when I too had company."

"Oh. That is something that I did not know. But I must tell you that Jose has been sitting at my table for breakfast," she told her sister animatedly.

"Another wedding in the offing?" I asked Gale.

She just stared blankly.

"A 'wedding' is the old word for our Ceremony of Harmony," Lincoln enlightened her sister.

"Aaahhh…but Jose is just a friend."

"Sounds like he fancies his chances with you Gale."

"Fancies his…"

"*Likes* you."

"He likes me as a friend maybe. But…"

She raised her eyebrows, and smiled cautiously.

"…but I am hoping that he will learn to like me more."

That glint in her eye was the first that I had seen of Gale's impish nature, and I hoped that I could learn more about my sister- in- law now she had joined us.

Back at our base, Lincoln showed Gale our unpretentious bivouac, and, climbing onto the grassy mound nearby, instructed her to take deep breaths of the pure sea air. Afterwards, Gale spied the music- box and mentioned that she liked it.

"It was a gift for me from Lincoln after the Ceremony," I explained, "and it shall stay by my side until I'm gone from this life."

We breakfasted- later than usual- on an abundance of the berries that Lincoln and I had picked only the day before, but, healthy as they were, we would need more than berries and once more our talk turned to fishing as we would need to keep our protein levels topped up.

"Well, we've got our new net, Linc. Let's move onto the beach and have a go."

No sooner had I finished speaking, than Lincoln bent down to prise off her shoes, then stood up again, undid the buckled fastener on her sash and let it drop to the ground. Naked again, she jumped from the mound and went to fetch the net.

"Come on, Gale, come and leave your footprints in the sand!" I said.

I cleared the hillock, and ran towards the foreshore. I tripped onto the dry shingle and ran to the wetter sand, and could hear Lincoln's feet patting the beach as she chased after me. I turned to see her perfect bronze frame gaining on me. Just before I reached the water's edge, she caught up with me, and, tossing her net to the sand, she threw her arms out to me. As she touched me, I stumbled backwards onto the soaking sand.

"*Ummphh!*"

"Ohh…I have caused you to fall."

"It's all right, Linc," I reassured her. She crumpled to the sand and rolled on top of me. I caught sight of Gale looking at us.

"Come on, Gale!" I yelled, egging her again.

"Gale. Come!" Lincoln echoed, as she slumped from me.

We sat on the sand with the wavelets teasing our lower backs, and watched as Gale stood up.

"I am coming now," she responded.

She walked calmly from our enclosure until she reached the shale. She still wore her sturdy shoes as she walked onto the shore, but, once she reached the wet sand and realised how difficult it was to walk evenly on the squelching surface, she bent down and prised them off, discarding them there. Then she carried on walking uncomfortably, with a pained but resolute expression on her face, as if she were braving white- hot coals. Every now and then she glanced down at the sand, and her eyes widened as she marvelled at the peculiar imprints that her feet were leaving in the muddy surface.

"Gale!" Lincoln said.

At last she reached us, and knelt down by the water's edge.

"Do you like the beach?" asked Lincoln.

"It is…strange," she said, her thoughts etched on her brow.

"Want to come in the sea with us?" I asked her.

"I...I do," she said.

"Come," Lincoln added, throwing her arms in both directions, "There is room for all of us!"

I went first, and waded out several yards from the shore. With the endless ocean bobbing pleasingly about my shoulders, I turned and trod water as little salty splashes taunted my face.

"Come *o-n-nn!*" I cried.

Lincoln stood and held out her hand to tempt Gale to follow. On seeing her sister's outstretched palm, she stood up and briskly removed the outfit that I have described earlier, and, once Lincoln had picked up her net, she followed her sister into the waves that lapped against the sand.

It didn't take Gale long to find her sea legs, and Lincoln encouraged her by splashing her. Gale responded jovially. As for Friday, he was just content to bound up and down the grand shore and run into the surf occasionally. The sight of the two naked girls dousing each other enthralled me, and, for a brief moment, I likened myself to Hylas with his Nymphs, although I trusted that I should not suffer the same fate! Once Gale had grown accustomed to the water- a world apart from the brook at Mentarea- we fished the retreating tide as if there were no tomorrow. Every time we filled the net, one of us would slosh to shore and pad back to the camp where we would deposit our catch. Having joked that we had almost depleted the sea of its stock, we moved from the water and, whilst the girls basked like bashful seals under the midday sun, I retired to a shady spot for a while. Some time later, I strolled back to the girls as I'd had a sudden idea.

"I know that you two will never have built a sandcastle!" I trumpeted.

Lincoln was mystified.

"A *sandcass*...what do you say?"

"A sandcastle- a building made of sand; something everyone should do at some time in their life," I remarked.

"You wish that we build here on this sand?" Gale asked doubtingly, brushing the sand from her breasts.

"Yes...well, back nearer the water, where the sand is damp. The tide will come in again later. But first, we need a spade. We need a piece of wood, flat preferably, but I doubt we'll be that fortunate- a thick piece will be fine though. A branch will do...it needs a stout end though."

"I will find the wood, but I do not understand what we will do with it. I share the doubt of my younger sister. At your school, you were taught that the wise man builds on *rocks*. To build a place *here* would not...be right. I have seen how the sea returns. I am thinking that we will be drier and warmer over there."

She pointed back to our gorse camp.

"Oh, Linc! No, no, no. I still talk as if I were back there, back in my own Time, don't I? We're not going to *sleep* in it...it's just a something to do together- a bit of fun, a child's game! Crikey! To build a castle big enough to sleep in, I'd need to build until..."I paused, "...until Eternity!" Well, it felt like I had that long. I certainly had an abundance of time on my hands.

Without further delay, Lincoln and Gale trotted back to camp and within a few minutes had returned with two slender branches.

"The wood is good?" Lincoln asked.

"Well...not flat enough really. Needed a spade shape- flat at one end- but they'll do for quick digging."

I took the piece that Lincoln passed me.

"Watch now," I said.

I began to scoop out large piles of sand, throwing them to one side. After I had excavated a substantial amount, I put my wood down and commenced the next stage.

"Right...we need to build strong walls now," I told them, and shoved the sand into a messy mound. It was good sand, damp and weighty, which, as every child knows, is perfect for the job- heavy sand for light-hearted construction! Then I flattened it slightly, and added more to one end, curving it gradually. Lincoln understood the idea, and Gale joined in too. I directed the girls to continue to form a circle with the sand, and we soon developed a system, taking it in turns to dig and build, the girls' slender fingers plunging into the sand, their palms then patting and flattening it. Once the rough circle was completed to a height of about nine or ten inches, Lincoln cried:

"It is like the wall of Mentarea!"

"Similar," I agreed.

"Inside we shall build too?" Gale asked.

"Of course, anything you want."

So Gale and Lincoln dropped little splodges of wet sand into the centre, crafting them carefully into splendid minarets and leaning columns. I added a couple of turreted features inside the perimeter on the seaward side, dwarfing the main wall and enhancing it so that it resembled an ancient fortification. Then I broke a splinter of wood from one of the branches, and pushed it into the larger turret where it doubled as a flagpole. I sat back to admire our work, and I think the girls thought we had finished.

"One more thing to do yet," I grinned.

I picked up the branch that I had used initially, the sand now encrusted on the end, and began to gouge a trench from the castle back to the sea.

"But the water will reach it quicker," Lincoln gasped, her face crestfallen.

"That's the idea! But the tide's not coming in yet. Let's go back and prepare that fish."

After we had cleaned the fish, we sauntered back to our castle where we awaited the rapidly approaching late- afternoon tide. We sat together behind our construction, the sand cool against our legs, and watched as the water began to trickle into the trench. The first flow entered, and ebbed, leaving behind a dirty dribble. Then it came again, merging with the thin stream, moving forward. Back it went, but the sand was wetter now. Again it came, then back. More minutes passed. Faster it came then, until it reached the wall, just nudging it; the kiss of death, but not enough force to destroy it. Just a few grains fell away, and I found myself thinking of the old town that we had visited only yesterday. I wondered how long after the Dark Angel had spewed forth his miserable bile before the first bricks had loosened and toppled. Nobody had picked them up and cemented them again as there had been no- one who cared to rebuild the town, for once incentive perishes, despair thrives. I recalled Edis's words from our first meeting and imagined that the people, depleted by the plague, had realised quickly that the old lifestyle had vanished forever, as the towns and great cities could no longer have functioned in the conventional sense. The whole economic system, from raw material to ultimate consumer, would have ceased. What use is shelter without food? The survivors headed for the countryside. They left forlornly, but decisively, in groups at first. They set forth purposefully like woodlice from under a raised stone. Then in pairs they would have shared superfluous adventure and diluted optimism. Finally, the town's sole remaining occupant would have hobbled away reluctantly, like the straggler who refuses to drink up after the landlord has called time, in search of...of something else. In search of *anything* else.

"Lincoln, quick…" cried Gale, immersing herself in the task at hand, and she scooped up a large handful of sand with which she tried to reinforce the wall. Lincoln copied her sister, and added another pile to the channel in an abortive attempt to dam it.

"Tsssk!" one of the girls uttered.

Forward it flowed again, and the sand was now at its mercy as the water lapped at the wall, smoothing out the faults, washing over it until it seemed to dissolve away. Further round the edges it came, as the channel filled, attacking slowly but remorselessly. Now it resembled even more the old town, crumbling, falling, defeated by a tenacious tide. But it was more than that to me, as I compared its state to my own hopelessness on that eventful day when I came to this bewildering place. I had been caught by an unknown wave, sprayed by a fine mist of fear and swamped by the breakers of dejection that followed. My defences pounded, I could have surrendered, fallen apart, foundered on the rocks of despair. But I was saved, plucked from that current by a beautiful maiden, and, with her strong foundations, she helped me to rebuild my life.

Over the edges the sea spilled, and into the middle of the collapsing structure it flowed.

"Ohh!" Lincoln cried, kneeling in the water, her hands dripping and with her arms plastered in sand.

"All our work…" sighed Gale, and straightened her legs again as she sat flat in the water.

"I am thinking that I was wrong," said Lincoln as she turned to me. The water was cool as it slapped my heels.

"Wrong? What about?"

"I said that the walls are like the walls of Mentarea."

"Well…they were."

"But now I am thinking that Mentarea will no longer protect its people."

"I don't understand. Why not?"

"Because if the walls of Mentarea are like those of our *sandcastle,* I am afraid that they will be washed away when next it rains!" she grinned. She looked at Gale and smiled; Lincoln was fond of what I can only describe as jocular sparring, and she had caught me with an uppercut again!

"I *hope* not! Come on, you two. Let's go back now," I said, as the froth licked my toes.

*

Back at our small but proud camp, we dressed and relaxed. Later on, Gale set off in search of some wood for the fire. She had only been gone about half an hour before she returned with her bag full of light branches and twigs, plus a clump of withered grass that she had uprooted. The fish had been prepared earlier, and, having started the fire (more successfully on this occasion), we dined once more on our perfect and freshly- cooked catch. After our meal we immersed ourselves in endless chatter and the time passed speedily. Lincoln chose a natural break in the conversation to ask me a question:

"At a time such as now, as sun is leaving to make way for moon, what would you have done?"

"Back then, at this time? Hmmm...I'd have gone out maybe."

"To pick berries?" piped Gale.

"No," I laughed, "not to pick berries. Out with friends, I suppose."

"Where did you go?" asked Lincoln.

"To my town centre for a drink...you know, a glass of wine or something."

"Who made the wine?"

"Who *made*...oh, Linc, it was just *there*. Not only wine though- beer, brandy, whisky, gin...lots of drinks!"

"Isaac would have liked it," Gale chirped.

"I don't doubt that he would have done."

We talked for a while longer, and gradually the flames dropped and the ashes began to glow emulating the westering sun as it sank behind the old town. A jaded Gale excused herself then as she tried to stifle a yawn. She had prepared a spot for herself behind a bush in the lee of the hillock, but some feet from our shelter.

"May the moon keep you in rest," said Lincoln.

"Have a good sleep. Goodnight, Gale."

"Until the new sun," she replied, and sloughed wearily away to her own private space.

"Once you told me of a place where you could go and eat a meal- a *ress*...restor...*" Lincoln carried on with our conversation as she edged up to me and settled her head on my shoulders.

"A restaurant. That's right, I'd have gone there at night too. I'll have to tell Gale about such things sometime. Anyway, why do you ask?"

"I ask because you sit by a fire in a strange place with a person from another Time, when perhaps you would rather be in the *ress-torront*.

Sometimes I feel sad for you," she said. A charred piece of wood popped at that moment.

"Oh, don't feel sad for me. Please don't. I've got you. And now Gale has come too. Anyway, *you're* sitting by a fire with a strange *man* from another Time!"

She giggled at my words.

A pause followed.

Then she said:

"And *I* sit in a place that is new to *me.*"

And I watched her sparkling eyes dance as they reflected the apricot glow from the struggling flames. It was a blissful moment of intimacy that we shared beside that fire. But we were hostage to the embers, and, all too soon, the whitening of the flickering ashes and the rapid blackening of both the sky and- naturally- Lincoln's eyes were signs that the day was over, and thus we retired for the night.

CHAPTER 18: *Trackless Sleepers*

Two days later, leaving Gale alone at our encampment, Lincoln and I ventured once more into the nameless old town, but, once we had reached the main street again, we deviated from our route by heading in what appeared to be a more interesting direction. It was a hot day. Not a sunny heat, as, surprisingly, the sky was a uniform dove- grey; it was a tight, oppressive heat, which caused us to shuffle lamely under the sustained clamminess. With little speckles of moisture coruscating on her unflurried face and, pearling beneath the shells that hung on a twisted blade of marram grass that had been worked by the girls' hands just the day before, were little beads of sweat which created a sheen upon the gilded flesh of her breasts. Lincoln looked hot.

"What...are those buildings?" she asked me, very excitably, as she pointed to a row of canopied structures that were visible through the greenery, across the crumbling walls and beyond the rubble field. "We shall look? Oh, do let us go and look!"

Well, we had been in this rotting carcass of a town just three days earlier and been eager to leave. But now, despite the humid and sunless weather, Lincoln seemed to be breathing a filtered air as she spoke with a happy ambition.

"Of course!" I cried, feeling somewhat sapped, and mopped my damp brow with my hand.

As we neared them, I could see that they were four in number, their curved smooth black roofs standing solidly under a shunned sunlight and looking as grim as a pew of cowled mourners. Behind them, poking teasingly through the trees, its grandeur long vanished, was what was left of a vast stone edifice. We picked our way across the ruins, again taking care not to cause ourselves injury on any concealed masonry or rusted framework, until we reached the first of the structures. But I had been so careful in my effort to avoid any man- made obstacles that I had been blasé to the natural foes that lurked on the ground. It was as I stopped that I felt the shy soft brush of a leaf against my bare shin. I shot a glance to the ground.

"*Tuuttt*! Blasted nettle!"

It was a huge, ungainly plant, growing by a log, and, in the absence of a gardener's glove, it had seized at the chance to thrive like all the other weeds to an obscene size in this dead place.

"*Ohh*...a nettle has stung you. I will look for the dock leaf. Always they grow nearby."

"No…no. It's all right. Let's carry on."

"I thought that would be your answer," she said, vaulting her eyebrows.

Although, as I conceded to the urge to scratch, I did think that perhaps I *should* have let her find a dock.

"Well I know what *this* place is. We're at the town's railway station!"

Lincoln stared at me. I had told her so much of my Time- her *past*- but realised then that I had failed to tell her of such a method of public transport.

"Trains…we travelled all over the country on them. They were a convenient mode of transport. Fun, too! Well…most of the time."

And sure enough, far back at the end of the hangars, stood huge inky shapes. They looked like cloaked assailants in that rayless obscurity, their sombre sides appearing to meld with the earth.

"Come on, Linc, let's go in and have a look- they're like no train that I knew!"

We trod our way carefully along the ground- there was no platform, and no evidence of there ever having been one- our route conveniently lit by huge gashes in the withered black material that enveloped us. As we spoke, our words rebounded under the cavernous old cover. And in the breezeless silence of the sultry morning we stood stock- still for a while as we laughed at our voices echoing around the forlorn boarding area. We reached the strange train (for, in the absence of any other word, that is what I would call it). It was dark blue, plain and perhaps even rather menacing looking in the close clotted air that hung dense around us. And this is the strange thing about it- it smelled! Not an unpleasant odour, and not musty like an unused bedroom or that old chamber stuffed with relics that lay back at Mentarea; no, more a stale, earthy smell- with a hint, imagined I don't doubt, of oil- where natural elements had been declined for too long. A small opening- where once Perspex or glass would have rested- was positioned about three feet above two circles- headlamps that were surprisingly still intact, each smooth with a tainted veneer. I bobbed down to look, surprised by their condition, and Lincoln crouched alongside me. I went to tap one, but found that my finger just pressed into it like putty. I pulled it out, startled, imagining in a fit of madness that the thing was alive.

"It moves?" asked Lincoln, her eyes as wide as, and brighter than, the very lamps. A line of sweat glistened on her fine nose.

"Mmmm...it did, and notice how, even in this half- light, they appear to shine? Wonder what causes that effect."

"*I* shall touch it, and I may be able to explain," she said quite assuredly.

Well, I have noted before how any challenge of mine would become Lincoln's too, and whenever I saw those blue eyes aflame beneath those soot- black lashes, and that display of those white teeth- as perfect as opals set in a ring- as she smiled, I knew that she was relishing every moment. So, still squat alongside me, with her left hand she shoved a froward tress of hair from her face and stretched her right index finger into the peculiar jelly- like substance on one of the lamps. It gave under the pressure and moulded itself around her fine finger. Then she sat for a moment, looking quite ponderous and just stroking her thumb over the surface.

"Ahhhhh...it is a strange substance fashioned by the hand of man, for I know of nothing in Nature like this."

She popped her finger out again, then reached for her utility- belt and from a pocket on the right pulled out her trusted blade.

"A challenge for Isaac when his hand holds no wine! I shall take a piece back for him."

She inserted the blade very delicately, just tearing the stuff, and then joggled it about as she sheared a slice from the odd mass. She withdrew the blade with the strange gelatinous substance quivering and glistening on its tip. I picked it from the blade and inspected it more closely. It was a queer, rubberised material, and if you imagine a polythene bag filled with water, you will have something of the general idea of its feel. However, it looked rather like a chunk of ice. I held it to the dull light that penetrated the broken roof, and the thing dazzled before my eyes.

"Those tiny strands...almost like shards...see them, Linc? I think they're splinters of crystal."

There was a myriad of criss- crossing hairs, each working as part of a whole, their purpose to reflect any natural daylight, or, more importantly, moonlight, and working in a similar vein to the old 'cats- eyes'.

"It is clever; I am thinking that we could light the whole of Mentarea in such a way."

I passed it to her and she repeated my inspection, and then squeezed it gently into a pouch on her belt for later perusal.

We explored the empty place, under the gouged canopy that lay stretched over hexagonal steel frames, past the strange train (a ghost train,

I thought), to an opening in the grey granite stonework that lay beyond. We walked through the opening. And what I saw next amazed me. Beneath our very feet were the remains of a beautiful tiled floor. Some of the squares were even still intact, their vivid carmine and ochre veneers looking almost as pristine and lustrous as the day on which they would have been laid; others were chipped about the corners, and the odd one had been rendered viciously in two. Upon the tiles, supported on two slender but secure columns, was a carved marble relief of an altered, but still familiar, outline. Even the youngest of school- children would have recognised it instantly; but to Lincoln, neither eyes nor imagination could assist her in deciphering it.

"What is it?" she asked, totally perplexed, yet, at the same time, quite mesmerised by it, for it was a stunning piece of craftsmanship. Each notable feature had been hewn in a different polished stone, and blue-green agate and turquoise quartz had been used to spectacularly creative effect; it was a carving of the British Isles, and, apart from a cleave across East Anglia, it was intact.

"That, Linc, is our country. That's where we live. It's where I *used* to live, and it's where I live *now*. With you."

"It...it is Otherland?"

"Well, I suppose it is to you...and to me now. But I know it as Great Britain- the United Kingdom. See that red stone there...no, that one...that's where I lived."

"And Mentarea? Do you know where Mentarea lies?" She was eager to know.

I laughed.

She looked confused.

"Oh, no. No, no, no. I just don't know. I mean...I've no idea. That's where I was walking, round there. Assuming I travelled..."

I talked as if my adventure were routine. Normalcy had been extinguished the day I awoke in Otherland. No, sooner than that, the day I departed from...

"Oh, do tell."

"Assuming I travelled to...or *in*, the same place, then Mentarea lies about...hmmm...just there."

"And where do we stand now? Where is the beach where Gale fishes and Friday splashes at this moment?"

That was the first time that she had called the dog by its adopted name.

"We walked in this direction."

I traced a line across the smooth surface.

"Then we reached the sea…Ohh, somewhere around here. But you have to understand the scale. If we're here, then Gale is just here. You see, Linc, this represents a big country."

I should have seen more of it. Now I never would. Not much more, anyway.

"Come on, let's sit awhile."

She sat down and leant her bare back against one of the pillars, eased off her boots and stretched out her legs. I sat down next to her.

I flicked off my footwear and rubbed my heels over the cool tile.

There we sat in a dead railway station, a successful symbol of a once-thriving kingdom. But there were no posters, no vending machines, no appliances and no furniture that I could recognise. And no trains would run again- oh, how I should have cried tears of rapture at that moment to hear the words 'leaves on the line' or – what was it again? - 'wrong kind of snow'! Millions of souls had striven for the gravy train, but had departed on the midnight train.

No barriers.

No route.

Not even a ticket.

Just herded like penned cattle, the electric signal replaced by the swath of the Reaper.

A scampering- so slight, so very soft- as the smallest of mice pattered past us.

Lincoln twitched her foot.

The creature tripped at that sudden movement but paid us scant attention, preferring instead to scoot across the floor and through a far doorway into the fauna that lay outside.

"You are quiet," she said in a low voice.

"I know, I was just thinking."

"Of what were you thinking?" She leant forward from the column and placed her hand on my knee.

"Oh, just being maudlin again."

"*Mawd…?*"

"Maudlin…sentimental, sad."

"Because of this place?"

She began to massage my knee affectionately.

"Yeah, because of this place, this dead railway station. You see, Linc, this should be a place of life. You could compare it to...say, a *heart*. Yes, a heart, with the healthy pulse of humanity throbbing across its floors."

She smiled at my analogy.

"And the train tracks- or whatever they ended up using- were like arteries, spreading out into the land, carrying people to wherever they wished to go, to do what they needed to do, so that they could maintain the vitality of the country. That's how it would have been a long time ago. Think of your Great Hall, all those people coming in and going out, talking, greeting each other; it would have been like that here, but many, many more people, most of them rushing for a train...ha! If you could only see the expression on the face of the man who has just missed his train, and lip-read the muffled utterance of his cuss, you'd know how important this place was!"

I slid around to look up at the huge marble map.

"Look- just look at it again. Imagine the distances."

She turned and squinted at the strange carving once more.

"We went all over the place."

I sighed and clicked my tongue, before continuing:

"I wonder what speeds we reached."

"Do not be *m...maw*...sad...instead, let us walk where the mouse ran. But first, we should drink again."

So, begrimed with sticky warmth, we swigged from our flasks, copious gulps of water between sharply salted lips. And then I explained to Lincoln how, in a far away Time, had somebody passed me as I sat here, wanting of socks and nursing a flask, they might have tossed me a coin. Perhaps a two- pound coin! But I described a nod to neediness that she would never comprehend, for she shared an oddly, but reassuringly, seductive world of very little in a land that historically had always proffered so much. In fact, poverty in this Time was as unknown as the apostrophe. Yes, Lincoln's cup was always full, spilling over even, and, like those of her townsfolk, it was refilled from the Well of Plenty. But the towels would soon be on the pumps. *Why?* I asked myself. *Why? Why must this Society perish?*

"It is like the rain arch!" Lincoln blurted.

We had emerged into a beckoning bright sunlight; as I had discovered already, on the rare occasions that it chose to, the weather here could alter in the time it takes to write a postcard.

"The rain...*rain arch*. What's that?"

"When the sun comes during rain," she said, as if I had asked a foolish question. She raised her hands above her head until her fingertips touched, then pulled them apart and swept them out and downwards again, each mirroring the other before continuing:

"It gives the colours of flowers."

I nodded, lips sealed with enlightenment.

"I see...of course, a rainbow."

Another word buried.

Centuries of earth.

Upon earth, and a new phrase born.

The bridge was built from blocks of stone; cubed, hewn, true, meeting tubular steel and ascending to a fine curve and then a feline curl before falling symmetrically to supporting masonry on the opposite bank.

The grey- jade waters of the stream scintillated, snatching the gleam from the steel apex, as they rushed underneath.

"That's a beautiful bridge," I said, whistling.

"You spoke once of such a thing. Now you have found one. Come, let us walk over it together."

And this time, I let her lead the way.

We had climbed up shining steps that were still fixed securely to stone pedestals. They, in turn, were approached by a brown clay path, barren, dry, uneven, textured with rubble. It was grand just standing there at the top of that bridge. Behind us was the rear of the old station, resting immobile and useless now up a bank of white-top dusted hawthorn, hollyhocks and gangly foxgloves. On the other bank lay tumbled walls of old buildings, and in front of them stood a row of slender slate monoliths, each tall, grey and tapering to a point. On each point was affixed a stone panel. We leaned against the rail, like two office- workers on a dinner break, and looked at our ripply images below.

"We see so much of us in reflection," Lincoln hazarded.

I smiled, for her usual collected manner had underplayed the intentional wisdom in her words.

Then I pointed to the odd columns.

"Wonder what those are, Linc?"

"The tall grey pillars?"

"Mmmm...strange. Maybe some form of transmission, power...I saw a few scattered around the other day."

"Perhaps they are…people- people who wait to cross this bridge," she mused lightly.

She slipped her arm around my waist; her hand was warm as she patted my hip.

"Ha! People who have stood for so long that they have turned to stone!" I exulted.

None of the other bridges had stood the test of time; in either direction, piles of masonry, emerald green with moss encrustation, lay toppled in the river.

Busy waters, redundant stone; stone cut by the hand of man.

By Nature absorbed.

"More bridges," she said.

"Yep, more bridges. But they haven't lasted. Won't be crossing *those* ever again."

She looked pensive.

"Linc…?"

"I am thinking. I am *thinking* that our love is like a bridge that cannot be crossed, but one that will last."

She turned to me.

"Oh, Linc. I like that, I really do. In fact, we should give this bridge a name."

"A name? You wish that we call it by a name?"

"I do."

"Tell me."

"No. Guess."

She puckered her brow.

"A name for a bridge…"

She blinked.

Then she added:

"I think I know."

I looked into her eyes. Fathomless. Captivating. Then I pushed aside her hair, black and smooth as boot polish, and whispered into her ear:

"Lincoln's Bridge."

And then, her bare skin against my chest, sweat on sweat, we kissed. A bee buzzed nearby.

On a bridge to somewhere, above a river in the sun with no- one else around, we kissed.

Two travellers, time on our hands and nowhere in particular to go.

"We shall return to my bridge?" she asked.

"Of course. Show Gale sometime, too."

So, in the afternoon sun, we strolled back to join Gale at the camp. We stopped only for Lincoln to gather a handful of dock leaves, fold them adeptly, and, with no less concentration than I should have expected, tend to the most irritating and infuriating rash on my shin.

CHAPTER 19: *The Weeds Of Wealth*

For once, I was up before the girls. It was a soundless dawn, devoid of gulls still, and I supped at the rare splashes of solitude so that I could reflect on my time so far in this new land. I was seated on our comfortable grassy knoll, scanning the horizon and making the most of an uncommon chill, borne on the incoming tide, which was seeping through the new morn like the inescapable draft from a badly fitting door. Lincoln had groaned as I stirred, but had not opened her eyes and I could see Gale's feet sticking out from behind the bush. My thoughts had wandered in all directions to the great cities and landmarks of my own Time and then to a period I never knew and no- one should have had to witness; the year 2120. How loudly had the last lion roared in Trafalgar Square? Who had waved farewell to that old seafarer Liverpool as he set sail on his final voyage? Who had listened as York, that aged and wise story- teller, recounted his epilogue for the pages of history? For how long had the Seven Sisters of the South resisted the tide until they crumbled, clothed in white until they perished like withered old spinsters? And who had sharpened the penultimate blade in Sheffield?

"Do you dream of another Time, or do you count the fish that we shall catch this sun?"

She had startled me, and I jolted.

"*Ohh*...morning, Linc. You're dressed; I never even heard you. Come and sit with me. I've always believed that an early morning mind is like the waste paper bin left by the cleaner- free and uncluttered!"

"I am thinking that it will take all of this new sun for you to explain *those* words to me," she said, screwing up her face, the tiniest of creases forming around her eyes.

"Some other time," I smiled.

She sat next to me and there followed a moment's pause before she said:

"I have my answer."

"Answer...er, to what?"

"The tree in the empty forest," she replied, running her pinched fingers along a thick blade of grass. The motion produced a raw, squeaking sound.

"Oh...okay, let's hear it then."

She shuffled and took a deep breath as if she were about to announce some momentous news.

"I am thinking that it *does* make a sound, but perhaps it is not known to be that of a falling tree."

"Hmmm…"

"During the storm we heard the branch crack," she continued.

"Yes, I remember…right behind us, too."

"The sound that we heard was the mental part. That is how we interpret it," she explained. She touched the side of her head. Her eyes were excited; I was just confused.

"The physical part is the vibrations in the air. That part is always present, so in an empty forest I am thinking that only the physical part exists."

"So you think…*what?*"

"The tree *does* make a noise, but it will not be recognised as a *sound* if no- one is there."

From Lincoln's point of view, *quod erat demonstrandum*.

"Linc! That's…that's very…erm…profound. You've never been asked that *before?*"

"I have not. What is *your* answer?" she asked ebulliently.

"I haven't got one…suppose I'd have just said 'yes, of course it does'."

"Ohh…" She sounded disappointed, but then added, "If you *are* asked, you may tell of the answer that I have given!"

Her teeth poached a sunbeam as she grinned, and her eyes shone with a sense of accomplishment.

"I will…I will, certainly. A mental *and* a physical part- I rather like that. Thank you."

"That is the mental part for this new sun," she elaborated proudly.

I pulled her closer and looked into those deep eyes.

"And when you tumbled headlong into the undergrowth that day, that was a different sound!"

"I experienced the mental part, and the physical one too! But I liked the part that followed, when you helped me."

"I did too, Linc…I did too. Have to remember to ask you the one about the man and the table in the locked room- that'll set you thinking!"

Then I kissed her, because, although I could not have deemed it possible, she was just that little bit lovelier than the day before.

"We shall have fish. Berries too. And afterwards, shall we journey around the land?"

She pointed to the cliff face, and the expanse of rock- pools and sand that lay in front of it.

"See what's there, you mean? Probably get into the town again that way too," I nodded.

"I shall wake Gale?"

"I don't think she'd want to miss out," I said.

She trotted off towards Gale, and I laughed to myself as I heard her say her sister's name not once but three times.

Back she walked.

"She comes now."

Clad just in her loincloth, Gale emerged from behind the bush. Her dark hair dropped neatly to her shoulders and she looked refreshed after her long sleep. Even the cut on her chin had paled markedly.

"A good sleep?" I asked her.

"I passed the moontime without disturbance," she replied, and then stretched her arms as she emitted a slow yawn.

"Linc and I thought that we'd go and explore over there. Want to join us?"

"I am…wanted…with you?" she asked cautiously.

I glanced at Lincoln who turned to me, and we both looked at Gale again.

"Not had a better offer, have you?"

Her face adopted an enquiring expression.

"Gale, we're hardly going to leave you here after you've walked all that way to find us," I said.

Nothing more needed to be said, for she ran back to her bag, pulled out her utility- belt (which, it should be noted, possessed fewer accoutrements than her sister's), fastened it around her waist, put on her shoes and said simply:

"I am ready."

"Er…shall we eat first?"

We breakfasted, and Lincoln and I prepared ourselves. Then we set off to tackle the new day's adventures.

We had caught the day with its defences down, for by the relatively early hour of just nine o'clock (I no longer checked as I relied on Lincoln to tell me the time) we had reached the foot of the cliff. The stony face of that tenacious watchman rose, scarred by the weather but undefeated by the tide, some fifty feet above us. Nesting in cavities and on ledges behind grassy tufts were colonies of kittiwakes, gulls and other sea- birds.

I thought I recognised a razorbill as it soared above the cliff top. We clambered over the slate- grey and tar- black rocky detritus that lay at its base- features that, to the sisters, must have been as delightful a sight as the toppings on a trifle. I urged them to take care and place their feet on parts where the seaweed was not strewn. We stopped at a small pool, and I crouched down to look for signs of life.

"Look, Linc. Gale, here," I said as I lifted a small flat stone encrusted with acorn barnacles, from the shingled bottom. They both mimicked my posture, and watched as a billow of sand squirted into the water, fogging the limpets, hermit crabs and anemones and causing the tiny fish to dart.

"Wait 'till it clears," I told them.

As it dispersed, a crab scuttled across the bed of the pool and stopped in the centre.

"It is alive!" Lincoln said.

"It moves…*sideways!*" Gale elaborated.

I reached into the pool, casting my eyes over the surrounding area lest I lost sight of the crab as my hand disturbed the water, and, once the ripples cleared, I placed my thumb and forefinger around its shell and lifted it gently from the water.

"Uugggh!" Gale cried.

"It's okay, it's only a crab, it won't hurt you…not unless you put your thumb between these." I pointed with my left finger.

"It is a strange creature of the sea," marvelled Lincoln, and asked me if she could hold it. I put it onto a rock, and she picked it up in the way that I had shown her. She raised it to her face, and peered at it.

"Crab, I am thinking that you are as old as the Earth," she spoke to it.

Yes, he was old all right, unchanged throughout the centuries, living in his own pool. Washed over by Time's tide, he'd never alter and once he died a new one would steal his place under that rock.

"I don't really know much about them, but I reckon they've been around for a long time," I agreed. "Longer than I have anyway."

She grinned, and Gale's features lightened as she began to take pity on the creature.

"He needs to return to the water?" Lincoln checked.

"Of course. Better put him back now."

We continued on our way. Had it not been for my unusual companions, I could have been on any beach on any typical summer's day in my own Time. The cliff face became less steep as we traipsed around it, and the beach gradually lessened, finally appearing to merge with a verdant wooded area that fringed the rivage as far as the eye could see. So we veered off the beach, and began our walk through the woods heading roughly in a westerly direction and back towards the old town again. It was becoming hotter as the morning went on, and we decided to take a rest at the edge of a stream that we had been following for some thirty minutes.

"Phew!" I sighed.

"It is time to rest?" Lincoln asked.

"I think so. Gale?"

"I am happy to stay at this place and rest," she said.

We placed our bags down, and nestled ourselves comfortably in the undergrowth that lined our route. Gale, whom, by now, seemed as if she had been with us throughout our travels, flopped down and gave a long and carefree moan. Lincoln sat next to me and put her arm around my waist. With armies of bluebells and rich red campion grouped in ranks in the shade behind us, we sat and did nothing but watch the water. Until that moment, I had never studied a stream in such detail before; it was one of those streams that did not seem to move, almost as if it were being stifled by the vegetation that grew from the banks. Compared to the brook in which we had fished back at Mentarea, it was positively sluggish. But dull and lifeless it was not, for the sun, penetrating patchily through the foliage, was causing the water to alter between hues of yellow- green and chintzes of lime- white. In fact, the whole surface of the water waltzed as if some ethereal underwater extravaganza were being choreographed, Nature's spotlights being focused from below on the drama of darting minnows and the pirouetting of teeming tadpoles. Every so often, little bubbles of air would travel to the top where they would fracture, the disturbance causing ripples to emanate furtively across the polished veneer. The area itself was alive with a myriad of sounds and somewhere close by I could hear the commonplace clicking of a grasshopper.

"Not a bad spot, eh?"

"It is a good place. Gale, do you...?"

But Gale was asleep.

"She sleeps," Lincoln whispered.

"Know what that means?"

"She is tired."

"True. But it also means that I can kiss you...properly," I said, and I placed my lips on hers and embraced her tenderly.

Gale had dozed until nearly Noon, and, once she stirred, we set off again. The undergrowth began to disperse, and to our left we noticed how the ground banked gently towards the top of the cliff that we had walked around that morning. We were still walking along the edge of the stream, counting the different insects, inspecting the plants and pulling at the leaves. And then suddenly, in no more time than it takes to change one's mind, Nature's carpet was swept from under our feet, only to be replaced by the split floorboards of bare reality. There it stood in front of us, grimy, grey, stark and severe. It resembled the skeleton of some huge behemoth, its concrete columns, although crumbling from neglect, were still standing and making gallant attempts to support it in places. But the gaping holes that peppered the structure suggested that it would not be long before it crashed in defeat to the ground.

"It's a...a motorway bridge," I said in answer to Lincoln's question. "Remember that I told you about the cars that travelled in my Time? Well, that's what they travelled on- or much of the time anyway. Looks a bit different to the ones I knew, but that's what it is...or was. Eight...nine, ten...ten lanes too! Did we *never* stop?"

It had broken where it had rejoined the land again, and I could see no trace of the road after that point. We tramped on. Gradually our surroundings altered, and we came once more to the ruins of the town, albeit a different part.

"It is...it is so old," Gale said. She had uttered barely a word since she had woken from her nap.

"All so old now, Gale," I agreed.

She stopped to look at the peculiar brickwork that had survived on one building, although the adjoining stonework had perished long ago.

"Ohh...so shining. Could this be *new*?"

"No, no," I smiled, "It's Manchester brick or Accrington maybe; good brick, made to last."

"Oh," said Gale simply.

"Oh...but...the pattern? It means something?" Lincoln asked.

"I don't know...let me see," I said, frowning.

Lincoln peered at the unusual design that had been incorporated into the bonding. It was a strange mosaic, for the broken pieces of brick had been placed intricately into position to resemble- of all things- a book!

"A page without words?" Lincoln posed the question.

"Maybe that's what this person did for a living, made his money from being...I don't know, an accountant perhaps, someone who managed another's finances. I wonder if that's how people ended up displaying their status- as glyphs on the walls of their houses? Strange!" I mused. But *was* it so odd? I thought that I had stopped thinking like that. *I* was the hiccup here. After all, *I* was the one with over four hundred years missing. Why *would* everything have carried on as normal? More to the point, why on earth *should* it have done so? I had only to think of Mentarea and the grave that Edis had shown me with the piece of hemp etched into the green glass; I had only to remember the disappearance of money; I had only to picture the incomparable lifestyle of Lincoln's people; there was so much to remind me that both subtle and major social changes could, and had, occurred.

"Yes, Linc," I agreed, "a page without words. Four centuries of unfilled pages torn and flung into the winds of Time."

We continued, cutting a swath through the long grass that had sprouted on what used to be a roadway. We stopped to look at the patterns in the brickwork of the ruins of the neighbouring buildings and I told the girls what I thought the images represented- odd machinery, the tools of craftsmen and even players indulging in sport (although I failed to recognise what must have been some strange pursuit of the future). And, in the distance, stern and ever present like prison warders, towered the lofty structures that we could see from our encampment.

"What is this place?" Lincoln asked, as we rounded a corner of the old town.

Shining walls sprang from the earth, in places so clean that they reflected the grass and almost rendered the place invisible, as it appeared to merge with its surroundings. There were small and slender spaces where once would have been windows. It was a huge square block, but only about three stories high and silver- white, smooth, clinical and constructed from blueprints that lacked any aesthetic imagination. But it did have a doorway.

"I'm not sure. It looks more modern than the other buildings, or what's left of them anyway. Shall we go in?"

"Of course," Lincoln replied.

"Ohh...I shall stay outside and rest," Gale said skittishly.

The edge of the door was flush against the stark wall, but there was a 'keyhole', although surely not for any conventional key.

"Almost as smooth as the cell wall in Mentarea, but this can't be cut," I commented as I stroked the surface. I whisked my penknife from the pocket on my shorts, prised the blade from its casing and inserted it into the hole. I scraped around, and as I withdrew it, small flakes of rust dropped to the ground. I tried again, turning the blade forcefully in the hole, flicking it up and down and then jerking it from side to side. The door, without warning, sprang open, belting me with so much force that it caused me to pancake to the floor and slam the back of my head on the ground.

"*Uummph!*"

I was glad that it was soft grass into which I fell.

"Are you hurt?" I heard Lincoln ask as I felt her fine hands shaking my shoulders.

"No …no…just…just winded, that's all. Think I…I saw stars for a second then," I gasped. I was aware of Gale gripping my right wrist.

"There are no stars yet. Perhaps you dream," Lincoln suggested.

"It's all right," I said, lifting myself up. "Thanks, Linc. Gale, you too. I'll tell you about the stars some other time. Now I'm *doubly* curious."

I hobbled over to the door. The apparatus inside consisted of a large spring that had been tethered to a firing mechanism. It was crude, but, as I had seen, highly effective and made from galvanised steel to which was smeared still the traces of an unidentifiable oil. It was meant as a trap, and, I imagined, at one time would have been rigged to an alarm. Had the contraption not been rusted so, I feared that the door would have opened with so much more force that it should probably have severely incapacitated- or worse- any intruder.

"Who would make a wall open in such a way?" Lincoln asked.

"Someone a long time ago."

I smiled, but not outwardly; it was strange to hear her describe the door as a wall, for I had almost forgotten the lack of doors in her world.

"And why?" added Gale, "*Why?*"

"In answer to your question, Gale, I should imagine that this was a way of protecting what was inside. Look at the windows- where they would have been- see how high up the openings are. It's a strange building, not like the others…"

I walked in carefully. *Very* carefully, lest that infernal door sprang shut again. But it didn't of course, for it was designed to deter, not imprison.

The sisters followed, Gale having had a change of heart. There was absolutely nothing to see, except for strands of grass, most of them wan and feeble from the lack of daylight. Those that had grown at the furthest points from the sun- facing apertures had turned a sour green or dismal ochroid in colour. Like a fine red wine on the best tablecloth, a large russet-coloured stain had spread across one of the metal walls, and vertical lines of rust had begun to bubble almost like an air pocket left in pasted wallpaper.

"Nothing here. Nothing *anywhere*. I think…"

"*What is that?*"

"Where, Gale?" Lincoln cried.

"There!"

"I see what Gale sees. The ring of a giant!"

The sisters were pointing to a large loop that lay, half- covered, in the fruitless earth. I walked over to it and kicked the dirt from it with my shoe.

"It's connected I think…yes, it's attached to the floor."

I clutched it and began to pull. No movement. Nothing was easy anymore, it seemed.

"Here Linc, grab it with me. Gale, come and pull."

We tugged and we heaved and we sweated until we finally moved the thing. It gave a wearisome and dull groan, like the dreamer disturbed from his adventures. We lifted it and pulled the plate, about four square feet, to which it was affixed. And as we did so, an incredible thing happened. I say 'incredible', but, if anyone were to hear of my tale thus far, nothing should any longer sound too improbable. So perhaps that is the wrong word to use. Nevertheless, we all three were astounded to see the chamber beneath us become bathed in a glossy artificial light!

"Ohh!" Gale put her hand to her mouth. "Light without sun, candles and blaze- beetles! It cannot be. What makes it?"

"I think I may know," replied her sister, her face frothing with enthusiasm. "I have seen light like this before. It is like the light from the…" she added, concentrating, "…the *torsh*."

"My torch, that's right." And carried always for her, I thought!

The morning of that first honey bath when she had brought that fine breakfast to my room, and been fascinated by my torch…it seemed so long ago now.

"Obviously rigged to a power source. Amazing it still works…an everlasting battery!"

I lowered the door again slowly.

"Watch."

The light dimmed and, as I all but shut the trap, darkened. Then I lifted it again, and the light returned.

"There's a wire…there, see it?"

"It makes the light?"

"Yes. Come on, let's go down and see what's in all those boxes."

I lowered myself onto the fourth or fifth rung of the conventional steel ladder and climbed down into the vault some fifteen feet below. Standing on the floor I found myself mesmerised temporarily by its pattern of seemingly never- ending interlocking circles. The hypnotic and somewhat maddening design of that floor started me thinking of the perpetual motion of Time itself, and the fascinating concept of going back and forth and returning to one's starting point. The pattern was without end…a myriad of variations…round and round…loops within loops…a tedious fascination…like the shadow of a tree on the floor of a roundabout. Where had I started? *That* one…no…it was…*could I ever go back*? Back, back to a Time before my departure, back to my favourite summer or back to someone else's summer? Take Lincoln and buy a place in the country? Ha! Even keep bees…"

"Shall we come?" Lincoln snapped me back into awareness.

"Sorry. Of course. Come down."

Her bronzed legs were swinging into view, and, with her nimble-footedness, she was by my side before I could blink. Gale followed.

We just stood and looked at the shiny unmarked crates that had been stacked three high against the characterless walls.

"We shall open them and look inside?" Lincoln asked.

"Definitely. What d'you think is in them?"

"Copper plates!" cried Gale.

"Doubt it. I think you have the last of those."

"Let us look."

"Okay, Linc, let's see."

I lifted the top box from one pile and was surprised by its weight. I placed it on the floor, and cut around the plastic seal with the handsome knife that I had brought with me from Mentarea. Gripping the lid with both hands, simply because that is what one does with unfamiliar property, I raised it carefully.

"What is it?"

"What *are* they?" Lincoln elaborated.

I reached inside and picked up one. They were smaller than I had been used to, and, although it barely seemed possible, thinner than wafers and even lighter. Had I closed my eyes at that moment, I should have doubted that I was even holding it. And it was so fine that I thought it might break. I bent it between my fingers, and it arched perfectly. Widening them again, it reverted to its original shape. There wasn't even the usual stress mark on its surface. But the hologram wording on its surface was the only clue I needed:

Bank of Europia County 29b:

20,000 credits

"I knew it by its everyday term as 'plastic'; a credit card. Remember my telling you of money that day, Linc...when we bathed together?"

"I do."

"That's what these are, credit cards...unless it's proper money...I can't tell. The difference was that instead of handing over real money that you'd been given because you'd worked for it, you could...er, borrow money...pay with this. It recorded how much you spent. Perfect until you got the bill!"

"The wealth of a dreamer!"

"Linc, that's a good description."

We opened another dozen or so of those boxes. Most of them contained the pliant little cards, although we did find, oddly, a few gold slabs. The bank had become worthless; once part of the heart of the community, it had become, at that tragic time in the past, no more than an untapped and surplus mineral seam in a plundered and abandoned quarry.

"Of what do you think?" Lincoln asked me.

"When the last supermarket has been looted, all trade in consumables has died and the designer labels unpicked at the seams, only then is it realised that credit cards and gold ingots are inedible. They had so much money, but not much of anything else and so little time," I sighed, and shook my head.

"For you it is different," she said quite emphatically.

I looked at her and she smiled as she put her arms around my neck.

"So little *money*, but so much wealth and so much time!"

It was nearing nine o'clock when we finally arrived back at our encampment. We had left the old Treasury of Europia, and its store of unused currency, to the merchants of Perpetuity. However, the slender gold tablets had given me an idea, and, absurdly cloaking any thoughts of theft, I had pocketed a couple of them. We had veered through the town towards the foot of the escarpment, at the other side of which we had stopped four days earlier and picked those splendid berries, and reappeared eventually in the vicinity of Johnson's Statue. In the dwindling light, we ate the remnants of our fruit, only too aware that we should need to develop some sort of routine regarding nourishment if we were to remain awhile at our camp near to the shoreline.

CHAPTER 20: *The Portentous Dawn*

I could hear the lively cries of the sisters scattering back to me, like ocean spray on the breeze, and I knew that it wouldn't be long before we sat down once more to our freshly grilled fish. Another sixty days had passed since our arrival at the beach (I had made a notch in some bark each day) and during that time we had enjoyed an extension to our carefree lifestyle. We had made just four further visits to the old town, one of which was to walk with Gale over Lincoln's Bridge. We searched and we trawled, we roamed and we inspected, but we found nothing else of any real interest. Apart from the aforementioned structures, it seemed like more than four hundred years was just too long a period after which to find anything. And so most of our days were spent quite decadently, although we all three were aware that, with no further excursions in the offing, we should be making plans to return to Mentarea. Edis had been right, for Lincoln's skill and knowledge had enabled us to improve our diet considerably. Most days we fished for prawns. Lincoln had fathomed that, by using her net when the tide turned and the water seethed and tumbled in the narrow channels by the rocks, the prawns would just drift effortlessly into captivity. Why, I was even surprised how much I enjoyed mussels too! And seaweed, for which we had passed many hours wracking together, when cooked- although clearly an acquired taste- had also become a staple requirement. Lincoln, who found any challenge intoxicating, had become erudite in algology, and was of the opinion that the brown weed in particular that grew in the rock pools, and was therefore always submerged, possessed all manner of nutrients absorbed from the ocean, such as calcium and the 'fruit goodness' (which I presumed to be vitamin C). When boiled in water, she also believed it to be somewhat of a philtre; I saw no reason to disagree! But not once were we tempted to eat a crab, that surviving pedireme from antiquity that had fascinated Lincoln and Gale on our walk that day. We had been fortunate enough to find some apple trees and a small 'orchard' of very old pear trees too, and, needless to say, we had access to an endless supply of blackberries, raspberries and even gooseberries.

I let out a large yawn, stretched and sat up. There was an element of chill in the air, and I noticed that a fine mist was hanging like lacework between the ocean and the undersky. Scraps of cloud were strewn across the sky, resembling heel marks in the dew on an autumn lawn. I walked to the little mound of grass that had become, over the past couple of months, something of a thinking area, for it was there that I sat whenever I wanted time and space to dwell on things. I still pined for all that was no more, of course, and I had spent many an hour thinking of my parents, my family, my friends and even my lifestyle. I still thought about what had happened to Society and how it must have been for people when progress stopped and the power to the mighty engine of civilisation was disconnected. My thoughts were snatched from me by a shout:

"We have...caught many again!"

It was Gale, and she gave a cheery wave. Lincoln acknowledged me too, but I noticed that she didn't possess her usual sparkle.

They splashed from the water and tramped back over the sand to join me, with gleaming breasts and drenched like two marvellous mermaids. Shortly afterwards, we sat down to breakfast on the morning's catch.

"Mmmm...lov..ely," I said, chomping on a mouthful.

"You say that *every* suntime," Gale remarked.

"Well, if I didn't say it, you might think that I wasn't enjoying it. Isn't that right, Linc?"

No reply.

"Lincoln?"

"It is correct."

"Of course, that's not to say that I wouldn't enjoy a good fry- up once in a while," I laughed.

"A *friup*...?"

"Gale, you and Linc have never tasted..."

Suddenly Lincoln gave a peculiar whimper, and as I looked she started to sway as if invisible hands were trying to waken her from sleep. Still holding the piece of fish in her hand, she said suddenly:

"I feel...I feel wrong."

I noticed that her face had paled, as if the sea itself had diluted her bronzed skin. She gave a little shiver and dropped the mackerel to the ground.

"What's the matter, Linc?"

"Her face turns another colour!" Gale cried.

I gripped her shoulders just as she listed backwards.

"Whoa... okay, I've got you."

"*Ohhh*...Ohhh," she cried.

"Come and lie down for a while."

I helped her up and we walked to the rear of our base where I sat then with her as she lay on the ground. I stroked her hair, which was still wet from her session in the water.

"What's the matter, love? I thought you were going to faint then."

"Ohhh…I was about to fall. I felt…I felt as if I was spinning," she groaned.

I rubbed her arms, and then carried on brushing her hair with my fingers. Gradually, like ink clouding clear water, the colour returned to her cheeks. Gale was sitting by me with a look of consternation engraved on her face.

"I…I am feeling right again now," Lincoln said.

"Good…good," I breathed. I hadn't really given it any thought before, but we were a long way from Omas and the other 'Men of Medicine'. Then a thought struck me.

"*You* feeling all right, Gale?" I asked.

"I am well."

"I'm okay too…you know what's the matter, don't you?" I turned to my beautiful wife again.

"I…do not know," she answered.

"You ate too many of those mussels last night. I did try to warn you."

It is an uncomfortable feeling when one awakens to a strange sound. It was a violent yet helpless noise, and, although vaguely ordinary, I was unable to identify it immediately. Usually though, once perception surrenders to awareness, it's an instinctive human reaction to bounce, limbs akimbo, from one's bed to apprehend the situation. Having adjusted my eyes to the light, I looked past the gorse bushes to see Lincoln on her knees. I hurtled from that spot, and as I did so the realisation hit me squarely on my jaw.

Lincoln was being sick.

I was by her side in a split second, and I knelt on the ground to tend to her.

"Ohh…" she uttered on hearing my voice. There wasn't much vomit, just a small milky- coloured splattering. I wiped the mess from her mouth.

"Here…sit up…that's good, legs out…breathe deeply, Linc."

She stretched her head back and took a deep inhalation, then gently exhaled again.

"Okay now…feeling brighter?"

Then, in her typical fashion, she puckered her eyebrows and I surely knew what should follow.

"I am still...*phooo- ooo,*" she gasped, "... in the same sunlight...so cannot be any brighter."

I knew then that she would be fine.

"Now I know that it cannot be the mussels, for I was sick when I wakened the time before last sun."

"You were?"

"I was."

"Oh, Linc, why on earth didn't you say?"

"I did not want to cause you concern. If I had told you of my sickness, you and Gale would have worried and would not have been happy."

I was sitting with my knees bent and with the soles of my feet pressed against her thighs. "Oh Lincoln, Lincoln. Don't you see now? It wasn't the mussels, it wasn't even last night's meal that caused this. You're not *ill.*"

"I...do not feel as if I have illness."

I looked at her face, vibrant, lustrous, alive, and then to her naked midriff; she was, I knew, the very picture of tonicity. That gentle Lady with tresses of silk, who drifts across the land with random purpose, like a spore on a breeze, and scatters golden pollen on the bodies of women who dream, had already embraced Lincoln some weeks earlier. Familiarity, that immutable and comforting friend, who had been loitering about the camp, had now placed both feet firmly inside.

"No, you're not ill. No, no. In fact, you've never been better! Linc, oh *Lincoln,* you're pregnant! You're going to have a *baby.*"

Her blue eyes, uniquely bottomless, no longer just windows to her soul, were shimmering more deeply at that moment and had now become portals to her womanhood. And as she smiled, a breeze fluted prophetically from behind us causing my music- box to whistle, whilst all the time the sun appeared to shine just that little bit harder.

"I...am carrying a child?"

"You are."

She flung her arms around my neck and hugged me tightly; I clutched her cool back strongly, as if trying to support a sapling struggling against the wind. Then she looked into my eyes and we kissed. And, snatching at the chance of early morning privacy, as one might slink from a hushed house into the stony dawn, we made love with a clandestine fervour.

But an unspoken feeling pulled at our minds. I knew, and Lincoln knew too, that alongside her pregnancy stalked a dark shadow, an uninvited traveller that would share our journey over the forthcoming months. I knew that the first time I made love to her. And now I would spend the next months hoping that the sun would seep through the blackness, shine brilliant white through a prism to diffuse all fears and meld them into an intense spectrum of hope.

CHAPTER 21: *Garden Visitors*

We decided to leave the following day, and, our bags packed, we set forth in the virgin light of a cool dawn. One of my regular pastimes with Lincoln has been walking and exploring, but now we were returning. I was disappointed by our lack of any real finds- perhaps I had half expected to chance upon the skeletal remains of a plague victim cowering in a rotting cupboard. But things were very different now; Lincoln was carrying our child. So we walked on, chatting about all sorts of things that people do when they are on their return from a holiday- the weather (good, nearly all the time), food, the piece of carriage lamp and the bars of gold.

And Lincoln's pregnancy.

It was a strange thought to think that soon her waist would no longer be slender enough for that small loincloth. The pregnancy occupied everyone's thoughts, as the banter between the sisters was virtually relentless. Continuing an earlier conversation, Gale chirruped, "Your stomach will swell so much that it will block out the sun."

Lincoln was, as usual, honed in her readiness:

"But as I can drink no wine for my term of incubation, you may...ahhh...drink mine and then your stomach will grow so that it blocks out the light from a bright moon."

Gale laughed, but looked like she was preparing her retort. And thus we continued, fine spirits all three...or four, if I include Friday who was relishing the chance to stretch his legs again.

By noon on the second day, I knew we'd have to rest. Whilst my fellow travellers could cope, I could not. We were cresting a leafy hill, and I suggested that we go down to explore as the valley below was abundant with vegetation and a blue stream, blotched with green, was visible from where we stood. It only took about ten minutes to clamber down and soon we were resting under a very strange tree.

"These leaves are massive...I wonder what type of tree this is."

" I am thinking the same," Lincoln said, as she drew and snapped a leaf from the branch and flipped it over in her hands.

"Look, Gale," she continued.

"It is unusual, and I too have not seen one before," contributed Gale.

"In fact," I added, "there are loads of odd looking plants around here."

The flora was indeed aberrant, almost freakish. Ahead of us were some of the strangest looking fruits I'd seen, as bright as sherbet and as big as footballs. And one plant behind Gale had a flower at the *base* whilst above grew a reedy and useless looking stem.

Gale seemed more content to shuffle into a comfortable position as she realised that we would probably be resting for a couple of hours.

"I'll go and get the water bottlers filled. You coming, Linc?"

"I shall come, and I shall wash whilst we are there."

The stream wasn't far away and we could hear it coursing and singing through the leaves.

So, leaving Gale and Friday, we walked through the strange plants until we came to the stream where Lincoln promptly undid the single bow on her top, unclipped her belt, unwrapped her loincloth, removed her ankle- boots and splashed into the stream. She gasped with the cold.

"I'm not joining you. It looks a bit cold."

"Ahhh…so I cannot tempt you. I have an idea. If you ask me a riddle and I tell the answer, then you must join me."

She started to splash her way along the stream, away from the wrack and foliage that cluttered the edge. I followed along the bank.

"Hmmm…well I'm not going to lose *this* one. Let's see…"

I pretended to scratch my head and adopted a professor's frown, which caused her to chuckle.

"Got one! Made it up, I think: what has four legs and two arms, but can't move?"

"Ahhh…hmmm…let me think…"

She was mimicking me, and scrunched up her face in deep thought.

"I know you know."

"I know that *you* know I have the answer," she said, smiling. "You are correct though, for now you will find that the water *is* cold!"

"Let's hear it."

"It is a chair!"

"Too easy," I said as I pushed a wiry branch from my path. "You win. I'll join you in a minute."

"I will never tire of your riddles and…"

Her face! She was staring beyond me.

"What's wrong?"

I turned around and saw it.

"What the heck's that?"

She waded from the stream for a better look.

What we were looking at shouldn't have been there, not there in that lush valley. The thing was metallic and its silent white face shouted disharmoniously at the creeping greenery.

"I...I do not know. Perhaps it is a...a *house.*"

"Come on. Let's go and see," I said, already rushing towards it.

We walked alongside it, and, as I pushed through the vegetation in places, I realised that, by observing the angle of the patterns around the edge, it was projecting from the ground. But it was only when I discovered a door that I turned to Lincoln in amazement.

"This shape here...I know it. No, it can't be..."

There was a feeling of discomfort and something else- not fear exactly, more a benumbed and unnerving sensation like one gets when sorting sewing needles.

"I will tell...Ohh...I know this pattern. It is the same as..."

She faltered, but she knew. We both knew.

"... the one on your belt buckle," I finished for her.

"But how can that be so?"

"I don't know, Linc. After all, we're a long way from home. But that belt- buckle may be a key."

She was speculative, I thought.

"I will fetch my belt."

And she paced back along the bank.

Within no time at all, she was standing alongside me and together we held up her buckle to the grooves in the surface. We looked at each other, each expression of bewilderment surely echoing the other.

"Okay, let's press it in. Ready?"

"I am ready."

The door opened fluently, soundlessly, and I stepped inside. The instant I did so, the room began to lighten.

"Come on, Linc."

She held my arm.

"The darkness is vanishing. It is like the light in the...the bak...ban..."

"The bank. Mmmm. But this is different; I think this is activated by body heat. I think...what the hell are those?"

"Ohh!"she blurted.

Around us, stacked one atop another, ahead too, and all over, were strange cylinders. I went to inspect one. Through the clear surface, I could see its purpose.

Andy Loughlin

"It's some sort of bed. Someone was in here. Look- see that shape; that's where their head would have rested."

That perturbing feeling was stronger now.

I looked at her face, which was locked in an expression I had never seen before. Not on Lincoln, anyway.

I raced up the passageway, my heart palpitating peculiarly.

I didn't want to see what I saw.

I willed it to be something else because I thought my nightmares were over. But there in front of me stuck to the floor were four seats. In front of them was a bank of controls and circular screens.

"Linc, your belt- buckle! Pass it to me. That shape's here again."

I knew she was behind me and I knew I was being terse. We had always explored together and had fun in our discoveries. But something was different now.

She handed me the buckle and, once more, I inserted it into its correlating shape.

There was no noise, but in a hushed display of varicoloured hues, the screens in front came alive.

"Pictures before my eyes. What is happening?"

"I...I've just turned on the power," I answered.

One screen showed, presumably, the view outside. Another showed a picture, complete with illegible labels, of a plant, almost like a textbook illustration. The last showed a row of characters and a picture of...was it really the solar system? I pressed the small button under the screen. And a voice spoke, but the words were meaningless. Then a man appeared on screen.

Lincoln vented a small cry.

I knew why.

The man was bald- headed and he spoke in words that still made no sense. But he looked like Edis and many of the other men in Mentarea.

I shook my head and closed my eyes; I didn't know people really did that when in despair, but that's what I did. Then I opened my eyes and sat down. Lincoln sat on the floor by me and looked at the screen like a child as the man spoke.

"He- is- like- my- father," she said in staccato.

"He *is* like him. This is...this is incomprehensible."

"I do not understand," she said, in an uncharacteristically subdued voice.

Then a woman appeared on screen as planets revolved almost cartoon- like about her head.

Lincoln stood and moved nearer the screen for a closer look and stroked her hand across the surface. I think she honestly thought that she could penetrate that surface and step inside.

"Ohh! She looks like Gale. And like my mother looked. She looks like others in Mentarea."

She seemed to stiffen as she stepped back, back still further, and edged past my chair, still staring at the screen. Although I couldn't hear the pad of her bare feet, still I knew she had halted right behind me.

I stood up.

Then, turning to face her:

"And you, Linc. She looks... like you."

I felt my stomach seethe and my temples thrum with emotions of disbelief and revelation. I knew that my face had morphed into a sickening mask of incredulity and, I am ashamed to admit, repulsion. She didn't say anything, but I could hear her nervous breathing as she just stood there, her eyes afflicted with affright. I felt a tingling about my head and a deluge of dread wash over me.

There was a weighted silence.

I could summon no words.

But what did *my* shock matter?

She knew. No, not *knew*, she *understood*, as did I, what was unfolding.

Still no words came from either of us.

I broke the silence:

"Christ! This isn't anyone's bloody *home*, Linc. You sense...no, I think you *know*. Now I see it all. This is...this is a...surely it's not possible. No, that word's archaic here. Here *and* now. So this is the explanation; *this* is the final answer. I remember something that you said about the hives after Mankind has gone. Well, you can forget the decades that will follow; *here's* the silent hive. I came to look for something and I've found it. This is about you, now, Linc. It's not just about me anymore. Now we're both immersed in this mad mix- up. This is how you- not you, but your ancestors- came here. It's from Space!"

I ran my hand roughly over my face then looked at her.

She stood there and then she sobbed, her tears a concoction of emotions. This was the culmination of our journey. Not her pregnancy, but the unveiling of this implausible shroud. For once, I gained a warped satisfaction from seeing those tears, because they were a reminder to me that everyone is equal in their vulnerability not only under this sun but also under all the other suns that may exist. The well of fear and disgust continued to rise within me but stopped short of brimming over.

Then, I felt a stillness about my mind.

A serenity like the peace after a downpour.

And somehow her tears began to seep through my feelings like rain through a fissure. Acceptance found a way and as I looked at Lincoln, consummate in her nakedness, the yellow light of the place suffusing her features and tinting her smooth breasts, and the thought of our child growing inside her, my disbelief turned to calm credence and her face dissolved into its beautiful innocence once more. No, I couldn't suddenly hate Lincoln with a vile disgust. The girl whose love had penetrated so deep that she had seared my very soul couldn't suddenly sicken me. In my eyes, she was as human as any woman. Had we never come here, I should never have known. I hugged her and clasped her close to me, feeling her perfectly natural warm bare back with my hands. I tasted the real salt from her true tears, and ran my hand through her thick hair. I pressed my palm against her midriff and longed for this to all work out.

"I have to…I have to accept all that I see, but it is not…easy," she said through choking tears. "Now I fear that you will see me as…as you once described those on other planets, a hideous monster, and that your love for me will…"

She really meant it, and how pivotally paradoxical was our situation.

"Oh no, Linc. *No*."

"…will die like the shrinking red sun. I could not live if it did. Oh, do not…"

"Shhh, Linc. I'll always see you for what you have always been and will continue to be to me, the most beautiful and loveliest woman in the world. Any world! And I'll love you until the sun shrinks. And until it dies. And then *beyond*."

And I cried too.

Once we had found Gale (who had dozed off right where we had left her), we took her to the strange craft from the unknown reaches of space. We reconnoitred and found spores and seeds still sealed in their little cases, and dead bees still lying in their long defunct hives. Lincoln even discovered a tank full of the strange plant- like cotton material that hung in sheets to separate our cells in the Chapel of Rest back at Mentarea.

Only when it reached early evening, and having spent the afternoon watching the screens was I finally able, from just the images coupled with educated guesswork, to work out what had happened. We sat down outside the door, my hand on Lincoln's knee, listening to the timeless sounds of Nature preparing for the night.

"This is my theory:

Ages ago, this ship came from your home planet to look for somewhere else to live and adapt. We know that from what we can interpret from the screens. They were just like us…er, me…Another planet out there with parallel evolution, albeit superior technology and a different language. But their planet was dying, Linc. You know that now? You see that too, don't you Gale?"

"We understand," said Lincoln, looking to Gale to urge her confirmation.

"I do," Gale replied.

"Anyway, they obviously selected a load of you- a couple of thousand, judging by the cylinders in there- to go on the journey. You could call it your 'Mayflower'; I'll tell you about that later. It was packed with various plants and insects. That's why here on Earth we now have the dogspaw plant and all these odd specimens growing around us. Maybe these grew from a seed spillage and thrived here in this sheltered valley. And your bees that don't sting- they don't sting 'cos they never could! They came here with your ancestors. Maybe it also explains the unusual butterflies I've seen and the fruit, as well as the oddly- coloured fish!"

Gale looked at Lincoln, then at me. I remembered how those fish had been the subject of Lincoln's remorse.

"And…and the blaze- beetles!" cried Lincoln.

"Mmmm. Then there's your technology- forgotten except for the magnasule, probably an offshoot of the technology lying behind us."

Lincoln smiled at that point.

"Do you remember how I stopped you from walking across the path of the magnasule?" she reminded me.

"Yes of course I do, just as we walked into your town. I was pleased that you'd touched me; I never told you that."

She rouged.

"I'm digressing. So they're on their way cruising around the stars looking for somewhere and they enter our solar system. Then they spy Earth but something goes wrong. I don't know what, it's irrelevant now. But they crash. They crash right here."

I stopped to ponder upon what I had just said, about how outlandish it all sounded.

"But 'The Passing', what of that event?" queried Gale.

However, it was Lincoln who answered.

"I am thinking that there *was* no 'Passing', Gale. There was no plague carried by rats."

Her eyes were shining.

"That's right, Linc. *This* is the cause of the plague. This ship carried a germ, a virus or whatever, obviously something harmless to your people but fatal to mine. It spread. Maybe it was airborne. Who knows? Now the situation is reversed; *your* people are dying through a long- term inability to adapt to this new environment. After hundreds of years, you're dying out."

"But 'The Passing'..." Gale said once more.

"No, Gale. A lie. Let's call it the biggest white lie ever told. Your ancestors were taken immediately to an isolated town, one that was emptied in readiness. The scientists here on Earth no doubt decided to segregate them, so they built the wall as quickly as they could. That wall wasn't to keep people out!"

Lincoln shuffled.

"It was to keep my ancestors confined."

"Yes, Linc. That's right- to stop them leaving. Maybe they were to be watched and monitored, even studied. But my people got no further than teaching them English and basic farming methods and stocking up the place with historical records before the virus became apparent. But those travellers *had* no virus. Like I've said, it was probably carried on their craft from space. There never were any 'waiters by the wall'; people would've kept as far away as possible from your 'town' as they thought you were the cause of the virus. Then the scientists amongst your ancestors realised what had happened, thus they perpetrated the story of 'The Passing' to assuage the guilt that they felt at having inadvertently destroyed another race! The lie died with its conspirators and the truth was never passed on. Only a rhyme was handed down to children. What was it? Something about 'a stealthy game' and 'a plague of death raining'? Only we three know the truth."

And that was the way we decided it should stay. I knew that the truth would fade like the rapidly vanishing blue of Lincoln's eyes.

*

Around ten- thirty that night, with Gale sound asleep and Friday curled up at her feet, Lincoln and I lay down together and I stroked her dark hair whilst I looked into her eyes. She spoke:

"You have reassured me that the findings of this sun will never take away your love for me. My heart burns even stronger for you now, for the boundaries of Time and Space cannot separate us. We have even more in common. I too feel as though I am a stranger, for this is *your* planet."

"No, Linc. It's *your* planet too, and it's now *my* Time as well."

She smiled, and, before she shut her eyes for the final time that night, I looked into them, and, in the yellow artificial light of our fantastic surroundings, I fancied that they were even deeper, perhaps radiating with the glow of a galaxy of stars.

CHAPTER 22: *A Time For Gathering Stones*

More than two- dozen new moons have waxed and waned since Lincoln gave birth to our twins, or, as she refers to them, our 'beautiful butterflies' that 'were born in the hive'. I don't know what caused Lincoln to have those symbolic dreams; call it her feminine intuition working surreptitiously within her subconscious- or some strange alien visionary power. Or, if imagination evades you, just bland coincidence. Her dreams came true though, and they give hopefully more than just a spark of promise to the cinders that are the Future. Anton, the elder of the two by three minutes (Gale held the watch and timed it exactly, shortly before the battery expired), is distinguishable from the few other boys in Mentarea on account of his shock of rich black hair. He's a boisterous little lad, and, like his father in another life, seems to be ten minutes ahead of everyone else. Cleo, on the other hand, is calmer of spirit but, even at her tender age, examines everything she sees and attempts to argue with chattering logic and clarity beyond her years. We all need not have fretted like we did over the period of Lincoln's pregnancy, for it could not have been any less complicated and the nine months culminated in an almost textbook delivery by Omas. Still with hair as dark as coalfish, and a pearly grin as open as the shore, Lincoln has conceded neither follicle nor tooth to the births. She has donned the cloak of domesticity and earthiness around her spirited shoulders, revelling unflinchingly in her role of motherhood, and already has begun to verse our children in the fineries of courting Nature. The twins even have a five-week old cousin, May, born to Gale and that certain young man who graced her table regularly at breakfast time and with whom she underwent her own Ceremony of Harmony just over a year ago.

Breaking with convention, we now live in the tower with the base of Portland stone and the three weathered - cracked now- steps that we explored shortly after my arrival in Mentarea. The name itself is derived from a broken sign that we discovered at the base of the wall. We soon found its other half; they read 'No Access- Government Area'.

I can't say that it's a restful life, not with two young children and the constant bustle of the crowds outside our house. But it's a good life, and a happy one too. We work hard within our busy community, and now I can turn my hand to many tasks. On a small wicker table in the corner of our 'bedroom' lie the few possessions from my old life; my wallet, my pen that no longer writes, an empty paper bag that once contained some sweets, the handful of loose change that I gave to Lincoln and a ten-pound note.

On a shelf stands our plastic soldier. Above the shelf, as if to remind me that there is always hope, hangs an odd copper etching of America's sixteenth President. And in the far corner of the room stands a taller wicker table, and on its small top, made by one of the town's more skilled workers from the two ingots that I took from the old bank that day, rests my gift to Lincoln, an exquisitely- crafted golden fish mounted on a slender serpentine holder. Sometimes, when the moon is bright, it tempts and dazzles the strange piece of train lamp that lies on the sill. And often, as we drift off to sleep, and the breeze decides to cavort across the town, we hear the soporific tones from my precious music box that dangles from a crooked hook outside our room.

Our friends from the town visit us regularly. Leo often walks from the Great Hall to our home with the most delightfully prepared platter of fruit, Ike sometimes asks for my help in the vineyard, and Olst and Frank call so that the latter can be regaled with my tales of the old world. And that whole- souled woman, Monet- well, she now makes clothes for the twins. Edis revels in his role as grandfather; I think it does him good, for, although I can still count on one hand the number of times I've seen him smile since that first occasion when he introduced himself to me, he *has* lost that rather disconcerting fiery countenance now! As for Isaac…well, I have tugged at his corners and revealed his feltside. He even calls in regularly for a drink…or two. On one intoxicating occasion, somehow he calculated the odds of both sisters surviving pregnancy and conceiving healthy children. I'd like to say that I could remember his mathematics, but I have never been one to see a man drinking alone.

I'm sitting in the honey- bath again now, and it's another scorcher of a day. With Friday panting at their heels, Edis has taken the twins to see the bees. Lincoln stands naked, and I see how she swells again around her midriff. She slips in gracefully to join me, the tiny scar on her left shoulder just visible as a crescent of white on a firmament of golden flesh.

"Ohh…that is good."

"I've another riddle for you, Linc," I tell her, "and it's *better* than last week's."

"Ah! The men digging half a hole! I liked that one. But I am prepared for a new one. Ask it of me now," she smiles, and ripples the water gently with her hand.

"Okay...here: *At moontime they come without being called, and by sun they are lost without being taken.*"

She pauses.

Then she frowns in that charming way, before grinning:

"I have the answer."

"Go on..."

"That is easy."

She looks around to ensure that no-one is within earshot, before continuing.

"They are the stars that my ancestors sailed past!"

I lean forward to kiss her.

"Do you want another one, or shall we wait?"

"We shall wait...save it. Yes, let us wait..."

She eases herself backwards in the water, pulling me with her.

She adds simply:

"...for another time."

Lightning Source UK Ltd.
Milton Keynes UK
13 October 2010

161230UK00001B/14/P